Finding Me and You

Ella McLaughlin

Publisher:
ASPG (Australian Self Publishing Group)
P.O. Box 159, Calwell, ACT Australia 2905
Email: publishaspg@gmail.com
http://www.inspiringpublishers.com

National Library of Australia Cataloguing-in-Publication entry

Author: McLaughlin, Ella

Title: **Finding Me and You**/*Ella McLaughlin*

ISBN: 978-1-922618-51-1

Chapter 1

PEARL BEACH

Chloe Clarke tossed her long golden mane back out of her captivating aqua eyes as she lifted her tanned slender arm to take a peek at the time. Raising her eyes, she looked around as she heard her name being called; people were waving and starting to leave.

"Bye, thanks for coming!" She yelled as she waved back. It had been an afternoon barbeque with friends on the veranda of the surf club. Chloe had won the end-of-year surf club raffle, a fourteen-day Mediterranean cruise, along with a small amount of spending money. Now, after an exciting wait, the time had come. She and her long-term boyfriend Craig Lamont were due to set sail in the next few days from Barcelona. Chloe had always dreamt about going to Europe, but never really thought that she could handle the trip being way too daunting. She understood her anxiety would never let her achieve her dream. So instead, she buried herself in work and volunteering at the surf club. But now, in one beautiful twist of fate, without a chance to change her mind, she was taking the trip. She had been building herself up for months doing meditation and yoga, along with a healthy diet; she felt she was in the best shape she had ever been. Both Chloe and Craig had recently turned twenty-eight; being the perfect age to go, to take in the culture, and at the same time, still young enough to enjoy.

She had walked away to take a phone call and stopped to linger a while, enjoying a peaceful moment on her own. What a glorious autumn afternoon. The leaves were starting to change colour and you could start to feel the slight chill in the air but it was still pleasant enough to be outdoors. The sun was setting earlier, and the colours in the sky at sunset were reflecting on the calm waters of the ocean. The salty smell of the ocean was lingering in the air. What a long hot summer they had endured; huge bushfires had savaged the bush and wiped out so much wildlife. Everyone was happy to see the end of the summer that year. The cool autumn air felt peaceful and was well welcomed. She cast her eye over the emptying beach. She loved the quietness. Taking a deep breath and breathing out slowly, watching the beach she felt it calm her. She smiled as she watched the last few dogs play with balls and frisbees before going home.

Umina Beach was one of the only beaches on the coast that was protected from the dreaded North Easters that battered the coast. It had great surf breaks for surfers and a calmer area for paddle boarders, even an area called kiddies corner, which was a safe area for children to play. It was tucked away in a corner near the rocks. If you walked around the rocky outcrop, within a few minutes you would come to another little beach called Pearl Beach. Being small, only about two kilometres long, with gorgeous golden sand but known for its dumpers and not suitable for surfers. That was where Chloe lived. It was a tiny town, which only had a small café, a restaurant, and a park for the kiddies to play. But that was the whole charm of the place. Usually it was a very quiet place, except weekends in summer when it got very busy.

She turned back to the veranda as she heard her name being called. It was Angie, her best friend waving at her frantically to come back. They had gone to school together, both primary and secondary, and had been in the surf club together since Nippers Angie had long wavy brown hair and warm brown eyes, the complete opposite to Chloe. She had envied her curls growing up and Angie had envied Chloe's long straight hair. She picked up her long pale blue, maxi dress with one hand as to not trip on the hill and walked back towards her.

"Oh sorry, I was taking a moment to myself. It's been such a hectic afternoon." She tossed her hair from her face.

"Are you ok? Is your anxiety playing up again?" Angie was aware of how Chloe sometimes felt at this sort of function.

"No, I am fine now, thanks." Chloe put her hand to her face to shade her eyes from the setting sun as her bangles clanged together, rolling down her arm. She was scanning the scene. "Where is Craig?" she asked. "I have not seen him in a while. Did he go home?" That would not have surprised her at all.

"Oh, I see him," Angie pointed as they spotted Craig striding towards two mates who had ridden up to the viewing deck on pushbikes.

"What in flaming hell are those two wombats doing here?" Bob had arrived, an older member of the surf club. He had come over after spotting Craig's friends arrive. He was well respected at the club, but everyone knew Bob was Bob; he could get away with things no one else could get away with. He spoke his mind, but you always knew where you stood with him. He had been there as long as Chloe could remember, probably before she was born. And he was still there almost every day, keeping an eye out over the kids. He wore his years of service proudly, with every line on his face, like a badge of honour. He had scars on his nose and balding head, where skin cancers had been cut out, and for that reason, was an ambassador for "slip, slop, slap." No kid, baby, or adult ever left the surf club without *slopping* on the sun cream, *slipping* on a shirt, and *slapping* on a hat. He still swam and worked out every day, to keep fit, but his days of being a lifeguard were well and truly over. He was just there for the kids now, and since he lost his wife a few years back, they had all become his family. He had a ladies' fan club with women of his age all coming for coffee regularly, hoping he would stop by at their table and spin them a yarn or two.

"Look at those idiots hanging out on the deck of excuses. Those two are good for nothing louts, fair dinkum idiots. I am giving ya that for nothing," he said, swatting an annoying fly then throwing his hands around in disgust as he walked away.

It really was called "the deck of excuses" where everyone would take the coffee they bought at the café, to drink, and watch the waves. Surfers would make up excuses why it wasn't a decent day for a surf, and others would linger, enjoying the view, having nothing better to do. Then there were also the eager beavers, the go-getters, who grabbed their boards and ran to the surf not even stopping until they reached the water.

Arriving back with a can of Aerogard, Bob was still keeping a close eye on Craig and his mates. He sprayed each arm, torso and then lifted each leg up one after another as he sprayed it all over him, not forgetting one last long spray down his back before offering it to Chloe. "No, thanks," she said as both she and Angie stepped backward, coughing and sputtering from the overspray of the overuse of the aerogaurd can. "How are you ever going to survive two weeks locked up on a boat with that lunatic? You two hardly spend any time together now. You're going to go crazy," he said, swatting a fly from his face. "He is about as annoying as these flaming things."

"I am sure we will be ok, Bob," laughed Chloe as she slipped her sunglasses to the top of her head to wipe her eyes that were still watering.

They leered at Craig as he walked back, tossing his curls back. Bob could not help but think, "What does Chloe see in him?" His lanky frame, blonde bushy hair, unkept and messy plus no dress sense at all, he had shown up today wearing corduroy boardies, a surf hoodie, and worn-out sandshoes. Bob was shaking his head in disgust as he watched him.

"I am going to shoot some pool and sink some beers with the boys. I will call around in the morning."

Chloe smiled and nodded. "No worries. Have fun."

Craig looked at Bob sheepishly, turned, and walked away quickly; he was aware what Bob thought of him, and wasn't hanging around for one of his lectures today. Funny, but Bob was usually a good judge of character, and if you asked most people around town, he was spot on the money about Craig. She watched as he jumped on his pushbike and followed them through the park, noting the sound of fallen autumn leaves crushing as he rode through them, scattering them in the air.

"I rest my case. No, I am not saying another word." Bob walked off waving his hands in the air. It riled Bob up seeing Craig at times; he knew he would never amount for anything, which didn't worry him, but Craig was hanging around with Chloe, and that's what he didn't like, she could do so much better in his eyes.

"I hate to say this, but Bob is right, Chloe. The two of you have been drifting apart lately. You never hang out together much anymore. Are things ok with you, guys?" asked Angie with a concerned look on her face.

"We are fine. He is going to hang out with his mates a while before we go away, that's all." The day was almost over, anyway; most people have gone.

"Why are you still hanging around with him? You do realise you can get any guy you want. They would all line up if you were single."

Chloe had a natural beauty, the type of beauty that girls were envious of, never needing make-up, maybe mascara and a lip gloss, but that was for special days only. "Oh, that is so lovely of you to say that, Ang. But we are ok. We both like to keep things simple, that's all."

The breeze was starting to pick up and you could feel the nip in the autumn air. The floral scent from freshly washed hair lingered in the breeze as Chloe tossed her golden mane, using her finger to swipe the last strand of hair that had got stuck on her lip from her face.

"He doesn't deserve you. You let him do whatever he wants. It doesn't worry you what he does, does it?" She laughed.

Chloe smiled. *No, what Craig did really didn't bother her*, she thought.

Bob sauntered back looking like he was about to announce something important. "I have an Uber on the way, Chloe, if you want to share a ride home. If that bloody pelican isn't going to look after you, then someone has to, and today that's me." He was looking at his phone. "It's on its way."

"Thanks, Bob, that would be fantastic. I will just say my goodbyes."

Bob lived around the corner from her, so it made sense to share a ride home. She hugged and kissed Angie, and promised to stay in touch and said farewell to the last few stragglers quickly, and was in the car park as the Uber arrived.

Getting in the backseat with Bob, she recognised the strong aroma of Aerogard. She rubbed her nose to stop it from tingling.

That was a smell every Aussie knew. The good old Aerogard. It did its job at keeping the flies and mossies at bay. It was always the first thing packed for a picnic or a barbecue.

Driving down the main street of Umina, she looked out as all the restaurants were setting up for the night. It was autumn so a much quieter town than it was in summer, but still had a warm homely feel. They drove up the sweeping road up above kiddies' corner, where you got a grand view of the beach below then around the headland towards Pearl Beach.

"I hope you have a lovely holiday. You deserve it. I was so happy when you won. You do a lot for the club and it is just what you need to get out of your comfort zone a bit. I just wish you took someone else along with you, other than the village idiot," said Bob as he turned his focus back on the scenery going past the window. He worried about her going with Craig. She suffered anxiety and even though it was only mild, going overseas with him was a huge problem. "I don't trust those mates of his, either. They were organising something with him today, all staring at that phone together, they were up to no good for sure. I am giving ya the mail now. If that flip puts one foot out of place, just let me know, and he will not only have me to deal with but half the bloody surf club as well."

"You don't need to worry, Bob. We will be fine, but thanks for your concern." Chloe sighed, patting his arm as she turned and stared back out the window. God, she hoped she was right, she wasn't sure who she was trying to convince more, her or Bob.

They made the turn down a long bushy road to Pearl Beach and before long, were stopped out the front of Chloe's place.

Bob gave her a kiss on the cheek. "Thanks for everything, Bob, trust me everything will be ok. I will send you an email, let you know I am ok when I land." He nodded and held her hand tight. "I will be waiting to see it. Take care of yourself."

Chloe lived in a cabin out the back of Mrs. Whitaker's house. A cute, little stone cottage that suited her perfectly. It had a gorgeous private courtyard out the back that opened up onto a bush setting. She had the safety and comfort of Mrs. Whitaker nearby and a beautiful private cabin where she enjoyed the wildlife that came to visit every day. She walked down the paved walkway and around the back to a pair of French doors that she opened up, and brought the outdoors in with an open plan kitchen and lounge area with a breakfast bar and a small cane setting for two. It opened up over the lounge area, which was a decent size for a small lounge, a coffee table, and her TV and entertainment system were hung on the wall. A little hall to the left led to a bathroom, a small study, and main bedroom that also had a sliding door that opened up to the back courtyard.

She threw her keys on the table and opened the courtyard doors, putting on some quiet music as she poured a glass of wine. This was still a pleasant evening. She decided to sit outside, grabbing a throw on the way out. She had decked it out with Balinese-style furniture. There was a day bed with a coffee table and two single chairs that matched. She flopped onto the day bed putting the throw over her knees and looked around; all her little solar garden lights were lighting up the plants she had scattered around, making it look peaceful and beautiful. Lots of Balinese statues were placed around to complete the style.

"Have you been waiting for me?" She whispered as she noticed the possum peering around the pole looking at her. She came to visit her every evening and Chloe would give her a strawberry or a piece of carrot, nothing too excessive, just a small treat. She gave the possum a strawberry and sat back and watched her eat. She would eat the strawberry all the way down to the green leafy bit on the end and then throw it away.

It made her smile, even possums were fussy. She usually had a bub on her back, but tonight, she was alone. As she finished eating, another little possum came out from around the corner. "Oh, you're getting big enough to be on your own now, are you?" She went and got another strawberry and watched them for a while before they went scurrying off back to the bush.

A wallaby came regularly to eat Mrs. Whitaker's back lawn, which annoyed her but Chloe secretly loved it when he poked his head into her courtyard to say hello. Along with the wallabies and possums came some unwanted visitors also, like the red belly black snake that sunned itself every morning of last summer on Mrs. Whitaker's back lawn. But they were aware it was there, and were cautious, and stayed clear when it was around. There were also lots of spiders, which came out from the bush, but Mrs. Whitaker had the house and cabin sprayed for pests every year, so that helped to keep them at bay. She looked at the clock; it was getting late she should grab some sleep. Tomorrow was her last day in town, before flying out, and she would feel better after an early night.

She woke up early to the sounds of the kookaburras laughing. They were so noisy in the mornings; they would always do a family chant as if greeting each other good morning. It must be 6 am, she thought. Looking at the clock she saw she was right. You could set your clock by them. She listened to the birds for a while, the king parrots were next to start singing. Then the magical sound of the currawongs. They had the sweetest sound of them all. She lay in bed and checked her phone; no new messages, and no emails that needed immediate attention. Ah, this was a wonderful start to the day.

Making a coffee, she took it back to bed, grabbing her "to-do list" for the day. She opened it up and grabbed a pen. Ok, Number 1, Go over her suitcase one last time and finally zip-up for the last time. Number 2, Visit Mrs. Whitaker to remind her she was going away, and Angie would be dropping by, to water the plants. And Number 3, Transfer another bundle of cash into her Qantas travel card. Seat selection was open today, but she would wait for Craig to do that so that they could choose the seats together. Easy, she would get the rest done now.

Dinner was at her sister's restaurant that night, with all the family. They ran Seasalt, the restaurant, right on the beach, a casual seafood hang-out where you could meet with friends and have a beer or a cocktail or a casual meal. Its deck ended right on the sand so needless to say it was hugely popular and outdoor tables were booked weeks in advance. They also hosted lots of birthday parties, events, and family celebrations.

Johnny, her sister's husband, was Italian, so it had all the wonderful Italian touches to make meals delicious. Hugely popular were the pizzas and portions of pasta. Johnny was from the farming region, his family had orchards and farmland. If his family wasn't growing food, they were thinking of food, and if they weren't thinking of food, they were pickling, baking, or cooking it. There was no way that Johnny could have done anything else, except become a chef. He did his apprenticeship at an Italian seafood restaurant in Darling Harbour, and that was where he had met Kait. She was waitressing at the same restaurant and living at an apartment in Pyrmont. They got on extremely well and had a few drinks after their shifts and Johnny stayed over a lot. They had an awesome relationship and married soon after. Chloe also worked at Seasalt, and then spent the rest of the time working at the café or spending time helping out at the surf club with Bob and Angie when she could.

She was looking forward to the catch-up with the family. It was always a fantastic night of fun and laughter. The restaurant had a great vibe to it, and as a family, they all got along well. She transferred the cash and then got out of bed and went to the study, where she had her luggage laid out on the single bed. Just looking at it was making her hands sweat. Pulling herself together, she started going over it once again. Once she was finally happy, she zipped it up, wiping her sweaty hands on her nightie and breathing out heavily. Her carry-on bag was all set, packed with passport, tickets, and compression stockings for the long flight, along with a few other essential items like chewing gum and a novel. Done, next on the list was Mrs. Whitaker. She had a quick shower and dressed casually for the day ahead.

She walked out of the courtyard and around a stone wall that led into Mrs. Whitaker's backyard. She spotted her, sitting in her sunroom, doing a crossword. She sat there a lot, looking out over the garden. She walked up the old stone steps to the door.

"Good morning, dear. Come in. I have just made a pot of tea, grab a cup, and join me."

"Thank you. I will."

She poured a tea and sat down. Mrs. Whitaker had been living alone for around three years now, after losing her husband to a nasty skin cancer. She was a sweet old lady that always kept to herself and never bothered Chloe. She had a son and a daughter both local, so they were always dropping in and doing errands for her. She enjoyed having Chloe around; it made her feel safe and not as lonely and isolated. Just knowing she was in the cabin made a difference.

Chloe had lived there for over a year now and they had built a close relationship. "I just wanted to remind you that I am going away tomorrow."

"Oh yes, dear, that has come around so quickly."

"It has, I know. Angie will pop around at times to water the plants."

"Oh, she is a nice girl. Tell her to pop up and have a cup of tea with me when she does."

She knew she would miss her so had already asked Angie to check on her also. "She definitely will. Now do you need anything before I go?"

"Oh no, my son is coming this afternoon. Thank you. Have a wonderful holiday. I will be waiting to hear all the news when you return."

Her son usually came once a week. He would do the lawns and run some errands and usually left with a basket full of homemade treats. You always knew when Mrs. Whitaker was baking by the smells that came out of her kitchen, and you knew it was the right time to pop up for a cup of tea. "I will. Thanks, Mrs. Whitaker." She gave her a hug and a kiss and left.

Chapter 2
THE LETDOWN

Knowing that Craig would not show till after lunch, she decided on a walk along the beach. Being such a lovely morning and all plus only a few streets away she couldn't imagine a single reason why not. She grabbed her sunnies and broad brim hat and set off. As she stepped onto the sand it made her smile. There was nothing better than the sand between your toes and the smell of the ocean. She closed her eyes and took a deep breath. She was instantly calmed and it bought a peaceful aura that made you feel as though you didn't have a worry in the world.

Everyone who passed you by had a smile and a good morning wish, and most were familiar faces. Being a small beach, it was an easy achievement to walk from end to end. There was a huge rock face at each end that framed the beach and looked like you were on your own private little beach. She stopped and had a peek into the rock pool along the way. She loved swimming there. Lots of locals came in the mornings and done laps, but there was no time for that today.

She started to head home, but stopped to talk to some neighbours that were sitting at the café having coffee. They chatted about the weather and the surf, and then she began to stroll home. What a lovely day. She was calm and relaxed after her walk. She had been quite anxious at times recently as the over-seas trip came closer. No one really understood, so she kept it to herself a lot. People thought that she was nuts suffering anxiety instead of being excited. She was managing to control her symptoms, and no one understood the true turmoil that existed inside her body. As she turned the corner to her street, she spotted Craig's kombi parked out the front of her place. He's early, she thought to herself, especially after being out with his mates. Great, we can organise the seat selection.

When she went inside, she found him making coffee. He offered Chloe one and they sat out in the courtyard. "You're early. I wasn't expecting you till later." He sat with his head bent, looking at the ground, not saying a word.

"What's wrong? You look like you have had terrible news. Is everything ok?"

He stared up at her. "Chloe, I can't do this," he whispered.

"Can't do what?" she asked uneasily.

"I can't come on holidays," he said glumly.

"But why? What are you saying?"

"I am saying, I can't go. I never really wanted to, but I was doing the whole thing for you."

"I don't understand. What, you wait until the day before we leave to tell me this?" She was starting to sound panicked; her eyes were wide and frantic.

"I am sorry. I wanted to go for you, but I can't."

They both sat in silence for a few moments. Craig had his head bent low.

"Craig, do you understand what you are doing to me? I have been so anxious about this holiday but I was being so strong and now you have ruined the whole thing."

"Yea, but you should still go, don't throw it all away because of me."

"I can't go on my own. If you do this to me, it is over, Craig. It is over forever, do you understand?" She said, infuriated. She was starting to lose control. She peered down at her shaking hands. "Just perfect," she thought.

"Yea, I do. I thought it would be. I think it has been over for a while now. We both know that. I am a jerk. I am sorry, Chloe, truly I am. Please go and have a fantastic time. You can do this, Chloe. You are stronger than you think."

He stood up and walked out the door, not looking back.

Chloe sat lifeless on the lounge. She was stunned. My God, what just happened? She sat for ages, trying to put everything together in her head. He didn't want to go. Why didn't he want to go? Why didn't he tell me that earlier? Why leave it till now? So many questions, yet no answers. Bloody typical of him, she thought. How could she possibly arrange for someone else to go with her? It was way too late. Impossible. She started to cry and pace the courtyard.

She grabbed her phone and with shaking hands rang her sister. "Kait, are you home?" Chloe asked frantically.

"Yea, I am at home. Johnny is at the restaurant. What's the matter?" She could hear in Chloe's voice something was terribly wrong.

"I am coming over. I will explain everything when I get there." Kait lived only five minutes away at Umina; she was on autopilot as she drove over the headland.

Kait was home. Great. And Johnny was at the restaurant, as usual. Perfect, she thought. She could talk in private. Johnny spent a lot of time at the restaurant, and Kait still worked as many shifts as she could, but they had a daughter Sophia now, who was two, and had started day care a few days a week, which helped. Their younger sister Chrissie babysat a lot at night, as she had a day job doing hair at a local hairdressing shop, and the extra money topped up a pretty average hair-dresser's wage.

Kait was waiting at the door when she pulled up. She was four years older than her, but they still looked very much alike except Kait had shorter hair to her shoulders. Chloe noticed the worried look on her face as she got out of the car and stormed up the driveway.

"Chloe, what's wrong?"

"It's over." Chloe was crying.

"What's over? You and Craig? What about the trip?" she said, stunned as she opened the screen door and they walked inside. Kait's house was in perfect order as usual. She had no idea how she managed to keep the place so tidy with a toddler running around. Perfectly filled with Ikea furniture, polished floorboards, and oversized scatter rugs, it made a beautiful room.

"Everything. Me, Craig, the trip. It's all over. Apparently, he does not want to go. Bob's right. He is a good-for-nothing bloody so and so, what a dirty trick and waiting till the last day to tell me." She was rambling and sobbing.

"Ok, slow down. Come, sit down." They sat at the kitchen table as Kait pulled out a chair and helped her sit. "Take a deep breath. Take it easy, start again, and tell me everything." Kait whispered, trying to calm her down. She quickly poured two cups of coffee from the coffee pot, bringing them back to the table and setting them down as she sat opposite her.

Chloe told her everything as she sat and listened quietly.

"Ok, wow." She took a deep breath herself, thinking quickly. "That's a pretty horrible story, but not the end of the world. Let's see if we can fix this. Who do you know that has a passport?"

Chloe stared at her with raised eyebrows.

"Listen to what you are saying. Finding someone with a passport that just so happens to have a few weeks leave up their sleeve the day before I fly out, you're crazy. I am not going."

"You have to go, Chloe. It is a trip of a lifetime, and you will probably have a better time without him, anyway," she said, pouring milk into their coffee cups.

"Go on my own? Are you nuts? I have never even been outside of Australia, remember? And you think it's ok for me to fly solo, halfway around the world, and board a ship that is so massive it could have its own postcode, and do all of this all on my own," she screamed. Looking down at her shaking hands, she started to wring them.

"Ssh! You will wake Sophia. I only got her down. Ok, wait here. I have an idea."

She watched as Kait tiptoed down the hallway and came back with a set of tarot cards.

"You are nuts, that just proves it. My life is falling to pieces and you want to play with those silly tarot cards." She stood up, ready to leave.

"No, wait! Before you say anything else, please sit down, let me explain." She put her hands on Chloe's shoulders and gently eased her back in her seat.

"If I do your cards and they show bad luck or bad fortune, then I agree, maybe you should probably not go. But if it's favourable, I think you should put on your big girl's pants and go," said Kait gently with a look of encouragement.

Chloe was aware that there was no way of getting out of this. She knew her sister all too well to argue with her over the tarot cards. She sat quietly with a frown on her face "Ok, let's give it a go, but I am still not going," sulked Chloe.

"That's because you're so goddamn stubborn. You live your whole life within a five-kilometre radius that you have never been outside of, ever!" She was glaring at her now with anger. Chloe annoyed her that she lived her life the way she did; she was more sorry that she had not experienced all the wonderful things that she had, the Sydney nightclubs, bars, and restaurants. She understood that it was her anxiety, but she needed to step out of her bubble and live a little. "I am sorry, Chlo. I want you to live a little that's all. I love you and want the best for you." She leaned forward and grabbed her on the hand. "You mean the world to me. If there was any way that I could go with you, I would, but I can't." She gazed at Chloe with her soft blue eyes.

She believed everything that Kait had said was true. She had struggled to be so strong and go; she had worked so hard on building herself up for this. Chloe grabbed the deck and held them in her hands. She took a few deep breathes and asked her nanna for guidance in the reading. She tapped the cards several times to spread the energy, and gave them a thorough shuffle, then split them into three sections, piling them back on top of one another. Spreading the cards on the table, she closed her eyes and selected three cards. She had been through this many times; Kait loved her cards.

Kait gently overturned the cards as she stared at Chloe. She sat quietly for a moment, taking it all in, looking over each card then glancing up at her. She had a stunned look on her face.

"What's the matter? It's all bad, isn't it? I knew I should never have let you talk me into this!" Chloe was getting jumpy again, wringing her hands to death, giving her sister death stares. But Kait just sat, staring back at her with the same stunned look.

"You have to take this trip, Chloe. There is something magical in these cards. I have never seen such a blessed reading in front of me, ever."

Chloe looked confused. "You're just saying that."

"No, no I am not. Let me explain your reading. The first card that you drew is the Ace of Pentacles." She picked up the card and showed her before setting it back on the table. "This is one of the best cards you could draw. It means a grand opportunity has, or is, about to land in your lap, and that you should grab it. That's your trip, Chloe." She glanced up at her, throwing an open palm towards her as she continued. "Your path is about to lead you to new heights. Amazing!" She picked up the second card, showing her before setting it back down again. "Your second card is the star. The star invites you to reconnect with your inner guidance, and the road in your past has been preparing you for an amazing journey that you are about to encounter. It's showing that you are exactly where you should be in life, and you need to go along with the flow. Then, as if all that wasn't good enough, you aced it, by pulling The Lovers card."

She sat back in her chair staring at Chloe who looked like she totally had no clue what she was talking about. "Chloe, when you pull this card, it means you are about to encounter someone with whom you will share a purely sensational relationship with, someone in which you find a true connection, the one who you will share a deep unconditional love with. Basically, your love life is about to be set on fire. All the stars in the universe are lining up for you, Chloe. You are about to encounter a magical experience, one that if you are incredibly lucky, you only ever get to experience once in a lifetime. You're about to meet the love of your life, Chloe," said Kait, stunned as she sat back in her chair as she threw the cards back on the table.

They both sat and stared at each other, both speechless. Kait did readings all the time and was shocked at how clear-cut her reading had been. The trip was the opportunity and Craig not going, which was clearing the path, for her to possibly meet the love of her life, and to find her own self along the way. Kait was stunned; one thing was clear: her sister definitely needed to take this trip.

Chloe was the one who finally spoke. "So it appears I have to go on this cruise." She looked scared and afraid.

"I would say you would be mad if you didn't," Kait concluded wisely in a slow soft voice.

Chloe knew that Kait was very serious when it came to the cards, and she would never joke about them. What she was saying made sense to her. She knew there was no turning back, not only would she be letting the surf club down, but she would be letting herself down also. She had spent months building herself up for this trip.

She heard Sophia starting to stir and went to give her a kiss and bring her out to play. She was a happy little girl who was very content. She had her mother's blonde hair but her father's brown eyes and olive complexion. She gave them the biggest smiles while happily eating a cheese stick Kait had given her. They sat and chatted, while Sophia happily played at their feet.

"Ok, I have decided, I am going. I have to be strong and go ahead and do this. Thank you for making me see straight, Kait. I will catch up with you tonight for dinner." She stood up to leave. "Well, at least I know one thing: everyone will be happy to hear Craig is out of the picture, once and for all," sighed Chloe. Kait laughed, leading her to the door. "Yes, Mum and Dad weren't too fond of him and that's putting it mildly."

Chloe arrived at the restaurant on time and instantly felt better. The Beach Boys were playing on the sound system, and the place was all lit up with fairy lights. She loved the atmosphere of the place. It was crowded, as usual, and she recognised a lot of familiar faces who called out to her as she walked in, taking her a while to make her way to her table, stopping and chatting along the way.

All of her family were waiting, her parents and both her sisters along with Chrissie's boyfriend Finn. Sophia was sitting happily in the booster chair, giving Chloe the biggest grin. When she saw her, she ran straight to her, giving her a big cuddle as she giggled. They all got up to greet her. They were all excited to see her. The dinner that night went smoothly. Obviously, everyone already was aware of what was going on, and they were very supportive of Chloe making the decision to take the trip on her own. Her mother moved over and sat next to her, giving her a warm smile. As Chloe studied her, she realised how beautiful she still looked for her age.

The girls all had her looks with the same features and blonde hair. She picked up Chloe's hand and placed a silver bracelet on her arm with a Saint Christopher medal to keep her safe. "This will protect you in your travels. You can do this, Chlo. You know you can. I am so proud of you." She was squeezing Chloe to death as she rocked her, whispering in her ear.

"I know, Mum. Thank you. I am sure that I will be fine. I am just a little bit scared. Thank you for my bracelet. It makes me feel better already."

The restaurant was open, so Johnny was busy in the kitchen, but he came and sat with them as soon as service was over. He had made them a platter of grilled seafood, which was a specialty of the house, as well as two of his best pasta dishes. Topping it off with a tiramisu to end the meal. Everyone was full by the end. They all thanked Johnny, and they sat and had a quiet drink with him after the crowds left. It was a nice time of the evening.

Chloe felt better about the situation after speaking with her parents. No one mentioned the tarot card reading, but she knew Kait would fill her mother in with all the details later.

Time was ticking too fast and it was getting late, so now was an excellent time to say goodbye. Everyone was in high spirits as they kissed her and said their farewells.

She found her little possum and baby waiting for her when she arrived home. Feeding them a snack and then pouring herself a wine, her head was so full from the day's events. She needed to unwind. Did all that really happen in just one day, she thought to herself. Her morning beach walk happened days ago, didn't it? She did a quiet meditation on the sofa before heading in for the night.

Chloe woke to the kookaburras again. She jumped out of bed and made coffee. Today was the day. It was the day she would take her first flight out of Australia. Time would go fast and she needed to keep a close eye on it. Kait was picking her up at ten and taking her to the airport. She jumped in the shower and got dressed in her most comfortable pants and loose jumper.

Two king parrots were sitting out in the courtyard. She took them out a treat and sat with them while she had her coffee. Birds came to visit her every morning; sometimes it was the kookaburras, sometimes the currawongs, and always a king parrot or two. She enjoyed their visits; they would miss her while she was gone. If she wasn't around, they always tried Mrs. Whitaker as their next port of call. Her stomach was in knots this morning but she managed to scoff down half a bowl of muesli.

Kait arrived right on time and Chloe was waiting out the front with her luggage.

"Ah, good, you're still going. I was half expecting you to be a no-show this morning," laughed Kait as she jumped out of the car to give her a hand.

"No, I have my big girl pants on as you put it. I said I was going and I am standing by my word. However, my stomach is in knots if you must know. I think I am going to throw up," said Chloe as she tossed her bags in the back.

"Well, I thought that might be the case. Get in, I have something to help that," yelled Kait. She opened the centre console and grabbed something. She handed her a coffee. "Here. take this, and pour two of these into it." She handed her two little plastic pots.

"What are these?" She read the label, unsure what she had been given.

"Oh, cowboy shots," she laughed, relieved.

"They will calm your nerves. I knew you would be freaking out."

She happily emptied them into her coffee, and they set off.

The run to the airport was easy going; peak hour was over and school zones out of hours so it was a clear run ahead.

"How did the shots go? Are they settling the nerves?"

"I actually think they have helped a bit, thanks." She smiled at her sister. She was grateful she had Kait, she was a wonderful sister and was always there for her.

They were at the airport. It had taken them an hour and a half, but that was with a clear run. It was starting to get real now. "Wait, before you go, here, I bought you a little gift to remind you of home." She handed her a small gold kangaroo.

"Oh, Kait, it's beautiful, thank you, I will treasure it."

"There is a latch on it so you can dangle it here from the zipper on your bag."

She helped her attach it before they got out. Kait helped her with the luggage, and after a long cuddle and whispered words of encouragement kissed her goodbye. Tears were in both their eyes.

"Go and have that trip of a lifetime. I am so jealous. And make sure you stay in touch. I will be thinking of you all the way. You are so brave, Chloe, you can do this!"

Chloe nodded and started walking away, tears streaming down her face, wheeling her luggage behind her. She felt like she was being sentenced to prison, not going on an overseas holiday.

She checked in, got her seat assigned, and went and sat at a bar. She had a drink and was surprised how quickly the time was passing; she had to find the boarding gate. She peered around, so many signs, where in the heck was the boarding gate. The airport was huge; it seemed to go on forever.

Finding the gate, she was feeling a bit more relaxed. Baby steps, she kept telling herself. She just had to board the plane, and then it would soon be over.

She was boarding in no time. Settling into the flight, she had been lucky enough not to have anyone beside her so she could stretch out. They were taxiing down the runway, getting ready for take-off. She couldn't remember a time that she had ever been more scared. She put on her noise-cancelling headphones and played some music. The engines roared, and they were off. Her eyes were closed and the poor armrests were getting wrung to death. It all went quiet; she heard the seatbelt sign turn off.

She opened her eyes and stared out the window. They were high above the water of Botany Bay and banking around. She was captivated. As she gazed out, she spotted the traffic on the M1 Motorway, all heading north, on their way to the central coast. Still watching, she noticed the beaches. Home, she could see home. This is fantastic, she thought. Take-off was smooth, completely different from what she had thought it would be, she felt like she was sitting in a lounge chair.

She heard and smelt that meals and drinks were on their way. She could see the meals being served across the plane. How much food can one person eat? There was no way she was able to eat all that. "Chicken or beef?" The waitress had arrived. "Chicken, please," she said happily. Studying the tray that she had been given, she couldn't believe her eyes. To start was a baby prawn salad, with apple and celery. Followed by a plate of baked chicken, with vegetables, and steamed rice. Served with a bread roll and butter, a little fruit salad, then to finish, a small ice cream bucket, fruit, and some peanuts.

She started on her feast as she peered out the window. She was starting to enjoy herself. She ordered a scotch to help calm her nerves. Everything was starting to fall into place. After dinner she laid her seat back and tried to relax, finding a movie to help take her mind off the plane.

The stopover in Singapore was quick; she found the next flight's boarding gate without any trouble and boarded. She was proud of herself. She had done it, just fourteen more hours and she would be in Barcelona. She was happy to see the seat beside her vacant again, so she would have a comfortable flight. She stretched out and organized herself.

Once again, meals and drinks were served soon after take-off. The food was plentiful and delicious. She ordered a glass of red wine to enjoy it with, and she was set. No wonder people like flying, she thought to herself. This is like being in a top-class hotel. It wasn't a huge seat, but hey, you can't have everything, can you? The lights in the cabin started to dim; time to settle in for the night. She finished her movie, took half a sleeping pill, put on her black-out eye mask, and pulled up the blanket. "I can do this, I can do this," she chanted over and over in her head, as she drifted off to sleep.

Chapter 3

BARCELONA

The flight was what she had been most afraid of, but she had proudly conquered it. Everything had gone smooth, and with a quick stopover in Singapore, she had no time to change her mind. The flight arrived in Barcelona in the early hours of a beautiful sun-filled morning. The transfer was waiting for her and after a quick drive, she had arrived at her hotel. She stood out the front and stared up at the building, It was stylish with white-washed walls, so European with lots of tiny balconies and wrought-iron balustrades. The driver took her bags, and as he passed her by, she followed him inside. The reception staff were pleasant and spoke perfect English. They informed her that her room was ready, so she got an early check-in, which was well needed. They handed her the key and she followed the porter who carried her bags to the room.

The room was beautiful. She opened the curtains and then the window and the sun immediately beamed in. Taking a big breath, she could savour the aromas of the city. The scent of coffee and bread baking from the café below, spices from paella's cooking, and the salty scent of the ocean wafting across from the marina across the road.

The big French doors had opened up to a Juliet balcony with the gorgeous wrought-iron balustrades that she had seen when she arrived. She smiled; she had been lucky enough to have been given a beautiful front room. Her bed was a huge king-size pillow top. Next to that a small table, with a lamp and flowers that had filled the room with a beautiful scent. She jumped on the bed checking its comfort level and spotted a coffee pod machine. She walked over and selected a pod and made a coffee. She closed her eyes and savoured the smell. "Oh, it smelt like the café at home." A tear came to her eye thinking about home, but she brushed the thought away instantly angry with herself that she let herself get upset. She was to stay focused on the trip and not think about home. She turned and walked to the balcony so she could gaze at the city below.

She spied people everywhere, some rushing, some just strolling along, enjoying their day. What were their stories? Where were they going? She drained the last bit from the bottom of her coffee cup and licked the froth from her lips, no one to rouse on her. She was alone, no serviette needed. She pushed the thought of being alone out of her head and stood turning to take her cup inside, placing it back on the coffee tray. Right O, time to be brave, and do what tourists do and go outside, she thought.

She gazed in the mirror. Her eyes had bags but a quick face wash and some concealer would hide that. She brushed her long blonde mane and smiled. Not too bad considering. She stared down at her clothes; she was wearing mid-thigh denim shorts and a floral buttoned top. That will do for a city walk, she thought, and slipped into her cork wedges, grabbing her bag and the city map reception had given her. Time to hit the town!

The day outside was glorious. It felt so wonderful to feel the warm sun on her skin. It was heading into winter in Australia, so the warm weather was a treat. Following the map, she soon arrived at the Las Ramblas. After reading so much about this place, she was excited to see it and experience it for herself. She stood in awe of the city. Finally, little butterflies of excitement danced in her belly. She sighed as she strolled along, looking at all the shops, restaurants, and bars.

It had an amazing vibe, packed with people all looking so happy, smiling, and laughing. She could hear people talking in different languages, and she loved every bit of the town. She shopped for a few hours. Looking in all the windows and sitting at the fountains, people watching and reading the monuments.

A boot shop took her attention away. Corbeto's boots, a sign hung proudly out the front, cowboy boots and accessories. "Oh, how I love boots. That would be a real treat." She thought "Spanish boots." Her RM Williams boots had been worn to death; she had even had them re-soled once. She walked over and stared through the window. Oh, what unusual and beautiful boots, all sorts of cowboy styles, long, short, embroidered, coloured, this shop had them all. The closed sign was up, damn, she thought. Oh well, probably a good thing, she should be careful with her money. She knew she would not have been able to walk out of there without at least one pair of boots. Maybe they sold them online. She snapped a photo of the sign; she would google it when she got home.

She walked on and came to a corridor on the right; she strolled down and found herself in a courtyard full of even more restaurants and bars. Suddenly she realised she was starving. The aroma of the food wafting in the air was making her stomach grumble. She found an empty table and sat down. The waiter came straight over and handed her a menu.

"Oh, could I please just grab a beer to start?" She instantly thought what if he doesn't speak English? Fear grew inside her.

"Of course. Grande?" asked the waiter. *Oh, phew!* Calmness took over her once again.

"Mmm ok, I guess." The waiter returned with the biggest beer Chloe had ever seen.

"My goodness!" Chloe was shocked at the size.

"Yes, grande," explained the waiter, chuckling at her surprised look.

"Oh, I see. Well, I had better remember that one." He placed a bowl of peanuts on the table.

"Oh, that is so lovely of you, thank you." She smiled up at him.

"This is what we do here. You order a drink, and we supply a small treat. Where are you from?"

"I am from Australia."

"Oh wow, wow, wow, so far from home," he said in a low deep voice like she had committed a crime.

"Yes, a very long way and this is my first day here, and I am feeling quite lost. What do you suggest for food?" She had a worried look on her face, flicking her hair and then clawing her stretched fingers through it as she read the menu.

"First day, well I will bring you a small plate of some of our local produce to try," he said, waving his hand to stop her from looking at the menu. She gazed up with a huge smile. Grateful he had taken the decision from her as she handed the menu back.

"That sounds fantastic!"

He smiled and walked away with his red rag in his back jean pocket, swaying as he walked.

Chloe sat enjoying her fishbowl of beer while she spied the scenery and enjoyed the music playing.

The waiter returned with a plate of cheese, ham, dips with bread, and an assortment of other small goods. It all looked delicious. He proudly showed everything to her, pointing to each item as he explained where everything came from, and what went with what. She wondered if a waiter in Australia would share his passion. She hoped to think he would.

A man came and sat at the table next to her. The waiter turned to him and he took his order of a beer. She heard that he had a Scottish accent and she smiled to herself. She instantly thought of her nanna. She had a very broad Scottish accent, always promising to take her back to her homeland one day before she died. But unfortunately, that never happened. She had loved her nanna a great deal. She smiled at the man, who was looking over at her. He was around her age and very good-looking but in a rugged kind of way.

Illegal street vendors caught her attention, with what appeared to be sacks made out of bed sheets with ropes on each end, tied together. They all had a spot in the centre of the courtyard where they laid out their sheets with goods spread out, hoping for a sale, yelling at people as they passed by. All of a sudden, they all grabbed up their sheets by the ropes, the sheets magically turned into huge Santa sacks as they yanked them up, and they started running, disappearing through a side alley. Mounted police entered the courtyard from an alley on the other side. What a funny game they were playing, she thought, and so amusing to watch.

The Scotsman was watching her as she spied the performance centre stage. She was more amusing to check out. She had a childlike look about her, innocent, gentle, soft. She was smiling as if she was watching a matinee at the theatre, eating her cheese and biscuit. He was staring at her and he knew it, but he could not take his eyes off her. She intrigued him. He tried to focus on the circus in front of him, but he was instantly drawn back to her. What was she doing here, and all alone?

She certainly did not appear to be a well-travelled woman, or a local, that was for sure. She looked like a little child on her first trip to a candy store; any minute she would be looking around for Mummy, realising that she was alone.

She gazed over at him and smiled gently before looking back to the centre stage. *Shit, she caught me staring!* He picked up his beer and took a long gulp. He tried to focus on something else but he was immediately unable to see anything else but her. He stared as she played with her drink coaster like a kitten playing with its ball of string. Playing with one corner then turning it around and playing with the other corner and then back again. No, wait, back to the other corner again. She put it down and took a sip of her beer; the moist drops fell from the bottom of the glass and landed right on her chest. Putting the beer down she started to wipe the drops off her breast. Oh God, don't do that! Did she have any idea what she was doing? She turned and busted him staring at her again, gently smiling and then turning back. She was like a little lost kitten. Sitting there meowing to him, drawing him in.

She was different from any other girl he had ever known. The women he knew were loud, forward, knowing exactly what they wanted and if they had seen him staring at them like that, he would have been slapped with a clootie by now and given a talking down to in a loud and rough fashion. You should never get into a tangle with a Scottish woman, he reminded himself.

The kitten started playing with its toy again, then put it down for another sip of beer. Drops started to fall again. Oh no, don't do that again! She looked down at her breasts brushing them gently. *Oh shit, she had no idea she was seducing every man in the bar.* The waiter had also seen and came rushing over, giving her a new toy to play with, but slipping it under her drink. She smiled up at him and graciously thanked him. *Phew, thank God for that.* He had wanted to do that also but seeing he did not know her, it seemed inappropriate. He needed to do something, he needed to move over close, protect her. Too late; he spotted a man walking towards her, as he had been eyeing her off from across the bar.

"Excuse me, Madam, would you like a cigarette?"

"No, thank you, I do not smoke," she said, looking uncomfortable.

"Can I buy you a drink, then?"

"No, I already have one." Panic was becoming obvious on her face.

"Oh, yes, so you have. I have one also. I will sit here with you while you finish your drink, seeing you are here all alone. I will keep you company."

The Scotsman leaned forward towards them

"She is not alone, she is with me." He said firmly as the man stared at him stunned.

"Oh, excuse me, I did not know."

He turned and scurried off quickly, not looking back. Chloe was rattled, her nerves were kicking in again, her palms were sweating and her heart was pounding. She sat up straight, hoping no one would know how she was churning inside.

"Thank you. He was a bit pushy, wasn't he?" she managed to say as she wriggled in her seat.

"I didn't mean to jump in like that, but some of the European men are so arrogant. I am sorry if I was out of line."

"No, I really appreciated that." She played with her ring and wriggled around again, uncrossing her leg and then crossing the other one.

The illegal street vendors were back, setting themselves up again as the police had left. She spoke English, yet it didn't sound American. He thought he had caught an Australian tone, but what would she be doing here all the way from Australia? He spotted another man itching to be next for a chance. He had no choice, he moved to the chair closest to her but still at his table; the tables were so close that he was almost right beside her.

"You do realise that every man in the courtyard is watching you," warned the Scotsman, still watching the vendors and scanning the courtyard.

She looked around with fright, as she was starting to fidget in her seat, playing with her hair.

"No I had not noticed, why are they staring at me?"

"They are trying to work out if you are single, a very attractive blonde, sitting alone. They all want a chance to pick you up."

"Oh what? No, I had no idea. That had never entered my mind." She scanned the courtyard horrified. "Thank you for saving me. My name is Chloe," she said, still looking around cautiously. She was Australian. He had spotted a little gold kangaroo dangling on her bag.

"Nice to meet you, Chloe. My name is Jack. So are you travelling alone?" he said with interest.

"Well, as it turns out, yes I am, not by choice, but that is a story I don't want to go into right now. I am boarding a boat in the morning for a fourteen-night Mediterranean cruise."

"*Pinnacle of the Seas*?" he said, surprised.

"Yes. You know of it?" She answered, sounding shocked. Her eyes lit up; they were soft, gentle, playful.

"Oh, aye, I am boarding the same one in the morning."

"You are? That's lovely. Are you also travelling alone?"

"Yes, by choice, but not of my own," he smiled as he played with the moisture on the outside of his beer glass with his finger.

She could see he was lost in thought for a moment. What was his story?

They chatted about the ship and the destinations for over an hour. She liked him; he was easy to talk to. He had relaxed her and she was feeling better. His eyes were so beautiful like the soft blue of the ocean on a clear calm day. She shared her food plate with him and explained every item to him just as the waiter had explained it to her. She was pleased to have company, someone to talk with, especially as they had a common interest, the cruise. She spotted a large clock in the centre; it was later than she thought.

"Oh, I can't believe the time, well I had better be off. I have a few things to organise before tomorrow." Chloe sprang to her feet.

"What part of town are you staying in?" asked Jack, starting to feel concerned.

"I am staying near the marina." He watched her fumble as she was organising her bag, double-checking she had everything before dusting herself off, one last time. He wanted to pick the little kitten up and tuck her under his arm and take her home, protect her.

"Me, too. I am heading that way. I can walk with you if you like, it would be safer for you," he added.

"That would be lovely." Chloe was surprised but extremely grateful. He certainly was charming.

They chatted all the way back; he had a lovely nature, she felt a lot safer being with him.

"Well, that's me, just across the park." Chloe pointed at her hotel. "I am sure I will be safe from here."

"Oh, we are close. I am just down the road," said Jack, pointing to a hotel not too far away.

"I can't thank you enough. You have no idea how grateful I am. I will keep an eye out for you on the ship."

"Aye I am sure we will meet again."

She turned and walked across the park. For some reason, Jack felt he needed to keep an eye on her. She could get herself in trouble quite easily, without even realising it.

"Wait, Chloe!" Jack yelled after her. He walked over to her. "Do you like paella?" He asked, hopeful.

"I don't know, I have never had one before," she said cheerfully.

"Well, that's the whole point, neither have I, and I was really hoping to try one, but they are always for two. There is a little restaurant just up the road, and if you don't have any plans, would you share one with me, no strings attached. It's not a date. I just really want to try a paella." Did he just do that? He just asked her out. What was he thinking? She will think he is no better than the men at the bar, all over her.

Chloe laughed. "Sure, I would love to. You don't need to explain yourself to me. I am scared and lonely also." He was grateful she didn't slap him and run inside.

"Oh, glad you understand. I didn't think travelling alone would be so daunting; it's the first time for me."

"What time?"

"Is seven-thirty ok for you? I will walk down here and meet you, if that's ok."

"That sounds amazing. It's a first time for me also. It's not as easy as I thought it was going to be. See you out the front here at seven-thirty."

He can call it what he likes, but she was on a date on her first night out of Australia, she chuckled to herself as she went back to her room. Wait till Kait hears about this. She did a little happy dance as she shut the door behind her. He made his way towards his hotel; he had things to do also. He had to call his mother to say he had arrived; she was the reason he was there, after all. She was determined to make him take that cruise, feeling it was exactly what he needed after all he had been through. His thoughts went back to Chloe—why was he so drawn to her? It was the strangest thing that had ever happened to him. He just asked a girl out and he didn't have to think for days about how to do it. The words just fell out of his mouth and even made sense. But best of all, she said yes. He could not wipe the smile off his face all the way back.

Chloe sent an email to her mum, her sister, and Angie, and then also, one to Bob at the surf club, just letting them all know she arrived safe and sound. She knew everyone would be anxious to hear from her.

She had a shower and put on a pair of jeans and a long-sleeved Aqua button-up cotton shirt. She checked herself in the mirror. Nothing too fancy, just neat and tidy. She checked the time. It was already seven-thirty. Wow, that went quick. She grabbed a cardigan and headed downstairs where Jack was already waiting for her. He loved the way she looked; her shirt made her eyes pop even more. It looked great on her tanned skin and she definitely looked fantastic in jeans.

They walked up the road together and found the little restaurant that he had been telling her about. It was a quieter side of town, with fewer cars, and people, and had a nice quaint feel to it, which she liked. It was a beautiful little traditional Spanish restaurant. The aromas coming out from inside were incredible and they both realised that they were in for a treat. He opened the door for her, and she stepped inside. As they entered, a waiter came rushing over and they were seated at a table that was neatly set for two. The walls were painted in dark red, and the flooring and furniture all dark wood with traditional Spanish paintings hung proudly on the walls. It was a tiny little restaurant but the atmosphere and service were fantastic.

They ordered the seafood paella and thought they should try a sangria being in Spain, after all. The waiter explained the paella would take twenty minutes being made from scratch, but it would be well worth the wait. She checked out Jack sitting opposite her as he was looking around the room. She noticed he had shaven since lunchtime and had left his hair out which was still a bit damp.

The conversation was light, keeping it about the cruise, Barcelona and their journey there, and no one pried into the other's private life. They were, as Jack had put it, just hanging out together to save being lonely. Jack liked his sangria but Chloe didn't feel the same; one sip and she had screwed up her face. Jack chuckled. "You don't need to drink it. Here, let me finish it. I will get you another drink." She ordered a glass of red instead.

He loved watching her. Her facial expressions were beautiful; it instantly bought a smile to his face. She was stunned at the quality of her wine, she was expecting something extremely bad as it was so cheap, but it was a lovely wine. Watching her face he instantly knew she liked it and he smiled. There was no need for words with her; you could read her face like a book.

The paella arrived at the table, and they both leaned in and smelt it and smiled at each other. It was as incredible as they thought that it might be. The aromas of the Spanish spices were delightfully appetising, seafood was loaded on top. "You know, I have read all about paellas and you know if it's a good one if there is a slightly burnt crust on the bottom called a *socarrat*," she said with a cheeky smile. Jack pushed the spatula into the paella to serve and took a peak. He looked at her and smiled. It was perfect. She smiled back at him, closing her eyes, breathing in deeply with delight. He could watch that face all night.

They ate their way through it all, devouring the prawns, mussels, squid, and clams. Sitting back in their chairs smiling, they had done it. The chef came out and checked if everything was ok, and they both agreed it was an amazing paella. Jack unable to resist, finished it off with a Spanish flan. They had a fantastic meal. They thanked the waiter and the chef came out to thank them for coming. It felt so special. Jack slowly walked her back to her hotel.

"Thanks for coming to dinner with me tonight, and for understanding. I am not usually in the habit of inviting girls to dinner after I have only met them for five minutes."

"I am glad that you did. I had a lovely meal and we can now both say we have had paella."

"And a sangria," he added. "But at least you know now that they are not your thing, right?" He laughed, thinking about her screwed-up face and bitter facial expression. He didn't want to say goodbye yet. He was having too much fun. "Hey, have you had a chance to check out these boats yet? Come over here and I will show you. I was looking at them today, some of these are worth an extraordinary amount of money."

They crossed the road and walked by the marina, he explained all about the boats and where they came from, and how much they were approximately worth. Chloe enjoyed his commentary; he seemed to know a lot about boats. She had a few wines and felt relaxed, enjoying the walk with him. They were back out the front of her hotel too quickly.

"Well, this is your hotel. I hope you get a good night's sleep tonight. We both have a big day tomorrow."

"Yes, I am very tired, it is quite late for me," yawned Chloe.

"Ohh, aye, I forgot you came all the way from Australia. I am sorry if I kept you out too late. It's not too bad for me, only a few hours away but I am also feeling weary."

"No, not at all. I had a wonderful time," she said, yawning again.

"So did I. Well, I guess I will head off now, but I will keep an eye out for you on the boat."

"I am sure we will bump into each other somewhere over the next few days. Thanks again, Jack, I had a fantastic night."

"As did I. Goodnight, Chloe."

He turned and walked back down the street to his hotel. He turned back as she was disappearing into the doorway. Why was he feeling so attached to this girl? He had only just met her, but there was something inside that was making him excited to meet her again. In fact, he was busting to meet her again.

The next morning, Chloe woke at three in the morning, jetlag still in her system. She made a coffee and opened the shutters. The city was still alive. There were numerous cars and taxis coming and going. The moon was shining on the water and also the boats, making the whole scene beautiful. A memory she will always carry, she thought. She spotted lots of bikes with little carriages on the back as they peddled along the pathway. Maybe electric, she thought. The people in the carts had blankets over their knees and the bikes were all lit up with pretty lights. How beautiful. Where are they all coming from? She would have to come back to this city one day. It had certainly made an impression on her.

At six in the morning, she went downstairs to a café next door to have some breakfast. The traffic was easing and it appeared the city was finally going to sleep. She was about the only person in the café and found a table by the window. She ordered a coffee with a *jamon* and Manchego cheese croissant. With a choice of plain or Bailey's coffee, she decided seeing she was embarking on a huge journey today, Bailey's might help her relax. The meal also came with freshly squeezed orange juice, which she hadn't had since she was a kid. The croissant was delicious; they had been heated and the cheese had melted. It was the same cheese that she had eaten the day before. It was so creamy; she remembered the waiter told her it was named after the breed of sheep the milk came from. Delicious. She had never had such tasty ham, either. It took her back to a story she had once seen about Spanish ham, the black pig, and the distinct strong flavour that was delightful. All those travel cooking shows she loved to watch at home, she was actually here, doing it. Here she was, in Spain, eating *jamon*, she laughed to herself. All she needed now was Rick Stein to walk in the door and she would be in heaven. A man did walk through the door, but unfortunately, it wasn't Rick. She watched as he walked to the drink fridge and selected his drink and stumbled to the counter. Chloe had a chuckle to herself. He was obviously on his way home.

The sights of the city were changing. All the party-goers had headed home and now she could see markets being set up in the park. After breakfast, she decided to go for a walk. She wandered along the marina looking at all the boats and then turned around the corner. A whole new area was beginning to unfold. More bars, restaurants, cafes; they were closed, probably only just, she thought.

Walking back, the markets were open. A stand that had beautiful hats took her eye. She needed a hat for the cruise. She tried on a few and decided on a wide brim straw hat with a bow. She moved on and bought some tea towels for gifts. Almost at the end was a man selling paella spices. She selected an already mixed spice satchel, ready to go, and he gave her good tips on making paella. She instantly thought of Jack. He was such a nice guy, and great company; she was hoping she would bump into him on the ship. He would be good company for her. Happy with the purchases, she headed back. Time was getting on.

Chapter 4

WELCOME ABOARD

At eleven in the morning, she was waiting patiently outside the hotel for her taxi. The morning was beautiful, with clear blue skies, and not a breath of wind. You couldn't ask for a better day to board a ship. Her stomach was in knots again, but she kept pushing it from her mind. "Happy thoughts," she kept telling herself. The taxi ride to the port of Barcelona was quick. The taxi driver was chatting with her all the way. She was grateful he was keeping her mind active as he explained how the ship was the talk of the town. Everyone wanted to catch a glimpse of the biggest ship on the seas. Being on the local news for days, immediately reminding her again how lucky she was and how she had to push her insecurities aside and enjoy the ride that she was about to encounter.

As she got out of the taxi, she immediately understood why the ship had made the news and was the talk of the town. The driver helped her with her bags and couldn't resist grabbing a few photos himself before leaving. When she saw the ship, the butterflies in her stomach danced. She stood in awe, staring wide eyed at the size. It stood like an elegant lady sitting grandly, looking spectacular, waiting graciously, for her passengers. The sun was lighting her up like a beautiful sparkling diamond. Was she getting on that ship? She had to pinch herself to actually believe it was true. It was the inaugural journey for the *Pinnacle of the Seas*. The newest and biggest of the fleet. She stood fifteen stories high with the capacity of carrying over four thousand passengers and fifteen hundred crew.

How spectacular! Chloe didn't know if it was excitement or fear that she was feeling. It was a daunting experience, to say the least. She may have handled it better, if she wasn't doing this alone. She walked up to check in and was surprised how easy and smooth it all went. She was ushered to a room which resembled a huge café, with tables and chairs everywhere and overhead screens with information on who was boarding. Boarding pass 5 was boarding, she had been allocated 6 so she took a seat and waited. Looking around the room, she saw how everyone was laughing and chatting, all looking excited. At the next table were a husband and wife arguing over what bag some medication may or may not be in. They kept her entertained as she studied them and listened to them blame each other for anything and everything. Bingo, the board changed to 6. Taking deep breaths, she wandered up the ramp with the pass she had been given and across the gang plank and she was in.

"Welcome aboard, Madam. All the rooms are ready so you can go up to your room at any time. However, why not relax a bit and have a drink at the bar?" informed a cheerful crew member. He showed her which way to go to her room when she was ready.

"Thank you," was all that she managed to say.

She had never seen anything like this before. A DJ in a floating box near the grand staircase was playing music. She stared up at four floors of people hanging over railings. A huge cylinder-shaped fish tank with images projecting up stood proudly in the centre of the huge circular bar. She walked over and ordered a beer.

Wow was all she could say to herself. She walked all around, looking at everything. That beer was finished all too quickly. She was aware her anxiety was playing up big time; she needed to calm herself down, one more drink, and then she would take a look around the other areas of the ship.

She sat at a table watching what was happening around her while she finished her drink. The whole place was packed full of happy, cheerful people, lots of different groups; some wore matching t-shirts to promote previous cruises they had obviously been on. Cruising seemed to be extremely popular. She started a self-guided tour of the floating city she had boarded and would call home for the next fourteen days.

She walked the grand staircase, and at the top, the marble walkway was lined with lots of beautiful shops. They were all closed but were due to open later once they set sail. After a quick look around, she decided to head to her room before exploring the outdoor areas. She was almost at level 5 so she continued to use the stairs. She found her room, 5130. *Oh God,* she said to herself as she wiped her sweaty hands on her pants, *here goes nothing.* Slowly, she opened the door. She caught her breath; how beautiful. Tears sprung in her eyes. The bed was extremely welcoming; the bathroom even had a bath. And a coffee pod machine. She can lie in bed in the mornings, and enjoy a coffee watching the views from the huge window. No such thing as a tiny porthole, anymore. Right…what now? She thought a walk out in the fresh air might pick her up, so she took the lift to the pool deck.

The day was stunning, the sun was streaming down, and people were swimming and sun baking. The whiff of chlorine from the pool, along with the strong smell of freshly painted decks and railings filled the air. How could she be feeling so alone with so many people around her? She moved inside to the food area. *Lunch*, she thought, *I forgot all about lunch*. The food was endless. Taco bars, hamburger bars, roasts, salads, sweets, ice creams and on and on. A salad sandwich would do to settle her churning stomach. She had no enthusiasm, no spark. Was she going to feel like this the whole cruise? No, she would not let her anxiety beat her. She would win this time.

She thought about her mother and sisters. If only one of them had come along it would have made things so much easier. She sat and played with her sandwich, looking out of the huge window in the food area. People were still boarding. Most people wore smiles, some obviously stressed, especially the ones with kids in tow.

Lunch was done, half a sandwich eaten, another tick in the box. She strolled towards the other end of the ship. More pools, bars, and restaurants. She liked the fish bar, but she had already eaten, another day. She would have plenty of time over the next couple of weeks to try it all. Two hours till sail away; a nap might help her relax.

She went back to her room. She wanted to go home. She lay on the bed and sunk into the extremely comfortable bedding, she wiped the tears welling up in her eyes again, and then unable to control herself she began to cry, softening her sobs with the pillow. Whenever her anxiety was too much, she always took herself to bed to help. She was a wreck, not wanting to go anywhere; she rolled over and cried herself to sleep.

She woke up to noises in the corridor. Startled, she remembered where she was. She was sure she felt the ship moving. Had she slept through the sail away? The huge moment a ship sets sail on its first voyage, and she had missed the whole party.

She yanked open the curtains. Yep, she sure had. Ocean as far as the eyes could see.

Panic set in. *I am on this massive ship all alone. Oh no, what now,* she thought, *I am trapped, stuck on this boat.* She was wringing her hands and started to sweat. I can't do this. I am so scared. She started on her breathing techniques that usually helped. She sat breathing deeply and staring out the window for what felt like forever. She turned on the television and brought the itinerary up. Tomorrow was a day at sea and Marseille after that. Perfect, she needed to get off the ship there and grab a flight home. She would go down to customer service and buy some Wi-Fi and check flights and send emails back home of the details.

Straight away things seemed better; she had a plan. *Oh, home,* she thought, *I am so homesick I wish I was home right now.* What a silly idea this was. Tears were burning in her eyes again. She grabbed her bag and took the lift. The doors opened and she stepped out as she saw the amount of people lined up for customer service. It went for miles, everyone booking day trips and organising drink packages. She would have to come back later.

She went for a walk and grabbed a drink and sat at a table looking out to the horizon. The sun was setting. How long had she been asleep? What was the time. She found a clock: just after 6. *Wow, I certainly filled in that afternoon,* she thought. She sat quietly, planning her escape. She was envious as kids splashed in the pool, yelling, screaming, having the time of their life. Parents were sitting on the edge of the pool, laughing, chatting, and happily taking family photos. No more stress on their faces anymore. Everyone had settled in and was having a lovely time together. She peered around the other way: people lined up at bars, talking with friends and laughing. *Am I crazy for wanting to disembark?* She thought about the whole thing for a moment. Determined, she made her mind up again. *I am extremely anxious, homesick and very alone and I simply can't do this, I need to go home.* She had tried, given it the best shot she could, but it had bet her, anxiety wins, once again. What was she even thinking? It was way too much of a huge challenge for her. She hated every single minute of the whole trip.

Making up her mind to eat and go back to bed, she thought, *but where can I go for dinner?* No way did she want to sit at the grand dining room and have conversations with other people without bursting into tears. Thinking for a moment she remembered the fish shop. *Yes, that is a plan*, she thought. She would hide in the fish shop for dinner and go back to the room and have an early night. Tomorrow she would have all day to organise her flights home.

The shop was empty. *Perfect*, she thought. She sat at a table by the window.

"We have some lovely specials today. Please take a look on our specials board here and I will come and attend to you in a minute," said the man behind the counter.

"Fish and chips would be fantastic." Her voice matched her mood—flat and uninterested.

"Coming right up." He was a jolly fellow and he appeared to be Italian or French and wore a huge towering chef's hat.

She caught a glimpse of a man walking towards the fish shop. She couldn't believe her eyes— was that Jack. He got closer. Yes, it was Jack. He saw her and came over. "Well, we are both hiding in here tonight, are we?" He laughed. "How are you, Chloe? So nice to meet up with you again," he said, looking down at her with a warm smile.

"I could not face that dining room tonight," she said with a nervous croak in her voice.

Jack sensed something was not right. She was fidgeting and he heard panic in her voice and on her face.

"Are you ok?"

She looked up at him and saw he was concerned.

"No, I am not. I am freaking out. I am so alone." Tears started to stream down her face.

Jack pulled out the seat opposite her and sat down.

"I am sorry, what can I do to help?" he asked sympathetically.

Chloe broke down, telling him everything. She told him about Craig, the whole sad story right from the start until now.

He handed her some serviettes, and she wiped her eyes and blew her nose.

"Well, if you sit here upset like this, he has won," said Jack softly. "You need to pull yourself together and start having some fun."

She played with her bracelet while he stared, waiting for a reply.

"He is not the only issue here. I am leaving the boat at Marseille. I will get a flight home," she said, sounding depressed.

"Leaving? Hey, oh! Ay, ok..." Jack was thinking quick. He knew she wasn't thinking straight. She certainly wasn't the girl he had dinner with the night before. He needed to help her pull herself together again.

"Well, if you're leaving, could you at least hang out with me until you go? I am also alone and a bit lost, and that would help me out a lot."

The waiter arrived with the fish and chips; he had been holding back bringing them over, not sure what was going on.

"Can I grab one of those also?" Jack asked the waiter and he was gone in a flash.

"If you keep your days busy, time will pass quickly. But if you sit in your room and sulk, it will feel like an eternity."

"I am not much company at the moment," whined Chloe.

"Excellent! That makes both of us! Let's both sit here together sad, and eat our fish and chips." The waiter arrived back with Jack's order. He started to spread the tartare sauce over his fish.

She sat looking at him while he ate his meal. Why was he being so helpful and sincere? He seemed like a genuine guy. A very fit, strong guy, she noticed. He had sandy golden hair, shoulder length with a red tinge, tied back in a ponytail. His eyes were blue and always had a sparkle in them. He was so easy to get on with, so easy to talk to. What harm would it do, to have some company? And he was right, the days would be too long on her own. Plus, she knew that he was also lonely.

"This fish is delicious," she finally said, trying to be a bit brighter.

"Oh, aye, I love fish. My father and both me and my brother work on the trawlers so I eat a lot of seafood. I guess I am lucky," he said, happy she was coming around. She nodded, squeezing more lemon on her fish.

"There is a little village next to where I live where all the trawlers fish."

A smile appeared on her face, thinking of Patonga. "Where are you from?" Chloe asked with interest, chewing on a chip.

"I come from a small seaside town near Aberdeen called Fraserburgh. My father has worked the trawlers all his life, well until recently; he died in a boating incident."

"I am so sorry, I am a bloody idiot. Here I am spilling out all my problems, and you have your own. I am sorry. Is that why you are here?"

"Well, in a way, yes. But there's more, lots more, but that's another story. And I am trying to cheer you up here, remember?"

"I feel awfully silly right now. My problems seem so childish and I sound like a spoilt brat."

"You're simply just plain old homesick. Come on, let's get out of here. Let me try to bring some smiles to your face tonight. There is a show on that I wanted to go to. We can hide in the back row together if you like. It would be no fun to go on my own," teased Jack.

Chloe smiled and pushed her plate aside. "Sounds like something we both need."

The show was crowded but they managed to find two seats right at the back as Jack had suggested. "Wait here and save our seats. I will grab us some drinks."

She glanced around the room, realising they were lucky to find a seat. There was a hum in the air from everyone chatting. Jack was gone for ages. She wondered if he had decided she was a sad sack after all, and left. *I would not blame him if he did,* she thought. But then she saw him climbing up the stairs to the back.

"I only realised when I got to the bar I don't know what you drink, but I remembered that you were having a beer at the bar the other day. But the beer on this ship is so pale. I thought I would save you and grab a bottle of wine. Plus it is so crowded in here, I don't have to go back." He grinned cheekily.

He made Chloe laugh. "That is so funny I can't find a decent beer either. Wine is a perfect choice."

He poured her a glass of wine and then himself and carefully placed the bottle on the floor. "Here is to a sensational first night," said Jack. "Cheers!" He raised his glass and she did the same.

The lights went out and the show started. The scene was captivating from the start. The costumes were amazing. It was a Spanish show with dancing and singing and a wonderful story about two young lovers. Chloe took a deep breath and sighed; she was starting to relax. Not sure if it was the wine, the show, or Jack, but something was working. She turned to Jack and smiled then whispered, "Thank you." He gave her a wink and smiled back. There was that sparkle in his eye again. Such a happy-go-lucky guy, what was he doing here all alone? What was his story?

The show was over all too soon. The crowd went wild; the cast all bowed and left the stage. They had finished their wine and they were both chatting about how they enjoyed the show. They waited for the room to empty out and made their way to the door.

"Would you like a night cap before we go up? I could do with a dram of whisky," said Jack. He had been so wonderful to her, how could she not go with him for a night cap?

"Sounds like fun. But since you got the wine earlier, this is my shout ." They walked to the front bar area. It was crowded but they managed to get a table.

"How do you have your whisky?" she asked. "Oh, thanks, straight and a water on the side," he explained. "No problem. I will be back in a minute."

As she got to the bar, she had no idea what whisky to buy. *Oh god,* she thought, *I am buying whisky for a Scotsman, I better get this right.* She ordered herself a red wine to stick to what they have been drinking and ordered a whisky fit for a Scotsman. The barman smiled and said, "I know exactly what you need." He went to the top shelf. "This one will be appreciated."

They sat and chatted for ages. There were no awkward moments. It was as if they had been friends forever. He was telling her some wild stories about fishing and she didn't know whether to believe him or not, but they were funny stories and made her comfortable and laugh. "I have to ask, what whisky was that? What a lovely wee drop." "I am not sure. I got the barman to pick me the best." "Aye, well, he did that. It was lovely, thank you."

"In the morning, I will meet you for breakfast. I will be on the right side somewhere in the food eatery," explained Jack, organising them for the next day. She enjoyed having some sort of a plan. She thanked him.

"Let's say around seven. I am sure you are still getting up super early, with jet lag, and if you happen to sleep in, I will grab a coffee and paper and wait," he suggested. "OK, seven sounds a good time," she agreed. They walked to the lift and got off on their own floors. As she got into bed, she had a smile on her face. What a lovely evening. She was extremely lucky to have made a great friend like him. Sleep came surprisingly easy that night; it had been a long emotional day.

Chapter 5

DAY AT SEA

The next morning, Chloe woke up relaxed and refreshed after a sound night sleep. She went straight to the window and drew back the curtains. The sun came streaming in. It was a beautiful morning. The water seemed magical as the sun danced on it. It was calm, hardly even a ripple. She checked the time: 6:50. She squealed—*how could I sleep in this late?* she had been beating the sun to rise each morning. *Jack,* she thought, *oh god, Jack. I am supposed to meet Jack at seven.* She jumped in the shower quickly, put her hair up into a bun, threw on a sundress and ran out the door. As she reached the food hall, she spotted him. He was exactly where he said he would be, reading a paper.

"I am so sorry to be late, I slept in," she explained.

"Well, good morning, sleeping beauty, I am glad to hear that. It means you are starting to relax a bit," he replied with a smile as he got up and helped her to her seat. He sat back down and leant back to have a long look at her.

"Aye, well, you do appear a wee bit better today. Your eyes are blue, not red and puffy, and your face isn't as screwed up with fear as it had been," informed Jack.

"Well, thank you, I think. But yes, I am a hundred percent better this morning. What are you drinking?" she said, intrigued by the large cocktail-style drink in front of him.

"A bloody Mary. A fantastic way to start the day, sort of kicks you into gear, if you know what I mean. Would you like one?" He asked, eagerly ready to jump up.

"Oh no, a bit early for me," Chloe laughed.

"Well, I was sitting here alone, and started to think you might not show, so I went and got a drink."

She realised that he was already looking around at the food. And she could understand why. The smells coming out of the place were incredible. The aromas of fresh bread and muffins that were being baked, bacon and sausages being cooked, and even the smell of freshly squeezed juices and coffee pots brewing smelt amazing.

"But now that you're here, I will go and grab some breakfast. Are you coming?"

"You go ahead. I will grab some coffee first."

With that, he was off. She sat and glanced around. She wasn't as panicked today, thank God. There was a small number of people around, not too crowded. The food selection was extensive, but she needed a coffee. She found the coffee pot and poured a cup; she set off looking around and spotted a pot of porridge. She grabbed a bowl, added some fruit and yogurt, and headed back to the table. Jack arrived back shortly after with a huge plate of food.

"What a grand selection they have. There is even an omelette bar where they make them from scratch, with whatever you want. I had the two eggs, with the lot, of course." He leaned forward and whispered with a cheeky grin, "Then I topped it with a pile of bacon and chilli sauce." He sat back with a smile very proud of himself. He glared at her bowl.

"And what have you got, porridge?" he cried with disgust. He was still staring at her, unable to believe his eyes.

"Yes, I love porridge, and I am still a bit flat today, my stomach needs something a bit bland," she explained as she put a sugar in her coffee and stirred it.

"Aye, well you succeeded in that. You're on a cruise, lassie, with every food known to man, at your beck and call."

"Yes, it all seems wonderful. Maybe tomorrow." She was sipping her coffee and it appeared she had no intention even starting on her food.

"Well it is my job today to spice your life up a bit. I have a day planned for you that is so action-packed with fun you won't have time to run home," he proudly announced, wiping his mouth with his serviette.

Chloe smiled as she pulled the bowl in front of her and they ate their breakfast. She played with hers a bit, but he was a big eater, she could see that about him.

"I didn't catch you at the sail-out party yesterday. Wasn't it the best fun? That cruise director certainly had the whole place jumping, hadn't he? And when they sounded those horns, absolutely awesome," he said with excitement.

"I didn't make it up there," she said in a quiet voice, looking into her porridge bowl.

"You didn't make it up there? What do you mean you missed the sail-off on the ship's inaugural set sail?" Jack was shocked; he was staring at her like she had two heads.

"I fell asleep," she said quietly with embarrassment.

"You fell asleep," he said stunned. "Ok, am I missing something here. Is this a homesick lassie or is this the usual you, a bit quiet and a bit boring."

"Boring, no," Chloe was on the defence. "I have never been called boring, ever in my life, I am fun loving and popular."

"Aye, well, right now, I don't see any of that in you at all. Wait here."

As Jack walked off, she sat stunned. *My God, he was right.* Here was this guy who she hardly knew, running around, trying to show her a lovely time and all she could do was be a sad sack. She was embarrassed. *He thinks that I am a bore. No one has ever called me a bore before. It is his holiday also, and he is wasting it on trying to make me happy.* There was no way she wanted him to know about her anxiety. *You have to try and pick yourself up for one day, for him at least and then you can organise your flight this afternoon,* she told herself.

Jack arrived back at the table with two bloody Marys in hand. He placed one in front of her. "Trust me, this will brighten up your day. You are on a cruise, remember? You are supposed to be having fun," explained Jack.

"I am so sorry, I have been a stick in the mud. I promise that I will pick myself up and have a nice day. You have been extremely good to me and I owe you that much."

"That you do," he said with a grin. "Grab your drink and let's take a walk out onto the deck. It's a beautiful morning. We have been blessed with a glorious day to explore this ship."

Watching him as he started to tell her funny stories about Scotland, she noticed his rugged good looks and he smelt divine, too. Not too strong, just a hint of scent as you got close. She listened to his story but couldn't quite concentrate; his eyes were stunning, a deep blue that, danced back and forth, as he told his story with passion. Then he would flash her a smile every now and again, which was so sexy and made her melt. He was so full of charisma, and she could have listened to that accent all day. Was she crazy thinking of going home? She was quickly beginning to think that she was. No one ever in her life had gone out of their way for her, as much as he did, and he had only just met her. She felt a strange calmness around him that she also liked; it made her so comfortable and relaxed. She was starting to think she needed to get to know this guy a whole lot more.

"It's so beautiful," she said, looking around; no land was anywhere to be seen. Her stomach had the usual butterflies but she had started to get used to it.

"Aye, it is. Did you bring walking shoes?" asked Jack.

"Yes, I did. I thought I would probably be doing a lot of walking."

"Excellent. Then after our drinks we will go back and change, and then we will go up to the top deck and play some putt-putt golf and hoops and there is a walking and jogging track if we feel up to it," said Jack.

"That sounds like fun. Have you been up to see what it is like?"

"Oh, aye, of course, and the gym. I went before breakfast. I am no sleeping beauty, as you can see." She laughed. No, he was out there enjoying himself.

Soon they were up the top deck playing putt putt and having a lot of fun getting to know each other. Chloe had changed into shorts and a t-shirt and so had Jack for their morning games. She was starting to enjoy his company and wasn't as scared. They took a walk around the track and gazed out over the horizon as they enjoyed the different views from all angles of the ship.

"So, have you worked up an appetite yet?" said Jack, wiping his brow.

"Yes, I am a bit peckish. What would you like to do?"

"Well, I hope you like Asian food, because I booked us in at the Asian restaurant for lunch." Jack smiled. Chloe stopped dead in her tracks and glared at him shocked.

"You did! When did you manage to do that?"

"While they were making the bloody Marys this morning I ran next door and booked us in. If you haven't worked it out by now, I love my food, so I have to exercise every morning." He explained, rubbing his stomach.

Chloe could not stop smiling. *This guy is amazing, he thought of everything.* Craig would never have done anything like this.

"Yes, I love Asian food. That sounds fantastic."

"Then we will meet there in forty minutes. It's near the food hall on the outside. We will have time to freshen up before lunch," explained Jack.

He was waiting for her when she arrived. Happy to see her as usual, smiling. "I am lucky to take such a gorgeous woman to lunch." She blushed and he smiled. He loved making her blush; it was so cute. He was looking fresh, smart, and smelt amazing again, in tailored shorts, and a loose, buttoned-up shirt. It was unbuttoned just enough to make you want to take a peek at the top of the hairs on his chest. He secretly stared at her from the corner of his eye as they walked; she had worn a floral maxi dress with sandals and put her hair up in a loose bun which showed off her slender neck that he thought looked extremely sexy.

"A booking for two for Jack Maclean."

"This way, Sir," said the waitress. They were shown to a window seat and given forms to order their food and a drinks list.

"I think I will have a beer today. I will try a Heineken. Every other beer that I have had has been quite watery," explained Chloe, pulling a face.

"Aye," said Jack, having a chuckle. "It's American beer, it's quite pale. I am also struggling. We like a full-flavoured beer in Scotland. I think I will have a whisky."

They had a choice between beef, chicken, prawn, and other seafood, then a list of all the vegetables and a selection of sauces. Chloe settled for a chicken in oyster sauce, and Jack had a combination satay. The food was delicious and they chatted the whole way through, teasing each other about the morning games session. They enjoyed each other's company immensely not noticing the time, or the fact that the restaurant was starting to close.

"I am so full," she said, sighing and lying back in her chair, hands on her belly.

"Oh, aye, it was tasty food, wasn't it?" Jack asked as he pushed his plate to the side. The waitress eagerly came over and took the plates, obviously wanting to close. They were the last ones in the room.

As they were walking back to the lifts, Jack asked her if she would join him for a swim. He couldn't let her go and sit back in the room, plus the weather was glorious. It wasn't only for her; he was feeling a bit lonely also, and she was fantastic company when she wanted to be. She was so easy to be around. She was pleasant, laid back natural, and extremely beautiful.

He had enjoyed the day with her, and was hoping she had also. The thought of not having her around and doing the cruise on his own was now something he did not want to consider. He was having too much fun with her and she would make a wonderful travel companion.

Chloe put on her swimsuit and sunscreen and threw a short cheese cloth dress over the top. She slipped on her thongs, which were waiting at the door, and she was ready. Stepping out of the lift, she glanced around but could not see Jack. Then she heard him. "Chloe, I am over here," he yelled. "I have found us a beer. Would you like one?" Chloe laughed and nodded, giving him a thumbs up. She walked over to him. "I found Belgian beers. They are the best," he said with excitement. He grabbed the beers from the bar and showed her where he was sitting. He had two sun lounges with a small drinks table in between and a straw sun umbrella. They made themselves comfortable. He was wearing boardie's and no shirt.

He was right, he definitely did work out. She felt embarrassed, but could not help to stare. Lucky, he didn't appear to notice or care that she was staring. He was still telling her all about the Belgian beer he had found and how he had drunk it in a bar in Glasgow once. She took a sip on her beer as he watched intently waiting for her reaction. "Oh, that is a nice beer. Thank you. It has so much body and heaps of flavour."

His eyes lit up. "I knew you would like it. So glad that I found an Aussie girl to hang out with. Not all girls like beer, you know," said Jack with an "I don't understand why not" look on his face, scratching his head.

"Well, you have been hanging out with the wrong girls." She laughed, sipping on her beer and getting herself comfortable on the lounge.

"Aye, I worked that out, but I have found the right one now." He smirked that smile she liked. It instantly made her smile with him.

"In Australia, we drink a lot of beer in the day as it's hot, but we usually only drink light or mid-strength, which is nowhere to be found here. And our beer is so full bodied with flavour also, like this one. It is a nice beer." Chloe started to read the label on the bottle. "Eight percent!" She almost spat her beer out. Thank God she spotted that. *You will need to steady this up,* Chloe she said to herself.

"A swim would do us both good," Chloe said as she took off her cheesecloth dress. She was already up and walking straight to the pool. It was Jack's turn to try and not to stare, but he couldn't stop; she certainly had a beautifully tanned, gorgeous figure. Speechless, he jumped in after her. They stayed in the pool for a while, meeting a couple from America, they got along with them well, and so they hung around and chatted with them for a while.

It was getting late in the afternoon. They walked to the bar and grabbed another beer as they strolled along the deck. Startled, she stopped and turned to Jack. "I forgot to organise my flight home," she panicked. "I was hoping that you might have considered changing your mind about that." He looked hopeful. Chloe stopped and turned to the railing, leaning on it, looking out to sea. He watched her. It was amazing. It was almost like he could see her mind working. She lingered for a while and decided that she needed to tell him it wasn't him but her anxiety that was making her run away.

"It's not you, Jack. I enjoy being around you, but I have a problem. I suffer from anxiety and coming over here on this trip has made it peak and I don't know if I can cope. I am sorry." There, it was out, he had just joined a small group of people who actually knew. She never told anyone, she just hid it and hoped no one would notice. She stared back out to sea.

He knew that had taken a lot for her to tell him, He turned to her. "Oh, I am so sorry to hear that. Thanks for telling me." It explained a lot. He had noticed a few things over the last couple of days that had not seemed right. He was thinking quickly; he could not let her go home. He had to convince her to stay. "Well, you seemed to have fun today, so maybe if we take each day as it comes we could make it work. And if it gets too much for you then I will help you organise your trip home." He could see she was thinking hard about it all. "I promise that I will look after you and understand your anxieties, and I will 'never' let you be sad or scared ever again. It will be my job to be there for anything you need, because if you go home, I am the one that will be lonely." He made a sad face. *Wow, is this guy for real?* She just told him that she had mental health issues and he didn't run. In fact, he had embraced it and offered to help her with it. She liked him and didn't want to leave but she didn't know if she could handle it. He was right; she did have a wonderful day with him and baby steps might work. She wanted to get to know him more.

"Travel buddy, hey, mmm. We hardly know each other and we don't even know what sort of travel each of us is expecting." She swept a hair out of her mouth that the breeze had blown in.

"Ok, let's talk this out, then," said Jack. "What big ticket items do you want to see?"

"Well, that's just it, I don't really want to see anything, and I certainly don't want to have to line up and waste hours of my day to get into somewhere. I am more than happy to wander around and see the cities and enjoy their culture. So you might be wasting your time on me. My anxiety will hold me back from doing lots of things." She flicked the hair from her face again.

"So far that sounds perfect to me, I am not into visiting millions of churches or wasting time queuing up, either," agreed Jack.

"I like watching the scenery, and the people, and different foods and drink."

"Aye, a match made in heaven, we are. Perfect, you see, for me, it's all about the food." He flashed that cheeky grin that made her feel all gooey.

Chloe laughed. "Well, I have already worked that one out."

"Aye, we are already starting to know each other. We will make excellent travel buddies."

She studied him as he was standing, watching her, waiting for an answer. He looked so helpless, lost, with a look of sadness in his beautiful blue eyes that she was starting to love looking into.

"You would do anything to make me stay, wouldn't you?" Chloe smiled gently at him.

"Aye, of course. You would have to agree we had a perfect day and a fantastic night together. Plus, we get on *soo* well. Imagine how much fun another couple of weeks would be. All that I am asking for is two weeks of your time hanging out with me. After that, you're on your own. What do you say about that?" He asked hoping that he had sold it to her.

Chloe already knew the answer. She had enjoyed the day with him a great deal and was starting to like him a lot.

"Ok, you win. I cannot think of a single reason why we shouldn't be travel mates," she said with a huge grin.

As he leaned down, he kissed her on top of her head. "I won't let you down, I promise," said Jack sincerely.

Those words rung in her ears. "I won't let you down," but this time she honestly believed the person who was saying them, and she had only known him a few short days, not half her life like Craig, and the funny thing was, she believed him. They started walking again back to the sun lounges.

"We have Marseille tomorrow. Did you have any plans?" she asked all of a sudden, excited.

"The only plan that I had was to find the best Bouillabaisse for lunch. Other than that, the day is yours," he announced, throwing his hands out in the air.

"You are easy pleased. As long as your belly is full, you are happy," she teased.

"You got it. Bouillabaisse was created in Marseille, so it's something I would love to do. It is on my culinary bucket list," he explained, proudly sucking on his beer.

"Mine, too. Well, let's just wing it and see how the day unfolds," she said, feeling comfortable again. "Any day in Marseille is a good day, I would think."

"Sounds like a perfect plan to me," smiled Jack.

"Now that I have my travel buddy well and truly onboard, and you are not going to run away from me, let's go freshen up," suggested Jack.

They both went back to their rooms to freshen up for pre-dinner drinks, feeling very happy and content after a glorious day together. She spotted her suitcase still sitting lonely, near the door. Time to unpack. She was staying and starting to feel more and more comfortable about the whole idea every minute. She started to think about her wardrobe. What did she pack? When she was packing at home she was packing for a holiday with boring Craig. Now she was with a very interesting Jack. And he was making her come alive again.

She pulled out her dresses and hung them up. Not too bad. She had the lovely formal dress to wear on elegance night, which she had worn as a bridesmaid at a friend's wedding, loose flowing shirts, shorts, skirts…yea, not too bad, could do better. But good enough, she thought. She hung them all up. Well, that was another plus for travelling alone looking at all this wardrobe space—I have this all to myself. She pulled out her flannelette pyjamas. My God did she bring them along, and the cotton sleep dress. Next was the underwear. She stared at them and gasped. *Did I really pack those?* One by one she pulled out items that had obviously gone way past their expiry date and she laughed. No wonder her relationship with Craig was dead. When was the last time she had bought new underwear? When was the last time that she even cared what her underwear was like? They were going to Marseille tomorrow, France, lingerie capital of the world. She decided to go shopping and treat herself; she would re-stock her whole underwear drawer.

A new Chloe was starting to come alive. A Chloe she had never known existed before. A Chloe she was suddenly starting to want to get to know a whole lot more.

They met back upstairs on the deck. It was full of beautiful cane outdoor tables and chairs with umbrellas. The sun was starting to get low and the ocean was calmly reflecting the colours of the sunset. Jack arrived back with two orange cocktails.

"What is this?" smiled Chloe, looking intrigued.

"Not sure, but it looks like sunset drinks, don't you think? It's called Aperol spritz," he explained. "The waiter said it was a popular Italian drink."

She slurped on her straw. "Thank you. Oh yum! So light and refreshing. You are an amazing travel buddy." She laughed.

"Stay with me, lassie, and I will lead you astray. But you will be looked after every step of the way the way." He winked.

She gazed at him, smiling, sipping on her cocktail, cocking her head to one side watching him in the sunset; he was looking pretty good to her. "How are you still single? You have swept me off my feet all day. Do you treat all the girls like this?"

He turned to her with a cheeky grin. "Only the ones that make an impression on me." He winked. She could feel herself blushing. He smirked; he loved it when she did that.

"No, I am only joking. In fact, there is no woman in my life. Well, not now, I am recently separated."

"Oh, I am sorry, I didn't mean to pry." She was quietly extremely happy to hear that news.

"No, don't be. It is the best thing that could have happened to me. We had not been romantic in a very long time. I knew the day would come when she would ask me to sit and talk. And she did a few months ago."

"Where is she is now? I mean, was she a local girl?"

"Aye, she was local alright and right about now, I would say that she is probably having dinner with my brother and going over the books of our family business," he said bluntly.

"Wait, what do you mean, with your brother?" She sounded confused.

"Aye, well let me tell you the whole story. I told you my father died about 6 months ago." Chloe nodded, looking interested, waiting intently to hear the story. She wriggled in her chair making herself comfortable.

"Well, Jimmy, my brother, started taking over the business. He was always the straight one, the one who never had any fun, just work, work, work. Me, I was exactly the opposite. I was always the one who didn't care too much about anything, except having a good time, of course. Mary was the same as him; she spent more time with Jimmy, trying to do the books than she spent with me. I didn't really care, to be honest. We had started to drift apart a long time back but neither of us did anything about it. I must admit I did wonder, quite a few times, about the pair of them, and I am sure lots of people did, as I look back now, anyway. One day not long after Dad died she sat me down and said it was over.

Everyone watched as she and Jimmy started a relationship and must have thought, poor me. Dad had left a chunk of money to each of us kids, which Mum had put away. And when Mum found the advert for this cruise, she said it was the best thing for me. I tried to tell her I was OK with it all, but she kept insisting. So I finally gave in and used Dad's money to purchase a ticket.

Dad had always wanted to travel; he was travelling when he met Mum. He had dreams of taking boats and touring the seas, but he got a job working on my grandfather's trawlers over herring season for cash. It was terrific money. It was just Mum and her father that lived there. Her mother had passed away years before. Her dad spent more hours at sea than at home, and she was always cared for by the fisherman families in the neighbourhood.

Well, he fell in love with Mum, and the rest was history. He gave up his dreams of travel for the love of his life. They lived in a tiny fisherman's cottage in Broadsea, where all the fishermen lived. The women and children were in and out of each other's homes and the men were hardly there. Well, he married her, and they had us kids, so they moved to a bigger cottage in Fraserburgh, which is not that far away, and where we all grew up and still live today.

He would always say that one day, I would be the one to travel. He had passion in his eyes when he spoke of it. Sometimes I am not sure if Mum was pushing me to travel for myself or for Dad. Anyway, I gave in, I could not stand looking at Mum's sad eyes anymore, so a few weeks ago I went and booked myself a cabin and here I am." Jack looked up at her. "Now you know the whole story."

Chloe sat there shocked. "Wow, that's one hell of a story. So you did it all for your Mum."

"Aye, of course. She is a lovely lady, and I didn't like to see her sad. But I must admit I was a wee bit scared getting on that massive ship all alone." He smiled with a smirk and raised eyebrows.

There was that grin again. She felt a heart string tugged. She knew he was a nice guy, but she didn't know he had been through so much, and still, he was there, trying to make her happy.

He was incredible.

"I was scared also. No wonder we both ended up in the little fish shop." She laughed.

"I was extremely happy to see you there. I knew you were going through the same, but I didn't realise you were 'that' scared," he said with a shocked look on his face.

"Yea, I was freaking out," she admitted. "I have never been away from home, plus it was halfway around the world, and one hell of a gigantic ship. It made my anxiety peak out of control. I feel a lot better now, thanks to you." She played with her bangle staring at him.

"I feel a lot better also. We needed each other," he said honestly. He was a guy and had to be brave, but he was the first to admit it wouldn't have been too much fun if Chloe had run home.

"Yes, we did. I get what you mean about growing apart and not noticing. That was exactly where I was with Craig, but I did not notice. He had just become a habit and I was comfortable with it."

"Aye, I know all about that," he said understandingly.

"But you have to continue watching them together every day, and she will always be there. How can you handle that?"

"Aye, but that's what my mother does not understand. I have no problem with that. They are meant for each other, a whole lot more than we ever were. I may not choose to socialise with them, or choose to have anything to do with them, but it doesn't worry me."

"Then I am glad you bought that ticket, Jack. We are going to have a blast, and we need each other. To great mates!" She raised her glass and he followed.

The sunset was spectacular; there was something special about a sunset over water. They were both mesmerised by it. Chloe was taking it all in; the story that jack told her was amazing, and she had so much respect for him now. She looked over at him. He had been sitting there quietly, lost in his own thoughts, staring out to sea. Then all of a sudden, he turned to her. "Do you like steak?"

Chloe laughed; he was thinking about his stomach again.

"Yea, I do. Why? What do you have you in mind?" She knew he would have something up his sleeve.

"I heard about a steak house I have wanted to try. Are you hungry for a steak now?" He turned to her, hopeful.

"Hell, yea. I am starving after all that swimming." she laughed.

"Let me take you to dinner, Mademoiselle." He held out his hand for her and helped her up.

It had the best atmosphere; a duet was playing country-style music and the décor set the scene. Seats at the bar were saddles and the booths were leather and wood with lots of cowboy accessories hanging around the room. They grabbed a booth and studied the menu. It had the best cuts of meat from around the world, most aged for twenty-eight days.

"There is an Australian wagyu on here, Chloe. I would normally go the big cowboy steak but tonight due to present company, I will try her homeland steak," he said proudly.

"Well, I am sure you will be impressed. We have great meat in Australia," she said as she smirked proudly. "My favourite cut of meat is eye fillet so I will try the USA eye fillet," she said softly as she was still scanning the menu.

Jack got the waitress's attention and she came over straight away. He ordered the steaks along with side dishes of onion rings, scalloped potatoes, sautéed mushrooms, corn on the cob and two beers. Chloe stared horrified. "There are only two of us here, remember, Jack?"

"If you are going to hang out with me, I should let you know in advance, I get carried away when I order sometimes. I can't help it. I just want everything on the menu. That's why I need to go to the gym every morning." He smiled at her cocking his head to the side.

The waitress returned with the drinks.

"What time do you think we should set off tomorrow?" asked Chloe as she sipped on her beer.

"Let's just make it a slow day. Taxis will be waiting to take us into town all day so we don't need to rush."

"The next two mornings are going to be very early starts and very long days," said Chloe with a sigh.

"How about we meet for breakfast at around seven thirty and have a lazy morning?" he suggested. He certainly did not want to stress her out on their first day out and about. "The town of Marseille is only a five-minute drive from the port."

She nodded. "I need to find a café or bar somewhere that has WIFI, so I can send off a couple of quick emails. Just to let the family know that I am ok. My mum will be worried about me travelling alone."

"Of course, I totally understand. I also have some emails to send," he added.

"I would love to do some shopping also, but only a small amount and will not keep you waiting long, I promise." She was not like other girls; she wasn't a shopaholic, that's probably why her underwear was in such bad shape, she reminded herself. It was usually out of necessity and just at K Mart.

"So tell me about you. What's your story?" he asked, sitting back, resting his arm across the back of the booth. She didn't have a grand story like he did, but she told him the story as he listened intently. "I have two sisters. I am the middle child. My older sister Kait is thirty-two and is married to Johnny Fontana, and they have a little girl, Sophia, who is two years old. Johnny is Italian and they run the restaurant-bar on the beach called Seasalt. It is a casual beach shack serving sea-food, pizzas, and pastas. It had a very good reputation and is always packed.

Chrissie is my younger sister. She is twenty-six and a hair-dresser at a local salon. She has a boyfriend called Finn, who has been around about six months. He works with Johnny at the restaurant. She is always out and about with friends, but does a lot of babysitting in the evenings for Kait, so she can do the dinner shifts at the restaurant.

My mum and dad are Robert and Olivia, they also live local. Mum is fanatical about growing her own food, so the backyard is full of veggie patches and fruit trees. What she can't grow, she buys locally. Dad works as a council worker, working in the local parks mowing lawns, and keeping them tidy. He has a great job, it is easy and something that he loves doing, and he is always home at night for the family, which is important. He loves working in the garden on the weekends with Mum. It's a pretty simple life, really."

"We are pretty simple folk. I am a middle child also. I have a younger sister who still lives with Mum, and works at a local fashion shop, which she loves as she gets all the clothes at a reduced price. And you know all about my brother already," explained Jack as Chloe nodded.

The loads of food arrived at the table. "Hope you're hungry," he announced with a grin as he put on his bib.

Chloe sat looking stunned; so much food, they were never going to eat all that. They chatted all through dinner and then unable to eat another mouthful, they sat back in their seats and laughed. "We did it," he said, quite happy with himself, like it was a huge accomplishment.

"You did most of it," cried Chloe, scared she might explode; she usually did not eat anywhere near that amount.

"You two look like you have devoured a feast." It was the Americans they had met at the pool.

"Aye, and now we canna move," explained Jack proudly.

"It was very good food," explained Chloe, a bit embarrassed. "Please sit with us have a drink. I don't think we introduced ourselves properly at the pool. I am Chloe and this is Jack."

The waitress came over and took drink orders.

"I am Rocco and this is my wife, Danni. We are on our honeymoon."

They went on to tell them all about their wedding. As they talked, Chloe studied them. Rocco had tanned skin, brown hair, and brown eyes. Danni had a blonde bob and green eyes. Both looked well dressed and very slim. They were obviously very careful with what they ate. What must they have thought about their table of empty plates they walked into?

"What are your plans for Marseille?" asked Danni casually.

"Not much. We are just taking it as it comes and find a nice spot for lunch," explained Jack.

"For me, it's all about the food," he winked at Chloe.

"Well, for me, it's all about champagne," she laughed. "We are off on a day tour to Monaco. I wanted to go to the champagne region, but it's too far, apparently. I just love champagne," said Danni with pure excitement on her face.

"She wanted to drag me across the whole of France so she could have a champagne, can you believe that?" said Rocco and they all laughed.

The scene in the restaurant was changing; it was starting to become a bar and the music was getting louder. People were starting to dance. They all chatted for a while and then Jack managed to drag Chloe out onto the dance floor. They all let their hair down and had quite a few drinks. Their new friends Rocco and Danni were great company.

After a while they all agreed to call it a night, and headed back to their rooms. "I am walking you to your door tonight, Chloe," announced Jack with a slight slur.

"I will be ok. I am only one floor under you."

"Then there is no reason why I shouldn't, then." He wanted to make sure that she felt safe.

They got out of the lift and she showed him the way. "See, we are here already."

"Then now I am happy I have seen my beautiful new friend home. I had a great night with you tonight, Chloe, and I can't wait for tomorrow." He gave her a wink, blew her a kiss, and was off.

Chloe lay awake in bed, thinking of the night and how great her new friends were, and Jack. Well, she had to admit he was definitely starting to sweep her off her feet.

Chapter 6
MARSEILLE

The next morning, he was waiting for her at seven-thirty, as promised. Wanting to do something special for him, she went to the bar and ordered two bloody Marys. He spotted her walking in, and a huge smile appeared on his face and stood up to greet her.

"So you are as smart, as you are beautiful. Good morning," welcomed Jack.

"I am so excited about today. Can you believe we are in France?" said Chloe, bursting with excitement.

Jack was happy to see her smiling. "Aye, you do have a little spring in your step and a little sparkle in your eye today."

He was starving after all the dancing and too many beers the night before. She saw him eyeing the food.

"But first, breakfast." He went and filled his plate as usual and even Chloe came back with real food, as Jack called it. They were so comfortable with each other. It was as if they had known each other for ages. Her anxiety had subsided, and she was excited about the day.

"Danni gave me directions to a restaurant last night, and it is supposed to serve the best bouillabaisse in Marseille," said Chloe as she started to cut into her omelette.

"Aye, then lunch is sorted. How did you sleep after all your dancing?"

"I had the best night, thank you. You really are fantastic company and not a bad dancer, either." She winked at him teasingly.

"Glad I made an impression on ya. They don't call me a mad Scott for nothing, you know," laughed Jack as he shovelled a huge piece of bacon in his mouth. "So how about we meet back in the foyer in half-hour?" Jack wiped his mouth and pushed his plate aside.

"Sounds great. I am almost finished here."

"Don't rush. Sit, relax, enjoy your coffee." He put the sugar bowl in front of her and sat back, finishing off his bloody mary. "Unless, of course, you are one of those girls who take ages to get ready," he teased.

Finished stirring her coffee, she stared at him, pointing the spoon, ready to snap at him when he threw his hands in the air, laughing. "It's a joke! It's a joke."

Determined not to take long, Chloe quickly changed into camel linen shorts with a matching vest and white t-shirt and sneakers. One last check in the mirror and she was set to go. As she arrived in the foyer, she spotted him straight away. He looked amazing as usual in jeans and a blue buttoned-up shirt and sandshoes, his hair tied back.

"You're beautiful as always, my princess."

How does he manage to make me feel that I am the most beautiful girl in the world every single day. She was not used to anything like that, but she was starting to like it.

They were down the gangplank and outside in no time. Another glorious day; the sun was shining and the breeze was gentle. Dozens of taxis all lined up, waiting patiently for passengers to arrive. They grabbed one and headed for the city, and the driver chatted to them all the way, eagerly giving them as much information as he could about his city. He was definitely passionate about it, which was lovely, and they appreciated it and thanked him. He gave them a card and said, "Call me and I will pick you up when you finish."

The Old Port of Marseille was alive with hundreds of boats as far as the eye could see. Old buildings six or seven stories high, all very French styling, painted in cream and pastel colours lined the courtyard as they stared out over the port.

People everywhere, happily strolling along, enjoying the day or sitting around eating ice creams and drinking coffees. The weather was glorious with plenty of sunshine and not a cloud in the sky. The south of France was showing off in all its glory.

Chloe pulled off her sunhat and did a twirl. "I am in France!"

He watched her as he smiled. She looked beautiful today; he could not take his eyes off her.

"I am so excited! I feel like a champagne bottle that has just been popped."

"You know, growing up, it's every girl's fantasy to see France, well especially Paris, but Marseille will do for me any day," she said as she was looking around excitedly.

"I thought it was every girl's dream to have a wedding day."

"No, not for me. My fantasy was always travelling, but I never really thought that I would get here; I only ever thought it would be a dream." She spotted the fish markets. "Jack, over there, fish markets, you would love this." She grabbed Jack's arm and almost ran to the fish markets.

She was not the same girl he met days earlier, that's for sure. Maybe he shouldn't let her have those bloody marys in the mornings, he laughed to himself.

The fish markets were amazing. Lots of tables all set up, along the banks of the water, boats were arriving and bringing bucketloads of fish, spilling them onto the tables. The fish were so fresh, they were still flapping around on the tables as the fishermen threw fresh seawater onto them. Shoppers would flock to every newly arrived fisherman, making their selection of the flapping fish.

They saw lots of different fish, ones that Chloe had never seen before. Jack gave her a rundown on what fish was what, and the best way to cook them. Chloe was already thinking of recipes in her head for home. She loved cooking and bringing new recipe ideas to the café and to Johnny and Kait's restaurant.

They wandered the streets for hours, looking in the shops and grabbing some souvenirs for home. They came across a bistro, with small tables and wicker cane chairs set out onto the street. They decided that it was a lovely spot to sit and do their emails, as they had spotted a "free Wi-Fi" sign.

Jack went inside and came out with coffees and two little pastries.

"They look delicious," said Chloe, closely examining them.

"You should take a peek inside. There were so many to choose from. I wanted to try them all, but I knew we were going for lunch so I controlled myself." He smiled, quite pleased with himself.

"Well, I am very impressed with your willpower," she smiled.

They were two, very French, beautiful little pastries, filled with custard and dusted with icing sugar and almonds. The pastry itself was extremely light and fluffy. Both were nodding with a smile, as they bit into them. They tasted just as scrummy as they thought they would.

Content with their pastries finished, they started on their emails. Chloe wrote a letter to Kait and her mum, saying she had met someone who was also travelling alone. She had so much to tell them, but kept it short and simple; she was having an amazing time and was safe. That's all they needed to know right now. She attached some photos and pressed send. That should keep them happy for a while she thought.

The city was putting on a spectacular show for them as they strolled along with adoration. Both sides of the street had gorgeous old buildings. They were all so old, and the beautiful mouldings and wrought iron were truly a work of art. Totally incredible.

"Fountains, statues everywhere. Oh, I just love this city," said Chloe dreamily.

Jack smiled and agreed; even he was enjoying every minute. But in his eyes, it was because of the girl standing beside him. Never would he have wandered streets looking at old buildings, and actually be enjoying himself doing it. He imagined what the boys at the pub would have said if they saw him, especially his best friend Patrick. He had a chuckle to himself, picturing him laughing at him.

"Jack, that's the restaurant Danni was telling me about." Chloe was pointing to a little restaurant across the road. "She said a colleague of hers told her to go, but they were doing a tour." It was a pretty little restaurant, with a large covered veranda that overlooked the port.

"Well, it's lunchtime. Let's check if there is a free table."

They walked over and waited for the waitress.

"Bonjour, une table pour deux, oui," said the waitress.

"Je suis à un rendez-vous avec une belle fille que j'essayais de faire impressionner et s'ils pouvaient m'aider avec une bonne table, ce serait apprécié," said Jack in perfect French.

"Bien sur monsieur."

She showed them to their table. Chloe noticed it was clearly the best table in the restaurant. Right on the waterfront with undisturbed views and tucked in a quiet corner.

"You speak French, Jack. You never cease to amaze me."

"Oh, aye, I know a wee bit. We deal a lot with the French with the shellfish trade. They are frequent customers of ours," explained Jack.

"You managed to get us an extremely lovely table. What did you say?" asked Chloe, impressed.

"I simply said, I was on a date with a beautiful lady that I was trying to impress and if they could help me it would be appreciated," he explained with a little smirk. "They are very romantic, the French, you know."

Chloe blushed and he smiled. Ohh, there was that charm and cheekiness coming out in him again. She was hoping that he meant those words and wanted to impress her. She felt like that princess again. He was waking her up inside, and she liked it very much.

"Now, what are we going to drink today?" asked Jack as he studied the menu. "Let's take a wee look here…what do you say we start with a beer? French beer is very tasty, I have been told."

"Yes, French beer. I have also heard it is tasty."

"Now, food," they both opened the menu.

"Oh, no, it is in French," whispered Chloe, panic settling in.

"Aye, lucky you have me, then." He smirked. She instantly felt calm.

"Is there anything you don't like?" he asked.

"No, I pretty much eat everything."

"Ok, then let's grab a sample plate for entrée with calamari, mussels, oysters, prawns, and snails. I will save you from the frog's legs," he cheekily smiled over the top of the menu. She smiled back.

"And you simply canna come to Marseille and not try a bouillabaisse. So of course, a bouillabaisse for a main."

"All my favourite things. Well, except snails, but I am willing to give them a try. Sounds delicious," said Chloe excitedly.

The waiter arrived and Jack ordered in French. He turned to Chloe. "Y a-t-il autre chose que vous aimeriez, Madam," the waiter asked Chloe.

"No merci, elle parle anglaise," answered Jack.

"I am sorry, Mademoiselle, I did not know you only speak English. May I ask, where are you from?"

"I am from Australia."

"Oh, so far from home. Is this your first time in France?"

"Yes, first time anywhere. I have never been out of Australia before."

"Welcome then. I hope you enjoy your lunch here with us today," he smiled. "I will do my best to make sure you are well looked after."

"Thank you. I am sure I will enjoy every mouthful," she said cheerfully. He was back in no time with the beer.

"Well, here it is. Cheers to our first drink in France," said Chloe.

"Aye, one of many, I am sure" smiled Jack.

They drank beer, peeled prawns, and laughed in the sunshine. Chloe even loved the snails, much to her surprise. The chef then arrived personally with the soup. He set the bowls down and started to tie a bib around Chloe's neck.

"Welcome to Marseille. I hear you are from Australia, and you chose my kitchen to dine at."

"Yes, I am, thank you."

"It is with pleasure that I will introduce you to my soup. You have never had it before, no?"

Chloe nodded. "No, never."

"Ah, well, it is my pleasure to show you how to eat it. You see you have these croutons, and this beautiful rue. The trick is to take a spoon of soup. Here, let me show you," he put the biggest spoon Chloe had ever seen into her soup. "You get your croutons and dip them in the beautiful rue and put it on top of your spoon. Now you will get all the flavours together. Open wide." He shoved the huge spoon into Chloe's mouth. It all started to run out the sides as she took the spoon off him. Her mouth was so full of hot soup; she tried to chew it all down.

"Ah, see, perfect. You get a bit of flavour with every mouthful."

Chloe was stunned; she grabbed the napkin and quickly wiped her mouth, almost choking.

"I am so sorry. I only wanted to teach you how to eat my soup. You have a very tiny mouth, Mademoiselle."

The chef disappeared quickly back to the kitchen.

"Fair dinkum, does everyone around here think we don't know how to eat in Australia," whispered Chloe. Jack was rolling around in his chair with laughter. It was the funniest thing he had seen in a long time. Lucky Chloe was a good sport and started laughing along with him. The whole restaurant was looking but neither of them cared.

"So Jack, how does this compare with your mum's fish stew?" asked Chloe, happily slurping on her soup.

"'Oh, I think it's a wee bit better, but maybe the company and the location are what is making it so much better." He winked and smiled at her. She stared back at him, smiling.

Lunch was over way too soon. Chloe was on the lookout to do some shopping. She spun around and spotted a department store. That would do. It should have everything she needed. "I need to do some shopping, if that is ok. I won't be long. I will find you a watering hole close by to wait."

"A what? Where am I going? I am happy to oblige but I have no idea what you want me to do," he asked confused.

"A watering hole you know somewhere to sit and have a drink."

"Oh, aye, I forgot I was with an Aussie girl. You have some very excellent ideas for a girl, you know," she laughed and started to look around.

"Over here," he said, pointing to a bistro on the corner. People were sitting, having drinks and coffee.

She sat and had a beer with him before she left. They chatted as they watched the comings and goings. "Well, I will be off." She drained the last of her drink and stood up to leave.

"Take your time and enjoy your shopping. I will be totally happy here waiting for you," he said as he waved her off. They had the afternoon to do whatever they pleased and if shopping was her thing, that was fine by him. Besides how often did you get to sit in a bistro in France and have a beer.

She walked over to the department store and glanced around. It was huge. Her anxiety started to kick in, her palms were sweaty, and her chest was pounding. She was determined; she was not going to let this thing beat her. She had wanted to have this shopping experience, and it was an important step for her. She never did anything like this at home. The major shopping centre was a half-hour drive and she never went. She stayed local and only ever visited the K Mart store, so this was very exciting for her.

She took deep breaths and went inside. The lingerie section was easily found on the second floor. It was amazing; she had never seen such beautiful items. All laden with such beautiful French lace, and extremely sexy. She peered down at the price tags; so cheap, she couldn't believe the price. She was suddenly like a mad woman at the Boxing Day sales. She was grabbing bras with matching panties, cute little nighties and cami sets. She was having so much fun and surprised how well she was handling the whole experience. Looking around she was mesmerised. Her arms were overflowing and a saleswoman came over and helped her, handing her a basket. She knew she was buying too much, but didn't care. She selected a couple of tasteful but elegant nighties, one each for Angie and Kait and one or two for her also. Chrissie was a bit young for a French nightie, so she would buy her a lovely perfume instead.

Next was a visit to the beauty counter. Looking just as impressive, she walked over with stars in her eyes. All the French perfumes and lotions were sitting neatly on the shelves; she selected a few from the brands that she had only ever fantasised about. Vichy, La Roche-Posay both beautiful skincare lines, both using thermal spring water, she noticed. The lady at the counter spoke a little bit of English so she helped her. She explained La Roche-Posay used water that was filtered from the small town of the same name. Well, no wonder they are so nourishing for the skin, she thought. Eau Thermal Avene spring water spray, Embryollise, Nuxe, Skinceuticals and L'occitane. She finally selected some to take home as gifts and bought herself some as well.

The sales lady suggested beautiful Nuxe oil that was for body or hair and smelt divine. Why not? She thought. Her mind went straight to Jack sitting patiently waiting for her while she shopped; she decided his mum and sister would enjoy a treat also. She chose a lovely cream for each of them. The lady also showed her a cream that was extremely popular, used for chapped lips and dry winter-ravaged skin, Homeoplasmine. Perfect. She grabbed a few tubes for Jack; she knew it would come in handy for him working on the trawlers. Her arms were loaded up; she went to the cashier and paid.

Walking back, she saw Jack happily sitting, waiting for her, reading a newspaper. "Sorry I took so long, I have never had so much fun."

"You weren't long at all. And I enjoyed myself sitting here. Plus I caught up a little on the local news." He waved the newspaper. "I have never enjoyed a girl going shopping so much before. I am really enjoying your Aussie ways." He was giving her that cheeky grin again, and she blushed. He smiled. *I did it again*, he thought. *God, I feel like a school girl with a high school crush*, she thought and quickly defused the moment. "I bought your mum and sister a treat. I know any girl loves a French lotion and thought they would like one also."

He was staring at her, unable to believe what he was hearing; she had bought his family presents.

"Oh and I bought this cream for you. Awesome for wind-chapped skin. I thought it would come in handy for you on the trawlers."

He sat speechless for a moment. He was so impressed; she had blown him away. "I am speechless, thank you. You did not have to do that. Thank you." He leaned over and kissed her on the cheek. It was the most thoughtful thing anyone had ever done for him. She just smiled, but the kiss had made her turn as red as a beetroot.

"Right, well, let's have a beer to help you unwind after your shopping ordeal." He went to the bar and bought them a 1664 beer, while she composed herself again. By the time he came back, she had calmed and started to tell him all about the store, but never mentioned the lingerie section, of course. He told her all about the things he had seen as he sat and waited. They laughed about the lunch and the chef. "He had a wee crush on you," he teased.

"What? No, he didn't," she replied, embarrassed.

"Of course, he did. He couldn't stop fussing over you all day. Did you notice him at any of the other tables?" he asked, raising his eyebrows at her. "Hmm well, did you?"

"No, I didn't. He was just excited that I had come such a long way."

"Ohh, aye that's what it was, I see." They were both laughing now.

The time to head back to the ship came all too soon; they had enjoyed an amazing day out together, one that they would remember for a long time. They called the taxi driver and he arrived in no time. He asked about their day and they told him all about the fun that they had. He was excited to hear that they had loved his city and told them even more stories about the fish markets and everything else that he loved about his city.

Arriving back on the ship, they went back to their rooms before meeting back on the deck. She took out all her shopping and laid it all out on bed. She stood looking at all the beautiful lingerie: Simone Perele, Chantelle, Maison Lejaby. She had them all. She put away her gifts and washed hers and hung them in the bathroom to dry. She smiled as she stared at her purchases. She had never had such a beautiful shopping experience. Just looking at them even made her feel special. She knew now why French women always had that sex appeal about them. They had the beautiful lingerie and skincare, of course they felt sexy and they oozed in it. After fussing with her goodies, she made her way to meet Jack.

They had found a lovely table on the port side, so they sat and watched all the comings and goings at the port. The ship had refuelled and now all the cargo was being trucked in. They watched as lots of fruit, vegetables, and seafood, amongst other things, were loaded. So amazing to observe what goes on behind the scenes.

An announcement came over the speakers advising buses would be leaving the port tomorrow heading into Florence for those who have still not booked a tour. That was them; they still didn't have anything planned. So it suited them perfectly. They would catch the bus in the morning, and then take Florence slowly. Jack was worried Chloe would miss Tuscany, a huge draw card, and thought he should mention it, as maybe it had been something she had overlooked. Being so much quieter also, it would suit her with less stress.

"It is near Tuscany, Chloe, are you aware of that? Are you sure you don't want to visit the Tuscany region instead of Florence?" asked Jack with a warm smile.

"Oh, I have seen so many movies set in the Tuscan hills, and it looks so beautiful. That's so confusing. It would be fun to do both, I am unsure. What do you think?"

"I am thinking a wine tour. I read about one that goes through all the little Tuscan villages. I am not sure if there would be any spots left, but we could try."

"Ok, let's go and try."

They went to check seat availability on the wine tour, but they had left their run a bit too late. Totally all booked out, most of the tours were. Well, that made their decision very easy: the bus to Florence in the morning was booked. After that, they thought they had better take a look at Rome. They didn't realise things booked out so quickly. They had a quick browse over all the shore excursions, Vatican, Colosseum, Amalfi Coast, they were all too busy for them, and they wanted something quieter, easier, no line ups.

They were starting to think they would not find anything that they liked and then they spotted the train. A private train that left Civitavecchia Train Station, with a local guide but when you arrived, you were free to do Rome as you pleased. Bingo! That was the one. They went and booked the Florence bus and the train to Rome. All organised, they started to relax and enjoy the evening; time to set sail was fast approaching so they grabbed a drink at the bar.

The sail-off party was quickly into full swing. The music was playing loudly, crowds were arriving, and the cruise director had everyone up dancing. Chloe and Jack joined in.

"This is so much fun."

"Aye, I canna believe you skipped this the other day."

The ship's horns blasted four times and everyone cheered. They were off.

"Italy here we come!" yelled out Chloe above all the noise.

"And au revoir, France," added Jack.

Jack went and got their sunset drinks from the bar. Of course, Aperol Spritz. They sat and watched the sunset together, another perfect end to another perfect day. They had enjoyed Marseille and looked forward to what lay ahead.

"I don't want much for dinner tonight," said Chloe, stirring her cocktail. "I still need something, but it does not have to be anything large."

"Hey, remember the waiter in the fish shop told us the other night to make sure we come back after the French port, as they will have all the best produce from the markets at Marseille?"

"Ohh, aye, I do. Sounds wonderful!"

"We can have something light," added Chloe.

"Sounds too easy. I will grab us another drink before we go."

Jack jumped up and headed to the bar. They were not in any hurry, and certainly loved the view and another spritz would set the mood nicely.

When they arrived at the fish shop, they grabbed the same table near the window where they had sat at the night before. The waiter remembered them and came rushing over. "I am so glad you have returned. You have taken my advice. You will not be disappointed. We purchased some beautiful fish at the market today," he said excitedly. "Let me put a sample plate together for you, with all the wonderful produce." He was so excited and passionate, how could they refuse.

"Not too much," they both added. "We had a very big lunch today."

He headed back off to the kitchen, happy with himself.

"What is it with you and chefs? They fall all over you. I have to hang around you more often, and you get all the good things. You do realise he is going to bring out a grand platter," he teased.

She couldn't stop laughing "It's not me; he is just very passionate about his food."

They spotted him rushing back to their table.

"I almost forgot drinks, please excuse me. Can I recommend a lovely glass of Domaine Félines-Jourdan Picpoul de Pinet? It's a local wine from the Languedoc region, south of France and it is very popular."

They looked at each other and nodded.

"Yes, it sounds too good not to try." Jack leaned forward and whispered, "And we get all the best wines. I am definitely sticking with you. If it was just me here, I would be offered a house wine."

"It's not me, you wombat," she replied, laughing.

The waiter was off like a rocket, back to the kitchen, and appeared almost immediately, with their wine. He didn't leave until they both told him how much they loved it. "I will be back to refill your glasses soon." They both laughed. He was a funny little man, but so lovely.

The sample plate was incredible; the oysters were huge, accompanied by prawns, crab, calamari, fish, mussels, and cockles. It was a tad too much food again, but Chloe sat back and watched Jack as he devoured the lot. She smiled at him. "I told you I had a problem," he said with a mouth full of food. She laughed.

They went for a walk after dinner and came across a karaoke room. It seemed like a whole lot of fun, so they went in and grabbed a seat. There were acts that were bad, some that were good, and some that were really good, like the one that came on next. It was a Spanish couple; he was a Spanish guitarist and she had the voice of an angel.They were both strikingly good looking as well as talented.

They were doing a Fado song and her voice made the hairs on the back of your neck stand up. You could have heard a pin drop in the room. She wore the most beautiful tight-fitting dress of sequined red and gold, and it had a fishtail bottom with a sheer gold lace cape which trailed all the way to the ground. He was in all black, but his shirt featured some red embroidery on the front and sleeves. They got a standing ovation and won their hearts. They would return for the grand final.

They were both starting to feel a bit tired, and decided it was time to head back to their rooms for the night. It was a big day tomorrow; they would have to set an alarm to get up early. They slowly wandered back to their rooms. They had conquered their first port of call, and had so much fun; they were looking forward to Florence, but mostly, seeing each other again.

Chapter 7

FLORENCE

The alarm woke Chloe at 5 am. Startled, she sat up, then realised where she was. She made a coffee and pulled opened her curtains, still weary eyed. They were docked, she could see the port. It was still dark outside and sprinkling with rain. There were people everywhere, all running around organising waiting trucks, loading, and unloading the ship. Lots of buses were starting to arrive and being directed to all line up one after another, it was so well organised. *This is so exciting,* she thought. *Italy, my goodness, I am in Italy.* She jumped in the shower thinking of the day ahead. *How was I ever thinking of going home? I must have been crazy.* Thank goodness Jack was around; he had made me feel so relaxed and calm.

She checked the weather and it was a much cooler day today. She decided on pants and a long-sleeved top and packed a lightweight rain jacket. She had her black RM boots; they were comfortable, and well worn. She selected a bra and panties set she bought the day before and started to dress. They looked lovely on her and she felt pretty wearing them. It certainly lifted her spirits. She felt amazing, with confidence she had never had before.

Jack was waiting for her, as usual. He looked good for such an early morning; he had probably already been to the gym, too. He had on a lovely blue Chambray shirt, which brought out the colour of his eyes, jeans and a leather jacket hanging on his chair. She loved his smell as he came closer, a hint of aftershave. His hair was tied back and still damp. He was so damn good looking; she was definitely a lucky girl.

"Good morning, my sweet Chloe. You are lovely as always," he said as he jumped up to greet her and pull out her chair.

"Thank you. Good morning. Can you believe we are in Italy?" she said, unable to hide her excitement.

"Aye, we are. Now aren't you glad you didn't go home? Imagine you would be sitting on the jet for hours but instead you are here in Italy."

"I was only thinking that myself this morning. I was such a fool. Thank you so much, Jack. I owe that all to you. You have no idea what you have done."

"Aye, well let's eat, lassie, before we run out of time. You will have plenty of time to thank me later."

The place was full, you would never have guessed it was so early in the morning; in fact, the sun still hadn't come up yet. The hustle and bustle of people all blurry eyed was incredible.

They both only partially filled their plates. It was too early but they needed something. They ate silently and then he stood up, throwing his jacket over his shoulder, standing straight and looking strong. She smiled looking up at him.

"Ok, let's go visit Italy," said Jack as he took her by the arm.

Dozens of buses were all lined up, but it seemed extremely well organised and they were on their bus within minutes. As soon as it was full, it was on its way and they started filling the next one. The tour guide introduced herself along with the driver, and gave them a quick rundown of the day. The atmosphere on the bus was quiet, most people were catching up on their sleep like Jack; he had got up extra early for a quick work out.

Chloe could not take her eyes off the window. The sun was finally starting to come up but was still overcast. However, the rain was holding off. They were on a freeway. It was extremely busy, probably peak hour, she thought.

The bus stopped and parked next to a river. The guide advised they had arrived and to start making their way off the bus. Everyone was pushing and shoving but they waited till everyone was happily off and then got off. The sky was still overcast but not raining. The guide gave them a timeline and pointed out where they were to meet at 4 pm. Jack gave Chloe's arm a squeeze. "So exciting, we are here." They were both looking around, not knowing where to start.

"I hope you have some idea where to go because I am totally lost. Do you have any clue where you like to start, Chloe?"

"Well, I have been told that if we head to Piazzale Michelangelo, we can get a bird's eye view of the whole city from there, and it's free," informed Chloe happily.

It was a good starting point. They worked out which way they had to go, and hiked their way up a winding path to the top of the hill. Reaching the top, it was a spectacular view.

They stared out over the crumbling, old city wall in the west, to the Duomo, the Arnolfo Tower of the Palazzo Vecchio and the Uffizi across the river. There were souvenir carts and buskers everywhere and the whole place had a nice vibe. They took lots of photos and spent an hour looking around, before walking back over to the other side of the river.

"Let's go and visit this patisserie shop. It looks interesting. I could do with a wee drink." Jack was pointing at a tiny little place which had caught his eye, with a couple of little tables out the front. He had obviously spotted the two people having a wine.

"Ok, grab a table out the front and I will go and buy us a drink. Do you want a beer?"

"Aye, a beer would be greatly appreciated, thank you," he said, a bit puffed.

Chloe came out in no time with two beers and a little bowl of olives.

"We are on the Peroni's now, Jack. We are in Italy."

They were still raving about the beer in France they enjoyed yesterday but agreed the Italian Peroni beer was just as flavourful. The waiter came out with a bread board full of salamis, cold cuts, cheeses, and breads; he put it down in front of them. "Buongiorno," he said loudly with a smile obviously proud of his offerings.

"Thank you," said Chloe, accepting the beautiful board and placing it in between them.

"Prego," said the waiter and he was off.

"What is this, have I got your appetite in tune with mine now?" he asked, looking up at her with a sparkle in his eye.

"Ha ha no, I saw a lot of people enjoying it inside and thought you might like one," chirped Chloe.

"Like it. Oh my, look at this, simply amazing. Oh you know a way to a man's heart, Mo Leannan, this is fantastic."

And fantastic it was; they were both amazed how appetising the platter was. They were hungry, having such an early start they did not eat much back on the ship. This was just enough to give them the energy they would need to enjoy the long morning. The man who served them came back out to check if everything was good. He chatted to them about Florence, and how long he had been here. He had a huge smile on his face the whole time, which made you smile along with him. He had made their visit so memorable. She was starting to feel the same way everywhere they went in Italy; it was just one of those beautiful friendly places that made you feel like you never wanted to leave. Chloe pulled out her little diary she had bought along and made some notes.

They happily wandered off with full bellies. Soon, they came across markets where they shopped for souvenirs. Chloe bought some Italian wool scarves for the men at home, and some Italian silk scarves for the girls. Jack bought some for his mum and sister and said the others didn't count for a present. Chloe actually had to agree with that one.

A statue of a bronze bore called Porcellino caught their eye and as the legend said if you pop a coin into the jaw and rub its snout you would return to Florence. They both put one in together rubbing his snout, hoping they would return again together one day.

After a pleasant few hours' shopping, they came upon a beautiful building which was marked as "Mercato centrale." Wondering what it was, they went inside to see what it was all about. The bottom floor was a huge fresh food market. They went up the escalator and found a huge food court with lots of restaurants and bars around the outside and the centre filled with tables and chairs.

They grabbed a beer and found a table and sat down. They peered around, take-away-style restaurants lined the walls, serving anything your heart desired.

"Well, look at you, Jack. Your eyes are as wide as a plate, you must feel like a kid in a candy shop," she teased.

"Oh aye, and you have turned out to be a very interesting travel buddy for me, finding me such places as this." He was looking around in awe.

"What do you eat when in Florence, Chloe?"

"Bistecca alla Fiorentina," she said, replying in her best Italian accent.

Jack was staring at her blankly. She laughed.

"It's a steak, but not just any old steak, a huge extremely thick cut T-bone, usually shared by two people, cooked over flame grill and brushed with herbs and butter just before serving. I spotted a steak place over in the corner, they would have it for sure," explained Chloe.

"Will ya share one with me," asked Jack, almost pleading.

She could almost see his mouth watering. "Yea, of course, and let's try a Tuscany wine to wash it down," she said excitedly.

Jack signalled a waiter. "Do I order with you?"

"Ciao, I will take your order sir, and drinks as well."

"Oh, we would like to try a Florentine steak to share and we wanted to try a local red wine. Would you recommend a decent one?"

"Of course, I will ask the wine expert to pick you one to match your beautiful choice of a meal," said the waiter.

"How do you know so much about European food?"

"Well, I watch a lot of travel cooking shows. It was the only way I thought I would ever manage to see the food, but here we are."

"I am so glad that you are here. It would be boring sitting here without you."

"Well, it is all because of you, that I am."

The wine was served to the table.

"Prego," said the waiter.

Jack took a sip.

"Oh, aye, excellent. Thank you."

"It's Chianti Classico," advised the waiter. "A local wine from Chianti in the Tuscan region. The rooster on the neck of the bottle shows you that you are enjoying a wine from Chianti and authentic," informed the waiter happily.

The steak was served to the table about twenty minutes later. The waiter sliced and set it on a platter with the bone, and it was huge and looked amazing. Some bread, olive oil, and scalloped potatoes in a cream sauce were also set on the table. It was served quite rare but would have been a sin to have it cooked any other way with such a fine quality of beef. Plus, the chef would have chased them out waving his carving knife.

"That is definitely the best steak I have ever eaten," said Jack. "And that wine…my God, one of the best I have ever tried!"

Jack was eyeing off the bone. "Go on, eat it, Jack! Enjoy! Who cares what anyone else thinks? We will probably never be back again."

"You sure I won't embarrass you?"

"No, not at all. Go ahead. It would be a sin to waste." She watched as he gnawed until it was bare.

Wiping his mouth with his serviette, he sat back in his chair and stared at Chloe. "Mo Leannan falaich."

"What does that mean?" laughed Chloe.

"You're killing me," laughed Jack.

"Let's finish our wine and take a walk."

"Oh, I will try. But you might need to carry me. That was an amazing meal."

"I think you will be right. I have watched you eat way more than that," she laughed, pushing the plates to the side.

They walked to the river and strolled along the bank, happily taking in all the sights. They were starting to walk a little closer to each other every day. Jack seemed to always find excuses to be close to her. Taking her hand to cross the road and walking on rough surfaces in case she tripped. She didn't mind; in fact, she liked it.

They stopped to skim some stones on the small bank of the river. Chloe sat on a stone ledge and continued to watch Jack as he showed off his skimming stones talent. After he had entertained her enough, he came and joined her on the stone ledge.

"Do you know there is a story about two lovers who met and fell in love?" said Jack, as he leaned in a little closer to her.

"No, I have not heard that one, but do tell me."

"Well, their families forbid them from seeing each other. So they would sneak away anytime they could and make love on the banks of the river. After a while their families found out, and they were outraged. They managed to run away one more time together, and decided if they could not be together, they would rather die. So they drowned together, in their river. And they say on a misty morning if you look close enough you can see them embraced in a kiss hovering above the water," he gently whispered.

"Jack, that's a beautiful story. Was it here, in this river?" asked Chloe, mesmerised.

"Aye, not far from here in fact," informed Jack.

He wanted to kiss her there and then; she was so beautiful, so innocent, listening to his silly story. But he didn't want to ruin what they have. He knew it was something very special. She was taboo, off limits. He cared too much about their friendship. They were rapidly building a very strong bond.

"Do either of you have the time," said a voice from behind them. She had startled them. It was a lady who was on the path behind them.

Jack gazed at his watch. "It's a quarter past three," he yelled back. She waved a hand and headed off.

He grabbed Chloe's hand. "It's time for us to head back." They wandered back with plenty of time. The bus was waiting. There were always a few that never made it back on time and today was no exception. After a fifteen-minute delay they were on the bus and heading back.

The bus was quiet again, most people having a nap. Chloe could not help wondering if the story Jack had told her was true. *How would he know a story about a Florence river*, she thought to herself. Oh well, she decided, she did not care if it was true or not, she had loved it. She peered over and he was sleeping. She smiled. She was so lucky to have found him.

The bus took almost two hours on the return journey. The traffic was horrendous, and a traffic accident on the freeway had not helped. The driver advised us he was making a detour, but not to worry he would make it back on time.

He took them on a little short cut which seemed to help. The guide informed them to relax and not to worry; they were on a trip booked by the ship, so the ship would wait for us. As it turned out, they were right, and no need to worry, they made it in plenty of time, thanks to the bus driver's local knowledge.

Boarding the ship they bumped into Rocco and Danni. They looked exhausted as they had been on another tour. "How was your day tour of Monaco yesterday, Danni?"

"I was so impressed but what a long day. We loved the town of Monaco and Rocco was happy, we walked the race track. We went to the casino also. I could rave about it all day about how wonderful it was." She had obviously been on the champagne and was extremely chatty.

"Thanks for putting us on to that restaurant, Danni, it was fantastic," said Chloe, grateful.

"Oh you went, I will tell John at work, he will be pleased." Jack went on to tell them the story about Chloe and the chef and they were all in fits of laughter.

"We are having dinner in the grand dining area tonight. Why don't you join us?" suggested Rocco.

"What do you think, Chloe?" asked Jack; he didn't want to make her if it was too much for her.

"Sure, why not? That sounds like a wonderful idea. We have not ventured that way yet, and we still haven't caught up on today's news." She smiled at Jack and he smiled back; she was obviously feeling comfortable.

"Is half past seven ok? We have another huge day tomorrow."

They stared at each other and both nodded in approval.

"Ok meet you out the front at half past seven," said Rocco, as he dragged Danni off before she started on another story.

Jack glanced at his watch and realised time was getting on. They both went back to their rooms to rest and dress for dinner.

Chloe was frantically going through her wardrobe. What did they wear to dinner? *A dress*, she thought. She had a deep blue maxi dress and was happy. One of the throws she had bought in Florence at the markets matched it beautifully. Cream and blue with a dark blue embodied pattern. Happy she had found a dress. She moved onto jewellery, some matching earrings and bracelet, just costume jewellery, but they would do. She lay on the bed for a bit before she jumped into the shower mindful of the time.

Right on time, Jack was tapping on her door. He looked smart but casual in a dark blue long-sleeved buttoned shirt and a pair of cargo pants. They even matched each other perfectly.

"Let me escort you to dinner mademoiselle," bowed Jack.

She took his arm and they walked towards the restaurant.

Rocco and Danni were waiting outside. Danni looked lovely, wearing silk pants and a pale green silk shirt the colour of her eyes. She had matching gold necklace and bracelet and little diamond earrings. Rocco was in a casual linen suit, with a t-shirt and looked smart.

"I think we are a bit under-dressed," whispered Chloe.

"Never. We are comfortable and that's what I like about us," stated Jack as he led her inside. *There was an "us" now,* she thought, and had a little giggle to herself.

Arriving inside, they glanced around. The room was huge and there were large round tables set for ten scattered around, and then small tables for two lined the walls of the room. Jack was keeping a close eye on Chloe. He was happy to see that she seemed relaxed. They were escorted to a table where there were three other couples already seated. The four of them joined the table. They introduced themselves and sat down.

Rocco poured Danni a champagne as he told the table their story. "Well, we are on our honeymoon. We work in an advertising firm where we met and live in a small apartment in New York."

"Yea, it is a small apartment but we eat out most nights," Danni added, sipping her wine. "I hate cooking anyway so we go out socialising after work and are not home much."

There was a Scottish couple sitting next to Jack. They were a middle-aged couple. He had thinning sandy orange hair and a little beard with the warmest blue eyes. She was a busty redhead, with curls hanging to her shoulder; both of them were extremely jolly people, so full of life, and they introduced themselves next. "A big bonne greeting. My name is Paddy McDonald and this is my wife, Maggie. We are on a well-deserved holiday. We have run away from our four boys."

"Don't say that, no we have not. They have all left home," Maggie added, giving him a stern look.

"Thank goodness, we can now enjoy our empty nest together," he laughed, giving her a hug.

"Oh I will give you empty nest. You miss them, always winging and whining they are not around enough anymore."

"Aye, that is when work is to be done; I see enough of the buggers at the hardware store."

"We own a hardware store in Glasgow, where two of our sons work," explained Maggie, frowning at Paddy. "Aye, still hanging around to annoy me."

Another American couple sat opposite, and introduced themselves as John and Ava Buckman. They were a fairly young couple, both very much the casual type. John was neatly cut, brown hair, slim build with brown eyes, wearing stylish cargo pants and a rust-coloured buttoned-up shirt. Ava had brown eyes and long blonde wavy hair, which had a strawberry tone put through it. Her skin was milky white and her hair and makeup were done to perfection. She wore a sweetheart neckline dress that had little pink flowers on it, matching the tone of her hair. "My father owns a chain of barbeque and outdoor living stores called Bucko's BBQ'S and outdoor living. I manage the one in Florida where we live. Ava is a beauty consultant," said John, sipping his beer.

"Yes, I work at a day spa. We are on the cruise to celebrate John's thirtieth birthday in a few days' time," added Ava. John seemed to have a carefree fun-loving personality, and Ava was much quieter and very sweet.

Seated next to Rocco and Danni was the Spanish couple they had seen performing the night before in the karaoke room. They introduced themselves as Cruz and Catalina. Cruz had short slicked back hair, brown eyes, and slim build with an olive tanned complexion and dressed in all black again. Catalina had long dark hair, which she had swept up into a loose bun with brown eyes and wore a lovely burnt orange jumpsuit that suited her olive skin. She had a stunning exotic look about her, and you could tell just by looking at her she belonged on the stage.

"We saw your performance last night. It was fantastic," said Chloe, looking back at Jack for input.

"Aye, we thought it was very impressive." Said Jack intently buttering his dinner roll.Catalina explained the story of the song. "Well thank you, that was a beautiful Fado love song. My mother was Portuguese, we grew up in Lisbon. She sang Fado for years and was extremely popular. So I know and love Fado. Cruz is an excellent Spanish guitarist, having played since he was five, taught by his well-known, talented father."

You could see in her eyes she was crazy for him. He softly thanked her, refilling her wine glass. "We both come from talented musical families, not just me," he corrected her. "We have been together as a singing duo for four years, and have been in a relationship for around the same amount of time. We started going out with each other soon after we met and now live in Barcelona. The whole idea of being on the cruise is to pick up some work on the cruise ships. Since the performance last night, we have been asked to do a small gig in the lounge area the next sail day." Everyone was impressed and happy for them.

Paddy and Maggie were jolly and loud and played off each other extremely well. Jack and Paddy were getting on well. "I can't understand a goddamn word you two are saying," shouted John across the table to Jack and Paddy, laughing.

"Wait till they get a few drinks under their belt," added Maggie, but in truth she was just as hard to understand. All their Scottish accents were strong. Chloe was glad she had a Scottish nanna, who also had a very broad accent so managed to understand them easy.

Scanning the table, she was relieved everyone else was dressed quite casually; she decided Rocco and Danni must like to dress that way. They were New York executives and were probably used to being dolled up to the nines. The waiter had arrived to take their food orders. Chloe picked up the menu as he approached her and ordered the smallest meals on the menu she could find; she was still full from their day in Florence.

"Yes, could I please start with the smoked salmon for entrée, and the prawn linguini as a main and an espresso martini as a dessert."

She closed the menu and looked over at Jack, thinking he would follow her lead and opted for a lean meal.

"I will have the pasta for an entree, the steak for the main with extra tatties, and chocolate cake for dessert, please." Closing the menu, he looked at Chloe who was smirking at him. "What?" he grinned.

"Where are you going to put all that?"

"You just wait and see."

Chloe was chatting with Ava and Danni, having a lovely time getting to know each other. She was telling them about her shopping experience at the French beauty counter and both the girls added they also had visited a French pharmacy while in France. Ava knew all about the brands and gave her a quick lesson on French skincare; turns out she bought all the right products. Danni added she was an Elizabeth Arden fan and that made sense as she was from New York, after all. Ava agreed it was a great brand. She recommended another good brand from LA, from her hometown, Kate Somerville. Chloe wanted to see if the girls knew some Australian skincare brands and spoke about ASAP and Alpha H but no one knew them. She could have talked all night to them; they were getting along like a house on fire.

Jack was sitting there watching. He thought how lovely it was to see Chloe laughing and having fun, her cheeks were starting to get flushed from the wine. He was oblivious that he was staring with a smile on his face. He turned to see Paddy looking at him.

"Have you known each other for long?" asked Paddy, watching Jack as he stared over at Chloe.

"No, we met on the cruise. Well, in Barcelona, really, in a bar. We were both travelling alone so decided to hang out together. It's lucky we met, we seem to get on quite well," said Jack proudly.

"Oh aye, I can see that, Jack, my boy. You are both very comfortable together, like you have been together for years," laughed Paddy.

"You know what is weird. I have never got on so well with a girl before. I actually enjoy being around her, she is easy going and fun. It's all a bit spooky," he added as he continued to watch Chloe.

Maggie was then calling Paddy, giving him some friendly argument about something he did in Florence. They were off, giving each other lip, and they had the whole table in fits of laughter. He turned back to Jack. "She is my Maggie May, I still love her to death, even after all these years. Let me give you some advice, Jack, if you ever find someone that you connect with, I mean really connect with, with a really strong bond of love and friendship, don't ever let them go. You will never find that again. Trust me. True love is friendship set on fire; remember that one, Jack, my boy." He smiled, slapping him on the back and turning to look at Chloe.

Truth was, Jack knew what he was talking about. Paddy had seen what he already knew. She was perfect for him. He just had to take things slow; he couldn't get this wrong and lose her forever. He had to protect their friendship; they were having too much of a good time as friends.

The meal was almost complete and Chloe spotted Danni pushing her food around again, making everyone think she was eating and then throwing a serviette over the top just as the waiter approached and handed him the plate. Jack got up to go to the bathroom and Paddy moved over to talk to Chloe. "So, you are travelling alone. You are lucky to have such a laddie like Jack by your side."

Chloe agreed with him and went on to tell him the whole story even about Craig leaving her and how she had wanted to go home and then how she met Jack. "He has been so wonderful. I would never have been here if it was not for him," said Chloe admiringly.

"Oh, I know. I have only just met him, but I can tell he is a decent lad, and he will take good care of you," agreed Paddy. Jack had arrived back at the table, so Paddy moved back over to Maggie, but he continued to watch them through the night. He could see a spark there, that was for sure.

Dinner was finished and everyone was starting to leave. "Why don't we all meet back at seven thirty tomorrow night? I will ask them to hold a table for me," asked Paddy as everyone was getting to their feet. Everyone agreed the night had been wonderful and would be back.

Jack took Chloe by the arm and helped her up. They said cheerio to their new friends and he walked her home." I will see you in the morning, another early start," yawned Jack.

"Yes, I will see you at six. Thank you for a fun-filled day," she said as she closed the door slowly.

It took her a while to sleep as she remembered the day in her head. It had been a wonderful day. Danni and Rocco were such lovely people, and all the couples they met at dinner were so interesting. What an amazing time she was having, so different to life in little Umina. It was a whole new world that had opened up to her. She was so proud of herself. She had conquered another day without too much anxiety and was feeling more comfortable every day.

She chuckled to herself as she thought about Jack. She relived the day, his funny faces when he thought about food, and then smiled, as she remembered his story about the two lovers by the river. He was so much fun to be around. "Rome tomorrow," she sighed. "Can't wait." She rolled over, pulling the sheet up around her chin, closed her eyes, and easily drifted off to sleep.

Chapter 8

ROME

The bus took them to Civitavecchia train station where they waited on the platform for the train. It was one of the warmest mornings that they had experienced yet, with the hot sun streaming down on them as they waited. Chloe was grateful that she had her large brimmed hat. She had worn a cool shirt and loose pants with her Sketchers as she knew it would be another huge day of walking. Jack had a loose cream short-sleeved shirt with casual light cargo pants with sandshoes. She waved her fan that she had bought the day before as she waited. It provided a breeze that helped cool her face.

The little four-carriage train arrived at the platform. Jack took Chloe by the arm as he helped her step up onto the carriage and guided her to the first two seats on the right. The guide walked up and down the aisle once everyone was seated and counted them all in. The train ride into Rome was exceptionally comfortable so much better than the bus into Florence. The train was fast and Chloe enjoyed the scenery from the window as it sped along. There were lots of farms and cute old farmhouses, with farmers out attending to their small family-size crops. Some would stop and wave as the train passed by and Chloe would smile and wave back. She turned to tell Jack what she saw but he was taking the opportunity to have a nap after another early start to the day.

They were there in no time and the tour guide was funny and kept them entertained the whole way. Jack awoke and sat up startled, realising where he was. Rubbing his eyes, he grabbed the map and Chloe peered over his shoulder. "Any idea where we should start today," asked Jack as he covered his mouth, yawning loudly again.

"I had a browse while you were sleeping and I thought maybe the Colosseum."

The guide was yelling out they had to meet back by half past four and to enjoy their day. Chloe checked her wristwatch: it was only eight in the morning so they had a whole day to explore.

They reached the Colosseum easily without getting lost and were stunned by the sheer size of it. They wandered around, looking at it all from the outside but both decided they didn't want to wait in line to go inside. Jack told her lots of stories about the fighting and horrible ancient ways with animals. That alone made her more determined not to go inside. Just up the road was the Roman Forum. It was hot as the morning went on; the temperature was starting to rise. They stopped to check the map and realised they were on the right track.

They strolled onto the Trevi Fountain, stopping and looking at things along the way. They took a short detour to visit the Piazza Campidoglio designed by Michaelangelo himself. Eventually they reached the Trevi Fountain. Jack was wiping his brow while Chloe started fidgeting for coins.

"Here, Jack, we have to toss these coins in and make a wish."

"Ok, turn around and let's throw them in backward." They closed their eyes, counted to three and tossed them in together. Losing her footing, Chloe almost fell in as Jack grabbed her arm to steady her. "Phew, that was close. Thanks." They both laughed.

"Let's find a café to get out of this heat for a while," said Jack as he glanced around.

"Up there, up that laneway," she pointed and they headed towards it. "I need to freshen up. There is a toilet sign over there. I will be back in a minute."

Jack found a table and started to browse over the menu. The toilet was down a long alley. It was a tiny room with a strange lock that you had to turn quite a few times to lock the door. She washed her face and applied more sunscreen, feeling more refreshed. She went to open the door but it would not open. Chloe was starting to panic. "How many times did I turn the key to lock it? Oh God, now what? I am stuck." She kept trying and got even more confused. Panic set in immediately. She started to yell, "Jack! Jack! Help, Jack!"

After a few minutes, she heard his voice. "What is wrong, Chloe, are you ok? I am here."

"I am trapped, the key won't open the door."

She heard him talking to someone, and then he said, "Take the key out of the door and throw it out to me, above the door where the bricks are missing."

She tried to throw the key through the hole a few times and kept missing. She started to panic even more. *Oh bloody hell, I am trapped in this small dungeon*, she thought. Finally, the keys went through the hole and Jack caught them. "I got them, Chloe. Hang on."

The door opened and Jack and a chef were standing there, waiting for her. She fell into Jack's arms and sobbed.

"Oh mo leannan falaich, stay calm, you are with me now. I will never let anything happen to you. You are safe now." Jack caressed her back to calm her down, as she snuggled into his chest. He walked her back to the table where their coffee was waiting.

"I am such a fool," said Chloe. He patted her on the hand.

"Chloe, you are not a fool. I thought you were so brave being trapped like that. You didn't scream the whole place down, you just yelled out for help. And besides, you are obviously not the first one it has happened to, going by the missing bricks," comforted Jack.

"How do you always manage to make things seem right again and make me so much calmer," said Chloe, taking deep breaths. She was starting to breathe slower and calm down again.

"It was a promise I made to ya, remember, when ya agreed to be my buddy? I promised that I would take care of you, and never let you be scared or sad," he smirked.

The waiter appeared with two little pastries. "Compliments from the chef. We apologise, Madam."

"Thank you." She smiled up at him and started to stir her coffee.

Jack's eyes lit up and it made her smile.

"And you keep finding these magical ways for food to appear to me, and not any ordinary food, all the best foods in life. I think we are even," said Jack, eyeing off the pastries.

Chloe laughed as they enjoyed their coffee and pastries.

"Are you ready to push on to the Spanish steps?" He was hoping she was still okay to keep going. Something like that could have quite easily sent her into a spin.

"Yea sounds like a plan. And then maybe a late lunch at Trastevere."

He was happy to hear that she was fine. As they walked out of the café, Chloe stepped off the curb not looking to the left and Jack grabbed her arm and pulled her back without a second to spare.

"Shit, I nearly got ran over," said Chloe shocked.

"I did notice that," replied Jack startled.

"You had to bloody rescue me again," she was horrified.

"I am a total bloody walking disaster. I really don't know what is happening with me today." She was shaking and crying.

"Here, come and take a seat over here for a minute."

He settled her down on a chair outside the cafe. She looked up at him. Her face was full of panic and tears were streaming down her face.

"I can't do this. I have to go home. I am ruining your holiday. You should be out there having fun. Instead you have to look out for a flaming fair dinkum idiot like me."

He smiled at her gently. "Well, you have that all wrong. I am having a great holiday because I am with you. If you went home I would have a miserable holiday without you, so if you are worried about me having a bad holiday you had better pick yourself back up and come and enjoy lunch with me."

She sat and thought for a while before wiping her eyes and smiling, nodding slowly. "Ok, I will try and be more careful. I am such a bloody disaster."

"Well, I am going to take you by the hand today and not let go of you."

"You better hang on tight as I am a bit of a problem child today. I need one of those child harnesses on with a lead."

"Aye, and for such a sweet little thing you have quite a potty mouth when you are upset," smirked Jack.

Chloe laughed. "It is the Aussie coming out in me; I think that you had better start to get used to it."

Jack's hand was wonderful around hers. It made her feel secure and close to him which she liked. *Oh god,* she thought to herself, *I am falling for him.* It would ruin everything; they had the most relaxed but strong friendship that had been created in less than a week. It was something that she never wanted to lose; she could see them being lifelong friends and didn't want to sacrifice that, ever. But what's the harm in him holding her hand? He was protecting her, after all, wasn't he? But she knew the feelings she was feeling inside were more than that. *Enjoy what you have here today, Chloe. In a week he will be gone*, she reminded herself.

They wandered along taking in all the sights, going in and out of churches and piazzas, taking photos and happily chatting. They weren't just taking each other's photos, anymore; they were taking lots of selfies of themselves together. Well, her mum and sister were going to love these, she thought to herself. They were already getting curious about Jack. Both her sisters and her mum were over Craig a long time ago and seemed quite pleased in their comments that she had met someone new to share her holiday with.

Arriving at Trastevere, they spotted a restaurant that had a lovely corner table under some grapevines on a veranda.

"Will this be ok? It must be popular judging by the crowd," asked Jack, looking around.

"More than ok—it's perfect!" added Chloe happily.

They were both tired and hungry and definitely needed a beer after walking in the heat. It was a much warmer day than the day before. As they sat down, Chloe took off her sunhat and tossed her hair. Jack filled their water glasses from a tumbler the waitress had put on the table. "Any drinks to start" asked the waitress, looking around in a hurry.

"Yes, I think we will have two Peronis, please." He glanced at Chloe for reassurance as he spoke and she nodded, smiling. "Yes, please, a beer would be lovely."

They were in no hurry to order so they sat back enjoying the atmosphere and the beers, and observed what everyone was ordering. They intently spied each meal that went by and soon worked out what seemed to be the popular meals.

"It appears the pasta carbonara is popular here," whispered Jack as he spied another huge bowl of pasta go past.

"And the calamari, I think it's salt and pepper style, that is the third one that I have seen," added Chloe, watching a plate go past. Just as they thought they had it all sorted, they spotted a humongous spaghetti and meatballs go past. The aroma of the parmesan and mozzarella cheese melting on top was strong and smelt amazing.

The look on Jack's face was priceless. Chloe couldn't help it; she burst out laughing. "You're so funny."

"Will you share with me, Chloe?"

She already knew what he was thinking; he was ordering the lot. She didn't mind; he always ate most of it anyway, and she enjoyed having a smaller serving.

The bustling waitress was back. "Are you ready to order?" You would not have dared to say no. Without even taking a breath, Jack ordered, "Yes we are. Can we please have the carbonara, along with the calamari and the meatballs with extra cheese?" Sitting back pleased with himself, he closed the menu.

"More beers," she asked. "A red wine would be lovely with lunch if you could recommend one."

"I will bring you a Tuscan wine that is popular here."

They nodded as she spun around and moved to the next table. Moments later a wine the same as they had for lunch in Florence arrived at the table. She was certainly speedy. It was all delicious and they were getting spoilt with the lovely wine, and nothing cost a fortune. It took them a couple of hours to devour their feast.

"Have you seen the bathrooms, anywhere," asked Jack, looking around. "Oh, wait, I see them right up the back. I will be back in a wee minute."

Chloe nodded and sipped on her wine. A different waiter appeared who was more relaxed and more eager to linger and chat. Scanning the floor, it seemed his job was to make sure everything was running smoothly.

"How was everything? I hope it's all ok."

"Oh, it was delicious, and this wine is excellent also."

"What is your accent? Where are you from?"

"I am from Australia."

A man passing by stopped. "You're Australian?" he said, shocked.

"Yes, I am, and so are you?" She laughed. It is so wonderful to hear another Australian accent.

"So many Australians today, mamma mia," said the waiter as he walked off.

"It is amazing, alright. I am Matt."

"I am Chloe; I am here off the boat."

"Well, I leave your side for one minute and I am sharked," teased Jack, arriving back.

"Don't worry, mate, I'm not here to cut your grass, only stopped to say g'day. I'm Matt."

Jack seemed a bit confused. "Aye, Matt. I am Jack. Nice to meet you."

"I am sitting over there with my girlfriend, come and join us for a drink."

"Okay, why not?" Jack helped Chloe up out of her seat before picking up his drink and wine bottle.

They walked over to the table together. "Nat, I met another Aussie."

"Hello Nat, I am Chloe and this is my friend, Jack." They all sat down and got themselves comfortable. "We are off the cruise ship."

"Oh, lovely, we have been to a family wedding in Tuscany and now spending a few days in Trastevere."

The restaurant was busy and the waiter was hinting that they needed their table if they were finished eating.

"Hey, let's go for a craft beer. We know a hidden bar if you have time."

Jack checked the time. "Yea, we have an hour free."

They all drained their glasses, picked up their bags and sun hat.

"Ready" she said excitedly.

They followed them down a little cobblestone lane with all the usual Trastevere style with the vines and flower pots and washing hanging above them. Before too long, they stopped at a little doorway that had a few little tables out the front. There was one free, so Matt escorted them over there and they all sat down.

It was such a beautiful little place. The strong smell of beer was wafting out the door and the boys were off like two scolded cats into the bar.

"This seems like a funky place," said Chloe, scanning the place.

"We were so happy when we found it, we have been stopping here for a beer every day since," laughed Natalie as she spread out four coasters that had been neatly placed by the ashtray.

The door opened and the boys reappeared with the beers. Jack had a huge smile on his face. "You should see inside, it's fantastic. I must hand it to you. I thought a scot could sniff out a beer anywhere, but you Aussies win, hands down."

They all laughed as they put their glasses together. "Cheers!"

"Chloe, it's Belgium beer," he said, looking very excited. Chloe knew she had to be careful as the alcohol content would be eight percent. She warned Natalie as they were drinking the same. They were only having one, so it wasn't too bad. They happily spoke about their travels and got on well.

After the beer, Natalie asked Matt if they could have a look at a little shop around the corner. "Why don't you girls go and have a look at the shop, and the boys can blow the froth off a couple of beers while they wait?"

"Aye, we can stay at the watering hole," laughed Jack, impressed with himself that he knew a bit of the Aussie lingo. Everyone laughed.

"I will teach you a few more of those before the days out mate," laughed Matt.

"Well, I'm heading in to grab us a couple of coldies," said Matt as he walked inside.

"Come on, Chloe. We don't have much time," she jumped up. "Won't be long Jack," she said with a happy smile and they headed off.

Jack watched as they walked off. He couldn't believe she was so happy and relaxed; she didn't even hesitate to go. Chloe turned and gave him a smile as she reached the corner. He smiled back and continued to keep an eye on her as they turned the corner and disappeared. Matt was back with the beers.

"Here ya go, mate. Get this into ya. It's a German beer. The bartender reckons it's alright."

Jack took a sip eagerly. "Oh, aye, it is good," he nodded as he had another big gulp.

"So how long have you and Chloe been together?"

"Oh, we are not together. We only just met in Barcelona. We are travelling together."

"Oh, yea right O. I didn't come down in the last shower, you know. If you two aren't together you bloody well should be. I can see the way you look at each other. It won't be long until you are, if you ask me."

"No, just friends. Well I am not saying, I wouldn't mind, but she wouldn't be interested in me in that way. And plus, if I did make a move, and she doesn't like it, then I ruin the friendship we have."

"I'm tellin' ya, mark my words. You will be with her within a week. Any girl that lets a bloke hit on her constantly and doesn't mind is definitely interested."

"Hit on her, I don't do that," said Jacked, shocked.

"My bloody oath you do. You are forever touching her and basically all over her, and she is fair dinkum loving every bit of it," said Matt with a convincing glare, taking a swig of his beer.

"Oh, I don't know about that. I don't think I am hitting on her. I am just looking after her, that's all," Jack said already on the defence.

"Well, you can call it whatever the bloody hell you want, but I think you'd be a dead set goose if you didn't have a go. A blind man could see, she's crazy for you and she ain't too bad looking, either."

"Well, I would like to think that you're right, but I am not that sure. Plus, you're right, she's gorgeous, too good for me, that's for sure."

The subject changed as they saw the girls heading back. They had little bags of goodies and seemed quite happy chatting away and laughing. Jack glanced at the time. "Well, sadly, I hate to say but we need to head back." They all looked at their watch and sculled the rest of their beers.

"It's been the best afternoon. Wish we had more time," said Chloe, picking up her bag and hat.

"Here's our contact details. It would be fun to catch up again at home," said Nat.

"Thanks, we will," she popped it in her purse and they were off.

"Trust me mate. Have a go, see if I am wrong," yelled Matt out to Jack.

"Yea maybe," and waved and smiled.

"What was that all about," asked Chloe.

"Oh, nothing, just talking about sport." He smiled to himself as they strolled along. Well it's sort of a sport, a bit of a game. But he wasn't too sure about what Matt was suggesting; it all seemed a bit too risky. Maybe at the end of the cruise, so that if he was wrong it didn't matter.

He smiled at Chloe and she smiled back. Maybe it was that Belgium beer but he looked so sexy today. The walk back was fun, smelling all the wonderful smells that were coming from all the little restaurants. It had such a quaint feel about it and as they crossed the river, they both commented on how they had loved their time there, and it was sad to leave it all behind. They took more photos on the bridge, with the town as a backdrop, before continuing on their way.

They made it back to the train right on time. Everyone was waiting and mingling, chatting about their day. The little red and white train pulled up into the station and everyone got on, heading to the same seats that they were in on the way into Rome. Funny how people stayed within their comfort zones. Something she knew all too well.

The guide counted heads and they must have been short. She was yelling out, "Oh, mamma mia" as she frantically went through to the next carriage. Everyone waited and then she returned counting heads again and was happy. Everyone was on board and before too long the little train was off.

Chloe rested her head on Jack's shoulder and had a nap on the way home while he enjoyed the scenery from the window as it went past. He started to think about what Matt had said. Was he right? Did she like him? She was sitting there with her head on his shoulder...that must mean something. He wasn't used to picking up girls, he really only had two or three girlfriends.

Well, one at school if you counted that as it only lasted a few weeks, and wasn't sure if they even kissed. Then there was one just after school and then he had been with Mary ever since. But the girls he knew weren't the same as Chloe. He felt a feeling of closeness to her that he had never felt for a girl before. She could quite easily be his best friend; they got on that well together. But he knew it wasn't just friendship he was feeling. He was starting to feel things that he had never felt before. Just seeing her gave him goosebumps, and the way that she smelt when she was close was driving him crazy. Just the scent of her hair sent him into a frenzy. Like right now, as she had her head so close to him, the scent of her hair was driving him nuts. How was he supposed to control himself till the end of the cruise? He didn't know. But one thing he did know was that it was getting harder every day.

They were back on the boat and exhausted after a huge day in Rome. "I need to have a bit of a rest. It's been a hectic day," said Chloe, looking tired.

"Aye, it is the heat also. Well, for me anyway. I will pick you up at half past seven for dinner if that's ok."

"Thanks."

When they arrived for dinner, everyone was there and sitting in their same seats. They were happy to see each other again.

Paddy and Maggie had been on the same tour of Rome with Cruz and Catalina. "We are too old to be prancing around Rome on our own now," said Paddy as he poured Maggie some water. "We like to be chauffeur-driven in air-conditioned coaches now. And also, Maggie will beat me if I don't look after her. You know she carries a big stick in her bag, and hits me with it." He laughed, leaning away from her, expecting retaliation. Paddy had a very contagious laugh, when Paddy laughed the whole table laughed with him.

"And we have never been out of Spain and have no idea where to go and what an entertaining day it has been with these two," added Cruz with a smirk. "My jaws are hurting from laughing."

They had obviously had an enjoyable day together and were happy to tell the table of their tales. Rocco and Danni had been on an ancient Rome tour. "Oh, it was so hot on our tour, I was glad for air conditioning and champagne at lunch," said Danni.

John and Ava did the Vatican. Between them all, they had conquered Rome and the conversations around the table that night was informative and interesting.

Dinner was top class as usual with all the matching wines. Danni continued to push her food around her plate and pretended no one noticed. Paddy and Maggie played off each other all night keeping everyone at the table entertained and Cruz and Catalina were light-hearted and fun. John and Ava got louder as the night went on, but all in all, they had a great mix of company around the table.

Chloe glanced around at what everyone was wearing. They all looked so lovely. She was enthralled by all the wonderful fashion. Danni was dressed in a stunning plunging emerald and gold shirt with a pencil skirt and Rocco was in a casual khaki jacket with a white shirt underneath. Danni had a stunning huge aquamarine ring. *Well, I bet that has a whopping price tag,* she thought. She could not stop staring at it as it sparkled as she moved her hand. Ava looked sweet in a beautiful blue sleeveless A-line midi dress that had a pink pattern on it that once again set off the pink highlights in her hair. John was casual in a salmon polo and Catalina wore a V-neckline shift dress in cream with lace sleeves and a flowing sheer over the top with a butterfly and flower print, which she had bought in Rome and it was very stylish and looked stunning on her. Cruz was in his usual black, while Paddy and Maggie were just in casual pants and shirt. Chloe looked down at her maxi dress; this was a nice dress back at home. It looked like a rag here as she looked around the room.

She looked over at Jack and instantly felt better. Jeans and dark grey polo, he was just as casual as she was. *He could wear anything*, she thought as she watched him chatting with Paddy. That simple polo showed off his build perfectly. He lifted his beer to have a sip but stopped halfway as he spoke, which made his huge biceps move and they looked so bloody sexy. *God, he had an incredible body*, she thought.

She was brought back by Jack, getting her attention as he told the story of her getting stuck in the toilet in a true Scotsman's way of making it a grand story. The table roared with laughter. He had hoped Chloe would be ok with it as he had a few drinks and didn't even stop to think about how she might take it after it traumatized her and turned to check she was ok. He put his hand on her leg and gave it a squeeze and she smiled. Luckily, she was easy-going and was even having a chuckle herself at his story. He turned to her all of a sudden as he realised he didn't want to break all the good work she had done to over-come her anxiety, but all good, phew, that could have been a huge mistake. She was definitely his kind of girl. He was quite good at opening his mouth without thinking after a few drinks. And she seemed to be able to handle it.

Maggie was trying to talk to Jack across Paddy. He got up and walked around to her. Paddy moved across to chat with Chloe.

"You two get on very well, sounds like you had a lovely day, other than your incident, of course."

"Yes, we do, we get on very well. I am going to miss him after the cruise. Paddy, you may be able to help me, he calls me 'Mo Leannan Falaich' or something like that. Do you know what that means? I am not sure if he is cursing me or something else." She flicked her hair back and turned to him, hoping that he would have the answer.

Paddy smiled gently, taking her hand and patting it. "He is definitely not cursing you. Those are special words kept for someone you care about. He obviously cares a lot for you, Chloe. Don't waste this precious time that you have been given to share together. It does not have to end at the end of the cruise. Don't stop forming a relationship just because of that."

Chloe nodded in reply. She was happy it was something nice. She glanced over at Jack. How would they ever keep it together if they did start a relationship? They lived so far away from each other.

Everyone was starting to say goodnight. It had been two huge days and everyone was tired. It was Naples tomorrow, so not such an early start. As Jack walked her home they discussed visiting Naples.

"We are both so exhausted. Let's just go into Naples on our own and spend a quiet day enjoying the city. It is probably too late to book tours now, anyway," said Chloe, looking up at him.

"Ok, so a later breakfast around nine. I really need to go to the gym."

Chloe laughed. "I think we both do, yes, nine sounds a reasonable time. I spotted a yoga class that I would like to do. My anxiety is really good and a yoga class will help keep it that way."

He kissed her on the hand. "Aye, that is a grand idea. You have been coping so well, so proud of you, Chloe." As he walked back to his room he thought about going back and seeing if she wanted to go for a nightcap. He didn't want to leave her. He turned around and then thought better of it. She had said that she was tired. Before he had time to change his mind again, he turned and knocked on the door. "Chloe, it is only me," he said as not to startle her.

She opened the door.

"I was thinking of going for a nightcap, would you like to come?"

"Yeah, sure, we don't have to get up early tomorrow, sounds like a plan. I will just grab my things."

They headed to the main bar, and there was a three-piece band playing, and the dance floor was packed. They grabbed a drink and found the only spare table which looked like it had only just been left, judging by the empty glasses left on the table.

"I will go and find a waiter to clear this off for us."

She grabbed his arm. "It's ok. They will come and clear it soon, sit down and relax, let's just put them to one side and you can come and sit closer to me." She started stacking all the glasses and he helped her. All of a sudden those glasses were an asset, as he moved closer to her and they clung their drinks together.

"Cheers!"

"Wait wait wait," she said, shaking her head.

"What happened?"

"You didn't look me in the eye. When you say cheers, you must look the person in the eye."

"Oh, and I didn't."

Chloe shook her head. "Ok, let's try again."

This time, he stared into her eyes and they locked. The three-second delay before they both said "Cheers" was obvious to them both neither wanted to look away.

"That's much better." She was wriggling in her seat. They had both felt that they had just shared a special moment. Both of them were way too shy to do anything about it.

Chloe was tapping her feet and looked keen to dance. "Come on, let's have a dance." He stood up and before either of them had time to think about it he had pulled her onto the dance floor.

"You're a very good dancer," she yelled in his ear.

"You haven't seen anything yet. Watch this." He was pretending to be John Travolta, using all the moves while Chloe laughed before he grabbed her and started swinging her around. They were having a ball. All too soon the band announced it was their last song of the night and started playing a ballad. They looked at each other and shrugged and thought why not. Jack pulled her into his arms.

Oh god, he thought. *There is the scent of her hair, it's driving me nuts. Think about boats*, he thought to himself, *cars, anything but not Chloe.* She felt so wonderful in his arms. What about what Matt said? Should he try and kiss her?

Chloe was melting in his arms, her legs were like jelly, and she never wanted the song to end. There was that smell of him again. *Maybe, if I move in a little bit closer and see if he moves away, she could feel his heart pounding.* Oh God, he was like a great big security blanket; it felt so nice.

This is crazy. I have to make a move. He moved his hand down her back and was about to pull her in a bit tighter for a kiss—but then the song finished. *Damn it,* he missed his chance. He took too long and now it was too late. They were both very hot and bothered and were hoping it was not obvious to the other.

"It is so hot. Come with me, let's go outside and cool down a bit." She nodded and grabbed her bag. He held her hand showing her the way through the crowd, not stopping until they made it to the back of the deck. "Oh, look at all the beautiful stars, I have never seen so many." She was gazing up in awe. She looked so beautiful in the moonlight. *How can I handle this*, he thought. Matt's words were ringing loudly in his head; he glanced back at Chloe still staring at the skies, so innocent and beautiful. It was all too much. *I don't care anymore what happens, I am going crazy with desire for her.* He had never had feelings about any girl like this before; desire, yes, but not like this, this was different. *I have to make a move.* He put his arm around her shoulder and pulled her closer. Then out of the darkness, they heard a voice. "Hey, what are you two doing? Getting some fresh air, I see."

It was John and Ava. They spun around. Straight away John knew he had walked in at the wrong time. He had felt Ava pull him back when she saw them, but John had too many drinks and was too slow to realise. He had already yelled out before he worked it out.

"It's a lovely evening, so we thought we would come out and get some air. We have been in there dancing, came out to cool down a bit," said Jack uncomfortably, fumbling his words, trying to compose himself.

"Oh, we have been at the wine bar with Danni and Rocco, so came out for a gaze at the stars before going to our cabin." John was slurring and wobbling a little but always with a huge smile on his face.

"What are you doing for Naples tomorrow?" asked Ava quickly, trying to move the focus of John.

"We are just heading in and taking it as it comes. We need a quiet day. What are you doing?" answered Chloe.

"We have no plans either. Maybe we could tag along with you guys tomorrow for a few hours"

"Sounds great! Let's say we meet at ten in the terminal?"

They all agreed as Ava was dragging john away, saying goodbye. John was still chatting as he was being led backward by the hand. He was a funny guy and great company; it would be fun hanging out with them tomorrow.

"Let's head in as well, it is getting late," said Chloe as she yawned.

"Aye, I am a bit weary also." He smiled gently. He was very glad that they had appeared when they did. What if he had made his move and she rejected him, he would have looked like a fool and he would probably have lost his good friend. *Shit, that was close.* He needed to keep a barrier up. Definitely not get that close again.

Chapter 9

NAPLES

Chloe woke early and rubbed her eyes as she opened her blinds. She made a coffee and went back to bed to sit and enjoy the morning for a while. She thought about Paddy and had a laugh; he was trying to play cupid, she was sure of it. If Jack cared for her, as Paddy said, why didn't he make a move? Maybe Paddy had been making it all up. But then, what if Jack was just as scared as she was? They were having a fun time as friends and taking it any further could ruin it. But in the back of her mind, she wondered: if John and Ava had not turned up last night, would things have been different? She was almost certain he was getting in real close, ready to make a move.

She arrived to meet Jack on time; he was waiting with their now traditional morning drink and a lovely warm smile on his face, always looking so happy to see her.

"Oh, I love relaxed breakfasts with you, Jack," she smiled as she sat down, her bangles clanging as she threw her bag on the empty seat beside her. "You have been to the gym already, I am guessing."

"Oh, aye, ready to start the day. Cheers!" He held out his glass. "And you made it to your yoga class."

"Yes, it was just what I needed, I am a new person."

They enjoyed a lovely long breakfast together; they had an hour before they had to meet John and Ava. Chloe had a Mexican bean-and-ham burrito and Jack piled his plate the usual way. He glanced at his watch; it was time to make a move. They began making their way to the terminal. It was a beautiful morning. The sun already had a sting in it but they were both dressed for the heat. Chloe had on a cool floral peasant dress with sandshoes for walking and her hat. Jack had on a beige loose cheesecloth-style shirt with shorts and sandshoe-style shoes. He could wear anything and look great, and today was no exception; he had his hair tied back and sunglasses on to finish his cool but casual demeanour.

There were a few pop-up-market-style shops, so they strolled around while they waited. It wasn't too long before they spotted them coming off the boat. Ava was beautiful as usual in a rust-coloured spotted sundress, which looked lovely on her and her hair was neatly pulled to one side. She also wore a hat that matched her dress and huge pale pink sunglasses. John was just in shorts and a polo shirt with a peak cap, as usual. They all greeted each other and went to the bus area. There were lots of buses going into Naples so they grabbed one easily.

The bus ride was quick, and they were there in no time. Taking a look around they decided to buy tickets for the hop-on-hop-off bus. It was the prettiest city. The streets were all lined with lemon trees and they had an abundance of fruit on them. The boys helped the girls onboard and headed up the stairs to the open-air roof. Chloe sat in the front and Ava settled into the one behind her as the boys sat next to them. They were all busy fidgeting around, setting up their earplugs and choosing the correct language.

"I am going to speak Japanese today," said John in his best Japanese accent.

"What are you doing back there?" Jack turned to see what he was up to now, nothing would have surprised him.

"Mine is talking in Japanese"

"You have to change the language to English." Jack got up and helped him. "Here, it's fixed, am I going to have to look after you all day," joked Jack, sitting back in his seat.

"Oh, I was going to have fun being Japanese for a day." He was speaking in his silly voice again and they all laughed.

Jack bantered with him about it for a bit and John gave back just as much as Jack gave him. It was amusing to listen to them, and the girls were both having a laugh. All fixed, they were set to go.

Jack took some selfies of them on the bus and then put his arm around her shoulder. She snuggled in a bit closer. He did like her, she was sure of it. Jack was thinking the same thing; she didn't pull away or freeze—she actually snuggled closer. *Maybe Paddy and Matt had been right*, he thought. John was digging Ava in the ribs sitting behind them, and she was shoving him back and laughing. They both knew they liked each other and thought it was cute and funny to watch.

The bus travelled around the city and went all the way to the top where it stopped for photo opportunities. It was a spectacular sight. The bus driver took some lovely shots of the four of them together. They made a great-looking group and they would all cherish the photos forever. They took more scenery photos and then they were off again. They were back where they started in no time.

It was lunchtime so they decided to find a place to eat. Ava spotted a trattoria that had outdoor seating right on the marina overlooking the water. "How about that place? It is so nice with the pretty red and white tablecloths."

"We are not eating the table cloths, Ava, we want the food to be tasty and authentic," mocked John as everyone laughed.

"No, she is right, it is very inviting, especially that lovely terrace. Well picked, Ava."

"Oh, so the girls are ganging up on us now I see," laughed Jack.

"Well, if the food is bad we can blame them, not a bad idea," winked John as he started to lead the way towards the entry. They were shown to a table on the terrace shaded by a vine-covered pergola.

"Oh, what beautiful atmosphere this place has," smiled Ava as she took her seat.

"Anything for you my dear as long as you are happy," smirked John as he helped her.

Menus were brought out and they all studied them. "Naples is the birth place of pizza so we have to have at least one pizza," said Chloe as she flicked her hair and turned the menu over to see what was on the other side.

"Ok, that's easy, we will get their most popular pizza," said Jack who was still studying the menu. "We have to have a bruschetta and a seafood plate with prawns, oysters, and calamari to start," added John loudly.

Jack was instantly impressed. "Oh, aye that sounds wonderful. We can start with that and then have pizzas after that." His eyes darted around at everyone and they all nodded and agreed. He put his hand up and gestured for the waiter who came over immediately.

"What would you like for drinks?" he asked with a smile. "Is everyone happy with a beer?" They nodded. "Ok, peronis and now food."

"We will have some bruschetta and a plate of seafood to share as starters and a few of your most popular pizzas after that."

"Perfecto, I will take care of the pizza." He picked up the menus and was off. He was back with the beers in a flash.

The food was incredible, the bruschetta and seafood plates that arrived at the table were impressive, and they slowly devoured them, as they listened to John and Jack bantering off each other with their humorous jokes. They got louder with every beer. "This seafood is so fresh. The prawns and oysters are huge," said Chloe as she peeled another prawn happily.

"Oh, aye and you can still taste the saltwater on the oysters."

"I love the calamari. It melts in your mouth," added Ava, cutting it into tiny pieces with her knife and fork as they all watched.

"Just pick it up with your fingers, Ava, we are not in a five-star restaurant now," teased John and everyone laughed.

Another round of beers was ordered as they waited for the pizza. The waiter arrived with the pizza. "You are going to enjoy these and I even cut them into slices as you requested much to the disgust of the chef." They all laughed. It was not done in Italy; it was actually frowned upon. He placed them on the table and yelled, "Prego!" and left. They all enjoyed them and there was nothing left at the end. Jack and John decided on a lemon cake for dessert. It was a wonderful authentic Italian meal none of them would forget in a hurry.

"Would you like any other drinks?"

"No, just the cheque, thank you," said Chloe.

"Where are you from? I have been trying to pick your accent."

"I am Australian."

"Oh, I thought so, but that is so far away."

"Yes, it's a long way, that is for sure."

"Wait, I will bring you a surprise." He was back with four shots of lemon cello. "You must try. Complimentary lemon cello shots for everyone." He put them down on the table. "Prego!"

"See, this is what happens when you go out with Chloe, she always gets offered the best wines, the best food and offered treats. That's why I hang out with her," Jack teased.

"I don't think that's the only reason," said John smugly as Ava dug him in the ribs.

Everyone wriggled in their seats uncomfortably and Chloe blushed. Ava changed the subject quickly. "What's the rest of the gang doing today?"

"Danni and Rocco are doing the Amalfi coast with Cruz and Catalina and Paddy and Maggie are doing a tour of a lemon cello factory. They needed a quiet day," informed John.

After lunch, Chloe and Ava spotted a little souvenir shop next door so they wandered in while the boys fixed up the bill. "I can't believe how cheap the meal was," said Jack. "And the food was incredible, but don't tell Ava. I will never hear the end of it."

"I just need to grab something to take home," said Jack as he headed back in to the restaurant.

"I will go find the girls." As he walked back outside, John spotted a taxi holding a sign saying Pompei. Jack came out and spotted what John was looking at.

"That is one thing I would love to do, Pompeii. I wonder if we have enough time," said Jack, looking around at John.

"It is definitely on my bucket list also."

"Look, wait here I will go and ask." He went over and spoke to the driver, hoping he spoke English, while everyone waited patiently in the hot sun.

The taxi driver ensured them that they had enough time as it was only a twenty-minute drive. They agreed and jumped into the cab. On arrival, the driver gave them a card and told them to call him when finished.

The ticket lines were not too long and they were soon inside. They used the guide maps to find their way around. It was an incredible feeling that took over you as you stood in the streets and imagined the town as it was. They saw The Praedia di Giulia Felice, the forum, the ampitheatre, and the garden of the fugitives, and the boys were both enthralled with the brothel. They laughed and joked at the menu on the walls with carvings of women in different sexual poses.

They spent a few hours wandering around before calling the taxi and heading out the front to wait. There was a little gift stall where John spotted erotic calendars, featuring all the poses they had seen on the brothel walls. The boys could not help themselves and went inside to purchase them, laughing and joking with each other along the way.

"I am sorry if we disturbed anything last night," said Ava sweetly.

"No not at all, we were just looking at the stars."

"Oh, ok, I felt bad I tried to stop John, but he is hopeless," she laughed. "He really likes you Chloe."

"Mmm maybe, he's a super guy, that is for sure."

"You two make a lovely couple," she smiled warmly at her; they were becoming very close friends, Chloe felt calm around her. She had a soft gentle personality that made her relaxed. "Thanks for coming today. It's nice having you around."

The boys came out with their calendars still chuckling as the taxi arrived. They were back at the ship in no time and decided to have a cocktail on the deck for the sail-off before heading to get ready for dinner. It was elegant night tonight and everyone got dressed up for dinner. Jack said he had packed a suit and

Chloe had an evening gown. John and Ava left to go for a quick nap; it had been a big few days.

"It was an amazing day today, Jack, thank you," said Chloe as she finished the last slurp of her drink.

"It's not over yet," he laughed. "I can't believe we went to Pompeii. It was incredible, wasn't it? And the food at lunch, I couldn't get enough of it," he said dreamily as Chloe watched him and laughed. Food was definitely his greatest love. "Come on, let's go dress for dinner."

Jack was back at her door to pick her up at seven-twenty, as promised. As she opened the door she was impressed. He was so very sexy in his suit and he had let his hair out which fell neatly into place, resting on his shoulders. He had on the after-shave that Chloe recognised straight away; it was definitely starting to be her favourite.

Jack stood back and looked at her in awe.

"You are absolutely beautiful, Chloe." She instantly blushed and he smiled.

"Thank you, you look pretty damn sexy yourself," she winked at him.

He was staring again but couldn't stop. He loved the pale blue backless evening gown that showed off her beautiful tan. And no bra, shit how was he going to handle this tonight? "You might need a jacket or something," he heard himself saying. *What did I say that for? She looked incredible why did she need a jacket?* She grabbed a silk throw she had bought in Florence and put it around her shoulders. The scent of her hair as she tossed it out over the shawl filled the air. *This was absolute torture,* he thought. She had lightly oiled her hair with the Nuxe oil for shine and it looked beautiful as it fell loose down her back. She was very happy she had purchased it.

They looked like the perfect couple as he took her by the hand and they walked to dinner. "I can't wait to see what everyone is wearing tonight, especially Danni. She has a gorgeous wardrobe."

"She spends too much money on clothes, that lassie."

Everyone was at the table when they arrived. Danni looked stunning in an embroidered mermaid evening gown. Ava wore a soft pink cocktail dress and Catalina wore an emerald green evening dress. All the men were in suits except Paddy who wore his kilt and Maggie wore a pantsuit, which matched the navy in Paddy's kilt with a little tartan shawl. Everyone agreed with Paddy when he said they were the best-looking table of the night.

Jack helped her to her seat and sat beside her. She stared around the table smiling. They were all becoming great friends and got on well. She had been worried, leaving her safety net at home and venturing outside her comfort zone, but what she had never realised was you create new comfort zones and that was what she was creating with her new friends sitting around the table with her tonight. She could achieve anything now.

"What has everyone got planned for Croatia and Corfu?" asked Paddy as the meal was served. No one seemed to have planned anything yet. "Well, I have an idea to put to you all. Why don't we all throw in together and hire a boat for a few hours. It comes with a captain and is large enough to take us all comfortably and is very reasonable."

They all loved the idea and agreed it sounded like a fun day out. "Ok, I will organise it. I have a phone number a friend gave me but it was too much for just Maggie and me."

Chloe and Ava both joined Danni in pushing their food around their plates that night, both extremely full from a huge lunch. It didn't seem to bother the boys. They were still eating like there was no tomorrow.

After dinner, Paddy came over to chat with Jack. "Have you noticed how beautiful Chloe looks tonight? There are other men in the room eyeing her off, you know."

"Yea I know, I know." He glanced around as he took a sip on his beer. He couldn't see any but he would not have been surprised if he was right.

"Would anyone like to go dancing," asked Catalina and all the girls said it sounded like a fantastic idea.

Jack knew if he was going to have a chance with Chloe he had to make his move right there and then before he was dragged off dancing. He leaned over to Chloe. "Dinner is over. Why don't we leave early and have a quiet drink somewhere? It's a day at sea tomorrow, we can relax and enjoy the night."

"That sounds like a nice idea." They declined the invite for dancing and said goodnight to everyone. Jack stood and took her arm and they left.

John dug Ava in the ribs again and she smiled. Everyone was hoping the two of them would make the move. It was a joke around the table and John was taking bets on who would make the first move and when. Most had money on Chloe making the first move as Jack was too chicken.

They wandered along the hallway towards the main bar area.

"Wouldn't it be nice to have a nice quiet wine? Wish we had a bottle of that wine we love. I bet they don't have it on the boat," she said sadly. Jack thought all his luck had come at once.

"Well, I just might be able to help you out with that, but you will have to come up to my room. If you trust me, I promise to be a complete gentleman," laughed Jack, throwing his hands up in the air.

"Really, you have a bottle of that wine? That's amazing," she said shocked. He nodded. "You really are full of surprises. Yes, let's go."

He was both anxious and nervous taking her back to his room. Could he really handle this situation? He had just promised her to be a complete gentleman. Why did he do that? He was setting himself barriers he wasn't sure he could obey. He wanted to back out there and then, but didn't.

He opened the door and she stepped inside. She instantly knew that it was his room. It smelt like him. It was neat and tidy, for a guy travelling alone also.

He went over and drew the curtains.

"You have a balcony!" squealed Chloe.

"Aye. I had very limited cabins to choose from. I booked last minute, remember?"

Jack opened the balcony doors.

"Come out here and make yourself comfortable. I will pour us some drinks." He took off his jacket as she stepped outside. He quickly returned with a couple of glasses and a bottle of wine. He was shaking as he poured the wine.

"Jack, it really is our wine. Where did you find it?"

He loved how excited she got; there was that wave of non-control he was worried about. This girl was driving him nuts.

"Well, today at lunch I noticed they sold that wine so while you went next door to the souvenir shop with Ava, I asked for a take-away. I just put it in my satchel bag. I could not tell you as it was supposed to be a gift for you to take home to Australia. And maybe remind you of us. But when a very beautiful girl says she might come back to your room for the wine, well of course, I thought well why not. I will have to buy you another present now," he said with a little smile.

"You never cease to amaze me," she said with a chuckle.

He sat down and they stared out over the water. It was a huge full moon and it lit up the water, making it shimmer. Chloe stood and went to the railing for a better view.

"Oh, Jack, come here look at the size of this moon."

He came over and stood beside her as they drank their wine.

He was extremely nervous; he had her in his room. He had promised to be a complete gentleman and he would do his best to keep his word, but it was getting pretty hard. She looked incredible tonight. "Pompei was good today, wasn't it?" he said, trying to stop thinking of her. But shit, now he was thinking of the brothel sketches on the wall.

"It was a great day. I enjoyed it all so much and I just love Ava. She is so much fun." She was still looking at the moon, thinking how beautiful it was. She was also a bit uneasy; she was shaking a bit and hoped that he did not see. He looked and smelt so good tonight. She had butterflies in her belly all night every time he looked at her, and now she was in his room. *Bloody hell I hope you can handle this,* she said to herself trying to appear cool and calm.

"We just left Sorrento, so I guess that must be a Sorrento Moon. How beautiful is it? Do you know the song 'Sorrento Moon' by Tina Arena?" She rambled.

"No, what is a Sorrento moon? Does the moon have mystical powers?" Jack asked, teasing her, smiling with that grin that melted her.

"It might," answered Chloe dreamily, looking at the moon. "You will just have to wait and see." She turned to him, smiling.

"Well, I can't wait to find out," winked Jack, feeling tortured inside; she looked so beautiful.

He went inside to compose himself a little and came out with a packet of nuts and placed them on the table. He had his phone in his hand and after a quick Google he turned to her and said, "Is this your song, Chloe?"

"Sorrento Moon" was playing.

"Yes, that's it. Oh, it's so beautiful isn't it, and here we are witnessing a beautiful huge Sorrento moon while Tina serenades us. Oh, just incredible."

"Aye, and it is a very nice song also."

Chloe was leaning on the railing. Jack was watching her; he loved every bit of her. Her child-like beauty, her soft heart and her sense of humour. He wanted her in his arms instantly, to hell with holding back any longer.

"Come dance with me, Chloe." Holding out his hand, she took it gently. He could feel she was shaking a bit...or was that him?

He pulled her into his arms and they danced closely. She put her head on his chest. She could smell his scent and feel his body so close to hers. They swayed and moved closely together. Neither of them ever wanted the song to end. He was struggling, he had the girl of his dreams in his arms and he didn't know how long he was going to be able to hold back. The song came to the end. He had mesmerised her; she looked up to tell him how beautiful that all was and found him staring down at her. He bent towards her and the next thing she knew they were embraced in a kiss. It was soft and tender. She thought her knees were going to give way. It felt exactly the way she had dreamed it would.

"I am sorry, I promised not only myself but you also, that this would not happen," said Jack, as he moved away. "I apologise." He was raking his fingers through his hair and began to turn away.

"I am glad that it did," she pulled him back towards her and he moved his head closer to hers. This time the kissing was far more passionate. He pulled her closer to him and she could feel he wanted her just as much as she had wanted him.

She started to unbutton his shirt and put her hand inside, feeling his skin and muscles. She felt his breathing changing and moved slowly down to unbutton his pants. She slipped the fly down and put her hand in to softly caress him. His pants dropped to the floor and he stepped out of them, kicking them to the side.

He then undid her zip on her dress and slowly slid the straps of her dress off her shoulders. Her dress fell to the floor and she stepped out of it and kicked it to the side. He pulled her away, panting. *Let me see you.* His eyes went over her body.

"My God, you're beautiful," he said. He took her in his arms again and started to slowly touch her breast. He ripped his pants off unable to get them off quick enough and picked her up in his arms and placed her on the bed. He sat and stared at her before kissing her even more eagerly than before. He started to kiss her all over. As he kissed her nipple, her whole body started to tremble. He moved across to the other one and kissed it gently. She was frozen, as he gently kissed her all over her belly. He pulled off her panties as he moved down even lower, kissing her between the legs. She started to sigh; he had her body in a place she had never been before, and he let his tongue dance between her legs. Her moans were becoming more frantic.

"No, stop," she yelled. "I don't want to finish yet." She laid him back and started to kiss him all over also, the taste of his salty skin exciting her even more. She moved down slowly, heavy with desire, finishing between his legs. She pleasured him with her mouth and tongue until he was also crying out for her to stop. They were both breathing extremely heavy, the electricity running through their veins was unbearable. Unable to wait any longer he gently pushed himself inside her as they both sighed. They rocked together in ecstasy. He felt her orgasm and finally he also let himself go. They lay back exhausted; breathing so heavy, he thought his heart was going to leap right out of his chest. He pulled her towards him and she rested her head on his chest, listening to his heart race as he kissed the top of her head. *"Mo leannan falaich,"* he whispered, panting out of breath.

They lay together silent for a while, getting their breath back before he got up on one arm and smiled.

"My God, you are beautiful." He was still looking over her body. "You have an all-over tan," he said, sounding surprised.

"I have a private courtyard at home; I can sunbake naked," she said with a small smirk on her face.

"Now that's an image I will never be able to get out of my head." He was still staring at her, unable to take his eyes off hers. "I am sorry I don't mean to stare but you are so beautiful."

"I think I have done my share of staring tonight also. I now know why you go to the gym, your body is a work of art."

"You had me in such a state I thought I was going to explode. I have wanted you for so long," he said softly.

"You are an extremely good lover, Jack. I have never been treated with such pleasures before, and you think that 'you' were about to explode," smiled Chloe "I was electrified."

"Let's cancel the rest of the cruise. We can spend it here in my cabin naked. It would be the best cruise ever," he said all of a sudden, looking very serious. Chloe laughed; she knew him too well by now. "I think that you would starve. You wouldn't survive a day."

"Aye, I think you're right there."

"Tell me, what do those Scottish words you keep saying to me mean. I asked Paddy and he said they were nice words but he didn't tell me either."

"You told Paddy?" His eyebrows shot up, his eyes were as wide as plates. "Oh, well, that explains why he has been in my ear every night." He was raking his hair again with his fingers, feeling uncomfortable. "Well, you won't be hearing those words again because my secret is now out," explained Jack.

"What secret? What do you mean?" said Chloe confused. She felt scared, uncomfortable. She had done the wrong thing. *Shit, what did those words mean?* He sat up and looked her in the eye. She was comforted by the warm and gentle look that was in his eyes as he gave her a small, almost embarrassed smile.

"Well, it means my forever love, my secret love. But you now know how I feel about you, so it's not a secret anymore," said Jack in a quiet voice. She smiled at him looking into his eyes. He felt the same way she felt about him. It was too good to be true. She finally came out of the trance he had put her under and was able to speak.

"Oh, that's why Paddy has been in my ear every night also. Now it is all starting to make perfect sense."

They both laughed. "Paddy has been trying to match-make us together."

"Aye," said Jack. "I can protect you from anything, Chloe, but not from the spooky magical spells of your Sorrento moon or a crazy leprechaun like Paddy," smiled Jack, tracing his finger over her breasts gently as he looked over her.

"Wait, is he Irish? I thought he was Scottish," asked Chloe, looking confused.

"Well, you can't be that silly. Just being Scottish, he must have some sort of Irish in him especially with a name like Paddy," smiled Jack.

"Well, whatever he is, he is a lovely man." She started to sit up. "Let's get up and finish our wine. We have a day at sea tomorrow we can sleep in," said Chloe, never wanting the night to end.

"If I knew when I bought that bottle today the night would end up like this I would have bought a dozen," said Jack.

He put on his robe and offered Chloe the spare one.

"Come and join me outside, it's beautiful out here," said Jack as he pulled out her chair.

"Oh, it is beautiful, isn't it? I am so happy we are here together tonight."

They moved their chairs closer and Jack put his arm around her shoulder and they watched the moon shining on the water.

"I have a little secret to tell you too," announced Chloe softly with a little smile. Jack looked at her wondering what she might say next. He was hoping that it was good news and not bad.

"I have been wanting you also, Jack. You are my secret I have desired for almost our entire cruise. You have totally swept me off my feet."

"Well, it's lucky for both of us. The magical Sorrento moon cast its spell over us tonight," he smiled relieved and kissed her hand.

"I thought you were going to kiss me on the banks of the river in Florence," smiled Chloe.

"Aye, I was, but that woman interrupted us, asking for the time. Then I was happy that she did. I thought I would wreck everything we had if you didn't feel the same way about me. I was scared that I would lose your friendship. I was pretty protective of it. What we have is very, very special."

"I was feeling the same. You had me in such a romantic mood with your beautiful story. If you didn't kiss me, I was going to kiss you," she said with a teasing look.

"Then I was going to kiss you out on the deck last night, but John and Ava turned up."

Chloe laughed. "Yes I had a feeling it might have happened last night, but I am so happy we finally got it all together."

They finished their wine and Jack took her to the shower. Seeing her naked again made him instantly wild with passion. He gently stroked her body and kissed her breasts, while she closed her eyes and groaned with desire. He had never made a woman groan before and it was so sexy; his desire for her instantly rose to the next level. He entered her slowly and they rocked together until they were both breathing hard and moaning. They washed each other and then slipped into bed.

Chapter 10
DAY OF BLISS

Chloe woke the next morning with Jack wrapped around her as they spooned. She smiled. She had never been happier; he was a dream come true. She felt him stir; he was holding her breast and gently started to stroke it. She felt him harden instantly. "Good morning, beautiful," he said as he was kissing her back gently and rolled her over. "My God, I am the luckiest man in the world. I thought I dreamt this but you are really here." He started kissing her neck and then moved down licking her nipple which was erect, showing him how much she was enjoying him. He needed to hear her groan again, he couldn't believe he could do that to a woman. She didn't disappoint him. She thought she would orgasm then and there so she laid him back and went down on him while he groaned with pleasure. He pulled her up and she jumped on top of him, taking him, in and out rocking as they both exploded at the same time.

"I think I have died and gone to heaven, I have never had sex like that before," panted Jack.

"Me neither, you have turned me into a wild beast."

"We are great lovers together."

Jack, finally coming to his senses, realised he was starving. He kissed her and said he would be back. He got dressed and went upstairs to the food court. Breakfast was in full swing. He grabbed a tray and piled it with as much food as he could. Arriving back in no time, Chloe had made them coffee while he was gone and they set it all up on the outdoor table.

"Wait," he said as he ran back inside. He returned with a half empty whisky bottle and poured it into their coffee. "If you are going to hang out with me, then you better start liking whisky," he grinned.

"Where did you get that bottle?" asked Chloe surprised.

"I may have snuck one or two in my luggage," he smirked sheepishly. "I can't live without a dram in the morning or a dram at night," he admitted. "I guess it's the Scot coming out in me, if you ask Maggie I bet she would tell you that Paddy has one or two tucked away also."

"Well, I guess I better buckle up for a wild Highland ride," she laughed. There was no other place that she would rather be than by his side. She had never been happier in her life.

They sat and enjoyed their feast of bacon, eggs, toast beans, and fruit. They had the whole day to get to know each other and enjoy each other. However, she needed to go back to her room and change at some stage, but they were in no hurry. So after breakfast, Jack showered and changed and then followed her back to her cabin. He watched as she was carefully sneaking, without too many people seeing.

"What are you doing?" he whispered.

"I am still in my party clothes. People will know we have been up to no good," she whispered back. He laughed at how innocent she was and how it worried her so much.

Timmy met her in the hallway; he looked after cleaning her room. "Your room is done," he smiled at Jack as they went into her cabin. She could have died of embarrassment; she knew Timmy would know what they had been up to. Jack laughed at her. "He would have seen a lot worse, and my room is the one we should be worried about. It was obvious I wasn't alone last night," he smirked. She blushed and shut the door behind them.

She showered and changed while Jack waited and they went upstairs to the pool area and found a double cabana day bed.

Jack rubbed her down with sunscreen and she did the same to him. She felt his muscles as she rubbed him down and knew she was stirring him again, but she was enjoying the way his body felt and did not want to stop. He had turned her into a wild woman; she would never have acted in such a way, but she loved the way he made her feel. They lay together in the sunshine until Jack got thirsty and went to the bar and grabbed them a beer. They didn't even notice Paddy and Maggie walking past, as they were embraced in a kiss and Paddy just elbowed Maggie and they both smiled.

That night at dinner, everyone watched as they walked in together, holding hands. Jack pulled out the chair for Chloe and she sat. He sat down and looked around the table. Everyone was watching and smiling.

"What?" asked Jack, smiling, turning, looking at everyone around the table.

It was John who finally spoke. "Well, don't you two have an announcement to make?"

They looked at each other and started laughing.

"Paddy saw you two getting it on at the pool bar today," John smirked.

"Wow, news really travels fast around here." Everyone was laughing and Chloe was as red as a beetroot. "Ok, ok, well, yes as a matter of fact, Chloe and I have realised we like each other a whole lot more than just friends."

They all cheered and clapped. "We knew it, we knew it. Finally!" They were all up and out of their seats, walking around to congratulate them, as they also stood. Everyone agreed they made the perfect couple and joked about getting invited to the wedding. Danni ordered two bottles of champagne and glasses. "Any excuse to have a champagne." Danni laughed as she handed them out after the waiter poured them.

Jack made a toast. "To Paddy, the match maker!"

Everyone echoed, "To Paddy!"

Then Paddy made a toast, "To the beautiful couple, our friends!" They all cheered.

"Wait!" yelled John. "Who made the first move?"

Everyone was staring at them.

"What, why?" asked Jack, looking confused.

"We just need to know." They were all looking intrigued, waiting to hear the answer.

"I did," said Jack, looking very proud. They were all sighing and bantering with each other. Then Chloe talked over them loudly. "Yes, but then you backed out apologising and 'I' took it to the next step," she said with a cheeky smile.

Everyone roared. "I won! I won!" John was doing his happy dance.

"Wait, you bet on us getting together?" asked Jack, not believing what he was hearing.

"Aye, of course, the others lost days ago. John and I were the closest," laughed Paddy, joining John in his happy dance, slapping him on the back. "But everyone knew it would be Chloe who got it over the line, you're too shy," said John as he put his arm around Jack's shoulder, laughing. Everyone agreed laughing while Chloe blushed with embarrassment, gasping at how everyone bet she would be the one to make the first move.

Cruz and Catalina had to leave early as they had their gig in one of the bar areas and had to get ready. They would all be there to watch them and cheer them on. They found a table and settled in to watch the show. The men went to get the drinks and the girls all chatted, wanting to know all the details about how they had finally got together. Chloe told them as much as she wanted them to know as the boys returned.

Cruz came out first all dressed in black and sat on his stool, Catalina was right behind him. She was dressed in a black and red flamenco dress tight fitting at the top with a layered skirt pulled up at the side to show the beautiful layers and fastened with a red rose.

They played a few numbers and the crowd seemed to really enjoy it. Paddy got up, grabbing Maggie by the arm and led her to the dance floor. He turned to encourage everyone to join them. John and Ava were the next ones up and then everyone followed. They were all dancing the best Flamenco they could, stomping their shoes on the wooden floor. The dance floor was soon packed and Cruz and Catalina performed an amazing show. As it ended, everyone was puffing and sweating and sat back down. People started calling out for an encore and after a minute they came back out. Catalina had changed into the stunning dress she wore at the karaoke, and everyone cheered. They did the Fado number and once again you could have heard a pin drop in the room. The applause was deafening at the end and they asked everyone to join them on the floor for the last song of the night. They played a beautiful Spanish love song. Cruz's guitar work was spectacular and Catalina's voice was captivating. Everyone enjoyed a slow dance, especially Jack and Chloe holding each other tight.

"Mo leannan falaich, mo Chloe," whispered Jack into her ear.

"Oh, I love hearing you say that, please never stop," she replied dreamily, hoping she would hear those words forever.

Cruz and Catalina left the stage, joining them at the table for a drink to celebrate. They had received a very good response and had been asked to do another show later in the week. Everyone congratulated them and stayed around to share a few drinks.

Jack and Chloe were the first to leave. After they said good-night to everyone they started to walk back to their room.

"Would you like to come back to my room tonight?" asked Jack quietly. He wasn't sure how she would feel about spending another night with him. He was suddenly feeling very embarrassed asking her, and hoped she would say yes.

"Wild horses couldn't keep me away," she smiled at him; she had never wanted anything more in her life.

When they arrived back at his room, she went to the bathroom to freshen up while Jack poured them a quick whisky. He took the glasses out to the veranda and waited for her. He turned as she walked towards him, dressed in an extremely short French camisole. He almost dropped his glass. She walked over to him, put her arms around his neck and kissed him. He put his hand down her back, realising it was all she was wearing.

"You're very sexy tonight," he said softly, almost lost for words.

"I had this on under my dress, so I thought I would get comfortable. Do you like it? I bought it when I went shopping in Marseille."

"Like it? I love it. I can't wait to see what else you bought," he teased. He sat down pulling her onto his lap. He loved feeling her body as he slowly caressed her all over, passionately kissing her. They were both starting to breathe quite heavily. He took off her camisole and looked at her, sitting there naked in his arms. He was once again in awe of her. She took off his shirt and he picked her up and carried her to the bed. He undressed, while she lay there naked, watching him. Her eyes never leaving his body, a thin layer of sweat made his muscles glisten.

"I have been wanting you all night," he said as he crawled in beside her.

"Then come and take me," she whispered, full of desire.

Chapter 11

DUBROVNIK

The morning of their sail day in Dubrovnik had arrived. It felt like they had only just gone to sleep when the alarm rang. Jack leaned over and kissed her gently on the cheek to wake her.

"Good morning, gorgeous."

She squinted and looked up at him. "Good morning, I love waking up with you."

Jack drew the blinds open and the sunshine came streaming in. They certainly had a fantastic day for boating. He made them a coffee and crawled back into bed. "You were extremely sexy last night," he said lustfully.

"I don't know what comes over me when I am around you," she giggled. "I have never been that forward before in my whole life. I like the way you make me feel," she said.

"I looove the way you make me feel," he said as he drew her in closer.

They were all to meet at the port at nine. They arrived just in time after getting side-tracked in their new-found morning activities. They had to skip breakfast, but grabbed a muffin and some fruit on the way out. They had certainly found a way to shed a few of those extra holiday kilos.

Dubrovnik was a stunning port. There were hundreds of little boats all at the marina. They had walked through the old town with the limestone pathways and baroque buildings seemed to line the walls leading to the Adriatic Sea; its beauty was outstanding. It certainly lived up to its name of, "The Pearl of the Adriatic." They arrived at the spot where they were to get the boat. Everyone was waiting.

"Good morning," they all yelled.

"Paddy, you have done well if this is our boat," said Jack still eating a banana.

"Aye, Jack, she's a beauty, isn't she? I think we will have a fun day." Then whispered, "No time for breakfast anymore, I see," winking.

A huge cabin cruiser was waiting for them. It had a luxurious lounge area at the back which would accommodate them all with ease, and a huge sun deck out the front for sunbaking. They were welcomed aboard and shown around, the fridge was stocked with beer, wine, and soft drinks and they were invited to help themselves. The captain gave them a rundown of the day, and safety procedures talk and then took the stairs up to the fly bridge.

They set off on their way to the first island, Lokrum. The women looked relaxed in shorts, t-shirt and a sunhat and the men were all in casual boardies and shirt or t-shirt.

"Thanks for organising this for us, Paddy," said Cruz.

"Well, I am surprised myself it is a massive boat, but very relieved also. I get a bit scared sometimes when I organise things. If I get things wrong, Maggie hits me with a big stick."

Everyone laughed.

"Aye, that's true. I felt like hitting you with a big bloody stick after you threw me in the rose bushes the other week coming home from the pub."

No one knew if it was a true story or not but they were all intrigued. "Come on, Paddy, what did you do to our poor Maggie? Is that true?" asked Jack, opening a beer and handing him one.

"Aye, it is true, but it is not as it seems. You see, Maggie's shoes were hurting her feet as we had been dancing all night, so I was piggy backing her home, but I was a bit too wobbly for her weaving all over the footpath and she got a wee bit scared so asked me to put her down."

"Aye, that's right, put me down. But what did you do, Paddy? You tell everyone what you did."

"Well, I spotted a wee stone fence so I thought I would lean back slowly and place her gently on the fence to help her get off…"

"Put me down gently? What a laugh! You threw me in the bloody rose bush's!"

Everyone was holding back laughter.

"Well I tried hard but I lost my balance and you went head first over the fence. It wasn't my fault there were rose bush's over the fence. How would I know that?"

That was it, no one could control their laughter any longer as everyone was rolling around in fits of laughter.

"Well, you could have let go of me, you dragged me over the fence with ya, we were picking thorns out of each other all night," added Paddy.

"Stop it, you two," yelled out Chloe, unable to hardly speak. It took ages for everyone to finally control themselves. But just as they did, Paddy started again. "Here, look, I still have the scars," Paddy was showing his mostly healed wounds.

"Don't you start. I wore the brunt of the fall, I was covered in them," she started, showing her scars and everyone was laughing again.

"So the story is true" said Catalina, shocked.

"Aye, of course, lucky we had another whisky bottle that night, we bathed our wounds and drank the rest," laughed Paddy.

"No more, no more! Oh, you are making me spill my champagne," said Danni, laughing hysterically.

"Well, put the glass down, Danni, you don't have to fill it to the brim, you know," sighed Rocco as he wiped the deck with a cloth.

Everyone was still giggling. "You have a live one there to deal with, Rocco," said Paddy.

"If you are on your honeymoon why aren't you all over each other like Jack and Chloe?" asked Maggie, sipping on her wine.

"We have lived together for eight years," answered Rocco.

"Yea and a two-year relationship before that," added Danni.

"We hid our relationship during that time because Rocco had a problem with us working together," she said, rolling her eyes.

"Well, yes, what if it did not work out, it would have made things difficult," said Rocco, crossing his legs.

"Wait it took you two years to work out that it was the real deal?" asked Cruz, looking confused.

"No, it was me wanting to keep it a secret in the end, it was so sexy," teased Danni, giving Rocco a sexy look.

The skipper came down. "We are arriving soon at the island. You are all allowed an hour's visit to do as you wish, swim, shop, or walk the trail around the town. We will dock soon," he scurried back up to his seat. Most of them decided to do a bit of sightseeing as they knew they were stopping for a swim later.

The skipper, Nick, got them all back on board on time and they set off to a blue cave which was stunning and then stopped at a calm part of the sea where he put the back net out so they could swim. Jack, Cruz, and John jumped straight into the water. Rocco followed their lead. Paddy opened the fridge and poured the women a wine, grabbing a beer for himself. It was a lovely day, so relaxing. Ava and Catalina went off the back and onto the net. "Come on, Chloe," Ava was yelling. Danni had already made it clear she was not swimming and settled back in, pouring another champagne. The boys all teased her but she stood her ground and stayed with Maggie and Paddy.

The water was so warm and clear; Jack came over and joined Chloe on the net. They could see the fish swimming around them. After a while, Cruz and Catalina went to the front deck to sunbake.

After enjoying a swim, they set off to see more islands, coves, and caves. They stopped at Lopud for lunch. Nick escorted them to a lovely seafood restaurant. It was right on the water and their table for ten was waiting. Drinks were poured and they were told that lunch would be brought out soon; Nick had arranged everything, no need for menus. He went off to talk to another skipper at another table. No one could believe how beautiful the place was, they were seated, literally, right on the water's edge with a shade sail over them. The entree platters arrived and were overflowing with oysters, marinated chicken pieces, and feta dribbled with honey and herbs, hummus, and breads.

The main meal was huge platters of seafood and lamb. Prawns, oysters, grilled octopus, mussels, and crabs. Marinated lamb, Caesar and Greek salads, and more bread. The rose wine that was poured with the seafood was crisp and refreshing.

Chloe watched as Cruz left the table and was talking with Nick. He went inside the restaurant and returned with what looked like a Spanish guitar. Nick nodded to the staff and handed Cruz the guitar. He walked back to the table and stood beside Catalina.

"I have an announcement to make, please." Everyone turned and watched Cruz. "Today is my beautiful Catalina's birthday and I wish to propose a toast to her."

Everyone cheered and yelled, "Happy Birthday, Cat!"

Nick was busy handing out bits of paper around the table and then disappeared, meeting a staff member with a trolley filled with wine glasses and champagne. "So today, to honour my beautiful Catalina, the love of my life, I wish to sing her a song. This song I will be singing to her in Spanish so I have arranged for the words to be printed in English so you can see what my heart is saying to her. The song is 'Acuéstate Conmigo Para Siempre.' Lay with me forever." He started to play and Catalina stared up at him, smiling. The whole restaurant by now was all watching and listening, mesmerised by the beautiful song. Chloe read the words.

I prayed for you forever
And you knocked upon my door
I knew when I saw your big mocha eyes
My heart would want you more.

Lay with me forever
Entangled in our love.
I am forever trapped
In your invisible chains of love.

Dance with me forever
But never stray too far
Rock my body gently
As I play my Spanish guitar

Lay with me forever
As you pierce me with your dart
I am tranquilised forever by your seductive love.

Stay with me forever
And walk this path called life
Lay with me forever
Catalina,
Please be my beautiful exotic wife.

Everyone started to clap but then slowly realised there was more to come. You could hear a pin drop, as Cruz handed his guitar to Nick, got something out of his pocket and dropped to one knee. Everyone gasped.

"Catalina, you are the love of my life. Will you say yes to me and marry me, so I can hold you in my arms forever?"

Catalina had tears streaming down her face. He stood and she stood with him. "Yes, of course," she cried as she threw her arms around his neck and kissed him. There wasn't a dry eye in the crowd.

"Let's fiesta!" shouted Cruz and everyone cheered.

Nick started pouring the champagne. A Croatian musician came out and started playing to keep the atmosphere alive. There was cheering and clapping and everyone took turns to wish Cruz and Catalina best wishes. A huge cake came out and they blew the candles out together.

"I am so glad she said yes, or this was overkill for just a birthday," laughed Cruz as he kissed Cat once again. The cake was cut and handed out to everyone in the restaurant. Dancing had begun once again and everyone was having a great time. Paddy was keeping everyone entertained and at times had the whole table roaring with laughter.

It was time to head back to the boat and they were all happy to sit back and chat and relax. "Thanks for everything, Paddy," said Cruz. Paddy admitted, "I had a lot of organising to do with Nick, on your behalf Cruz to pull it all off, but it turned out alright." Everyone agreed he did a good job. "The proposal I knew nothing about, I thought that I was organising a birthday party." Paddy laughed. It had been a wonderful day.

When they arrived back at the old port they all went their separate ways. Jack and Chloe took a walk through the old town. There was a sign overhead that said "drinks" with an arrow pointing through a hole in a wall.

"Come in here," said Jack excitedly.

As they stepped through the wall, they were speechless. There was a path that led them down a rocky outlook to a bar perched on the side of a cliff. It was so beautiful. They made their way down carefully hanging onto the railing for dear life, and found a table to sit and enjoy a beer, taking in the stunning scenery, watching all the sail boats go by in the sparkling Turquoise waters.

"We don't have anything like this in Scotland. I now understand why my father wanted me to travel," he said, staring at the beauty in front of them.

"We have lots of beautiful places, but this has taken my breath away."

"Aye, let's sit for a while longer, I will get us another beer."

It had been an amazing day. Croatia had never been a place Chloe had wanted to visit, but so glad she did. It was certainly one of the most beautiful places she had ever seen, and the proposal just made it all the more stunning. She had put the song into her pocket to show Kait; she would have just loved it, she couldn't wait to tell her.

They all met for dinner again that night. Everyone cheering and clapping as Cruz and Catalina arrived. The girls were all fussing over Cat's ring. It was an exquisite emerald, oval in shape surrounded by tiny diamonds. The gold band had diamonds all the way down the sides. He had chosen it especially for her as he knew she loved emeralds. The girls were amazed how romantic it all was.

"So how did you two meet?" asked Danni, sipping elegantly on her champagne.

You could see the dreamy look that came into her eyes as she recalled. "We met in a bar in Barcelona, it was a place where all the musicians would go after work. We hit it off straight away, so within a week we were in a relationship and within a month he had moved into my unit, and here we are together, now happily engaged," she squealed with delight. "I knew it the day we met. I knew he was the one."

Chloe's mind was racing; so it was possible, it did happen. They had a relationship after just one week and living together after a month.

"What is it with these Barcelona bars? That's where you and Jack met, wasn't it" asked Danni.

"Yea and they were in a relationship within a week. Yoohoo! Chloe, it might be you next," said Ava excitedly.

"Yes, but they lived in the same town, not halfway across the world from each other," sighed Chloe.

"Long distance relationships can work, Chloe. It just means one of you has to the take the plunge and move," said Cat.

"Or meet halfway and move to some exotic location," laughed Ava.

"Well, who knows what is in store for us? I guess we will just have to wait and see. It might just turn out to be a holiday romance and fizzle out after we go home," said Chloe.

Everyone agreed it didn't look like that to them, and deep down, Chloe knew it was so much more than that also. One of them would have to move. That was a depressing thought. It all sounded too hard. She looked over at Jack. Was he worth it? Well, she really couldn't think of life without him now, so I guess the answer to that is yes. They would just have to take it all very easy and see what the stars have in line for them.

"Oh, look, what you have done, Cruz, all these women will be wanting us to sing songs to them now," cried Paddy. Everyone laughed.

"Well, Ava won't be asking me to sing. She told me to shut up last time," said John, smirking.

"If you have ever heard John sing, you will understand what I mean, and you were blind drunk and you were singing the wrong words," said Ava cheerfully. With that, Paddy reminded everyone about his plans for Corfu and everyone agreed that sounded like another fantastic day.

"One problem," John announced with a serious gaze in his eyes. "Tomorrow is my thirtieth birthday, and I pity poor Ava, how is she ever going to top that one?" Everyone laughed. "Ava, you will have to sing me a birthday song," he demanded.

"I will jump out of a cake for you, Johnny, how about that?"

"I am going to hold you to that one, my love!"

The waiter came out with a huge bunch of flowers and a bottle of champagne and glasses. "We have been informed there is a celebration on this table tonight." Drinks were poured for everyone. Danni was clapping and jumping up and down, watching the champagne being opened.

"Settle down, Danni," said Rocco. "It's not the last bottle on the planet, you know." He turned to the boys. "She gets so excited when she hears a champagne bottle popping, it gets a bit embarrassing at times." Rocco was sounding a bit uncomfortable.

"It's the most beautiful sound in the world," yelled Danni over the top of him. She had a few wines and was away, but that's when Danni was the most fun. Rocco needed to loosen up a bit.

"I will back you up on that one."

"Thank you, Ava. It's just like I think Paris is the most beautiful city in the world, but Rocco says New York, of course."

"Well, I would have agreed with you there, but after seeing Croatia today, I might have to disagree," added Chloe with a challenging gaze she turned to Cat who took the challenge.

"Well, for me, it's Prague. I have never been there, but that has always been my dream city."

"Oooh, that's one for our next trip, I also have always wanted to go. We should all meet again next year for another trip in Prague," said Danni.

Rocco shook his head. "Paddy, pour me a wine, will you, I need to catch up with her, this woman will drive me crazy, chasing her all over the world."

"Aye, but they are worth it. I could not survive without my Maggie May. Drink up, Rocco," laughed Paddy.

They all had their glasses filled and ready to toast Cruz and Catalina.

Everyone raised their glasses and Paddy made the speech. "To our new friends, we wish them every happiness in the world. To Cruz and Cat!"

"To Cruz and Cat!" everyone replied.

Paddy pulled Jack aside; he wanted to do something for John tomorrow. "I have a few ideas," whispered Paddy and explained what he was thinking. Jack was laughing and called over Cruz.

"I don't trust those three," John said to Rocco with a chuckle in his voice; he was watching them carefully.

After dinner, Chloe and Jack went for a walk outside on the deck. They went to the back pool area and found it was movie night. Greece was the next port so *My Big Fat Greek Wedding* and its sequel were playing on the huge outdoor screen. All the sun lounges were set up facing the screen with blankets provided. They smelt popcorn coming from the bar area.

"How about taking in a movie for a while?" said Jack.

"Why not, it will get us in the mood for Greece."

They found two sun lounges, which they pushed together. "Wait here, I will just go get some popcorn." He was back in no time and they settled into the movie. It was half way through the first show but as both of them had seen it before so didn't matter. Chloe looked around. It was pretty crowded and everyone seemed to be having a good time. Kids all lined the front few rows; some were already sleeping, obviously after a day full of activities.

The weather was warm, but comforting to have the little throw rug over you, as you ate your popcorn and enjoyed the movie. Every now and again someone yelled out something funny, which added to the atmosphere of the night. Once or twice Chloe and Jack looked at each other. "That was John, I am sure." That would not have surprised them if it was; it definitely sounded like him.

The first movie was over and Jack noticed Chloe had fallen asleep. He gently woke her up and said he would carry her to bed if she liked, but she just laughed and said she was fine to walk. She felt a bit embarrassed falling asleep like all the little kids.

They arrived back at Jack's cabin and he helped her undress and get into bed. He poured himself a whisky and got in beside her. She put her head on his chest as he sat up looking out the window. The moon was still full and was making it so light it was almost like dusk.

"I am just going to sit here quietly and have my night cap. You just go to sleep."

"Tell me about Scotland. What is it really like, and do you really wear kilts?" said Chloe sleepily. She wanted to hear his voice as she lay quietly. She loved his accent and his stories.

"Aye, well we do wear kilts, just not every day. It's more for celebratory occasions now. I have one of my grandfather's kilts and also one of my dad's. I am a Maclean, as you know, so our tartan is a red tartan and then we have a green tartan that is for hunting. The MacLeans were highlanders. My ancestors hated the MacDonald clan and fought many a battle, but don't remind Paddy of that, as he would never let it rest."

Chloe smiled as she laid happily and listened.

"Anyway, we still have a castle that is still standing as part of our history. I will take you to it one day." He smiled down at her while having a sip of his whisky. "I think that you would really like it. The sun doesn't shine much, but it has a different beauty in the rolling hills, covered with mist and wee little houses with smoke billowing out the top of chimneys as fires roar to keep the families warm. And when it snows it is almost magical." He looked down and she still had a little smile on her face, obviously still enjoying his story. "At night the wee streets are lit up, and the pub is standing there like a shining beacon that seems to draw all the men towards it, to enjoy their pints of beer. It's normally freezing cold but by the end nobody seems to feel it as they wander home, but now after Paddy and Maggie's story they beat any story of walking home from the pub hands down." He looked down again and she had finally fallen asleep. He smiled. "What a treasure I have found.

Mo leannan falaich I will love you forever." He gently kissed her and she rolled over onto her side. He sat and watched her as he finished his drink. He had certainly been blessed to have found her. But what will happen after the cruise? He pushed it from his mind. Where there is a will there is a way, they would work this one out.

Chapter 12

CORFU

They woke snuggled up together as usual. Chloe leant over and kissed him good morning. "I could get very used to this," smiled a very sleepy Jack.

"Good morning, my highlander. Thank you for my beautiful story last night, I think I went to sleep."

"Aye, that you did, but I don't blame you one little bit, my stories tend to do that, my wee dog at home doesn't even last as long as you did, you should feel proud," he said, smiling at her.

"You have a dog? What's his name?" asked Chloe, sitting up interested.

"His name is Jock, he is a little mixer dog, you know, a bit of this and a bit of that, but he's a loyal wee dog. He is getting quite old now. He has been with me a long time, he just wandered in one day, and never wanted to leave."

"Well, it sounds like Jock and I have a few things in common then." Chloe rolled over and noticed the time. "We have to make a move, we are going to be late," she said as she frantically jumped out of bed and went to the shower. Jack made them coffee and then joined her in the shower. A morning ritual for them, and something he enjoyed a great deal. A shower in the morning alone is not something he wanted to do ever again.

Chloe found his bottle of body wash. "Do you know how much the smell of this has been driving me wild?" she laughed.

"Aye, I will thank my sister Jeannie then. She bought it for me as a Christmas present years ago, first time I have used it."

"It's my favourite, it smells like the ocean."

"I will remember that one."

They all met at the table and chairs on the dock where Paddy had told them. Everyone wished John a happy birthday as he arrived; they were all excited for another day on the water. The boat was slightly larger than the one in Dubrovnik and just as stunning. The skipper came over and introduced himself as Jimmy. He was very much like Nick, loud and extremely funny. "Welcome aboard, please make yourself at home!"

They all jumped on board carefully. "Today, we will have a relaxing, fun day. We will cruise along to Antipaxos, stopping at blue caves and places to swim, then off to Paxos for lunch."

He handed out water to everyone and said to help themselves to any drinks in the fridge throughout the day. Before too long they were off. Jimmy had the music pumping as they left the port and lots of people were watching and waving, the surroundings were beautiful, the weather perfect.

Everyone was in a happy, relaxed mood. They cruised through the turquoise waters until they reached the blue caves. It was an incredible sight. Lots of little boats were scattered around. The water was so clear and such an amazing colour. Jack was doing the honours organising drinks. "I think we need an early drink today as it is our friend John's birthday." He handed out the beers and poured Danni and Maggie champagne.

"How are we ever going to return to Glasgow after all this, Maggie?" said Paddy as he looked out over the water.

"You will have to come and visit us in Florida," said Ava. "No way near as stunning as this, but it is warmer than Glasgow "

"I can cook you up a Greek pizza in my pizza oven to remind you of here," added John throwing a nut in the air and catching it in his mouth.

"You have a pizza oven?" laughed Rocco, crossing his leg.

"Of course, I have the biggest and the best pizza oven. I sell barbecues, remember? We have a massive house with a great outdoor area. And a table with room for us all plus Ava is a fantastic cook, you're all welcome," said John as he looked at Ava with a smile.

"You just have to keep an eye on John, when he has his barbecue apron on, he seems to forget about the meat when a beer is in his hand. We have had many a disaster," laughed Ava. Everyone knew John well enough by now to know it would be true. But everyone loved him and he could do no wrong in their eyes.

"I think it is a reunion we will all have to do. We will hold you to that one, John," said Paddy, swigging on his beer.

"Wait, last night I was getting dragged off to Prague, where am I going now?" asked Rocco.

Paddy poured him a wine. "Drink up, Rocco, you will enjoy the ride much better." Danni had a secret chuckle, thanking Paddy quietly.

"What about poor Chloe, she has such a long way to go," said Maggie. She liked Chloe a lot and it saddened her that she would be so far away.

"Don't you worry about Chloe," said Jack. "She is never leaving my side ever again, I am hiding her away with me forever in Scotland."

Everyone laughed, but the truth was, they were all dreading the end of the cruise. They would miss each other's company; they had all become great mates.

"You're all more than welcome to visit me in Australia," said Chloe, sipping on her beer.

Everyone was chanting out, "No" all together.

"Oh, what is wrong with Australia?" cried Chloe, sounding hurt.

"Too far!" they all yelled back.

They had stopped at a beautiful cove. The waters were crystal clear. Jimmy came down to inform them that the waters were safe for swimming and snorkelling.

"Where are we?" asked Danni, shading her eyes with her hand while looking out over the view.

"It's a place called Antipaxos. Beautiful, isn't it?" explained Jimmy.

"How stunning. I have never seen anything so beautiful."

Everyone was in awe of the beauty of the cove. There were little boats all around them, with lots of people swimming around the boats and a little rocky beach where lots of people were enjoying the water.

"I have come in as close as I can to the shore, its shallow waters close by and you can swim into the shore and look around town, or you can snorkel out here. The waters are very clear and there are lots of pretty fish to see," explained Jimmy proudly.

With that, John had ran to the front of the boat and was standing on the edge. He jumped straight in but landed very awkward.

"Ava, Ava, where are you? I need you come here and rub my balls, they're aching," he yelled with a screwed-up face.

Everyone was laughing and then it was Rocco who jumped in. "You all have to come in. The water is so warm."

Jack grabbed Chloe by the hand and they jumped in together. Paddy was next and Jimmy threw out some noodles and floating devices.

Catalina and Cruz grabbed the snorkelling gear and decided to join them.

Everyone was trying to coax Danni and Maggie in, but they would not budge.

"Don't worry about your hair, Danni, jump in and come and have some fun," teased Rocco.

"Maggie and I are just fine. You don't need to worry about us," she said as she popped another bottle of champagne.

Everyone was having a wonderful morning. They swam and snorkelled for well over an hour before Jimmy said it was time to move on. Jack and Chloe grabbed a beer and headed for the front deck to sunbake. They all let them have some time for themselves. Rocco and Cruz went up to the fly bridge to chat with Jimmy and the others enjoyed a small morning tea Jimmy provided.

"You could not get a more perfect day," said Chloe.

"No, it's certainly stunning. It sure beats Fraserburgh. I really don't know how I am going to go back. This is heaven," said Jack, swigging his beer.

"In Australia, we have a saying: you wouldn't be dead for quids."

"Oh, aye that's a good one. We say, you're a long time dead, meaning enjoy yourself to the fullest."

"Well, we are certainly doing that," she laughed.

He pulled her closer with his arm around her as they enjoyed their beer and the spectacular views. Soon after Jimmy arrived. "We have almost arrived at Paxos. We will be walking to a taverna not far away where we will have a prepared meal like in Dubrovnik."

"Oh, I loved our lunch there with Nick. I am so eager to see what Jimmy had lined up for us," said Chloe, getting up excited.

It was a beautiful restaurant with huge courtyard that was enclosed with stone walls and floor with lots of beautiful plants and vines. It had wooden tables and chairs set up and they could see that the big table at the back was theirs. Even though it was lunchtime the whole courtyard was filled with fairy lights all under a beautiful canopy of bougainvillea. They could only imagine how beautiful it would be at night. A small trio played soft Greek music in the corner. The whole scene was magical.

The entrees came out quickly after drinks were served. There were large platters of grilled octopus, stuffed peppers, haloumi drizzled with honey and mussels cooked in ouzo. All of the food was delicious. The main meal was slow-cooked Greek lamb, grilled fish, Greek salads and bread. While they were eating the meal, Jimmy was running around making sure that everyone was happy. Jimmy was bantering with the waiter as everyone laughed at them and had great fun.

After lunch, the plates were cleared off and the band started to get into full swing. Dancers came out and the whole place started to clap and join in. The wine was being poured and desserts were served on dessert trolleys for anyone who still had room. People started to get up and dance. Paddy got up and grabbed Jack's arm, taking him with him. They started with some sort of their own version of Greek dancing and everyone was laughing and clapping. Next they were doing Scottish dancing and started on with a song for John bringing him up onto the dance floor. The waiter gave them a small shot of ouzo to keep them dancing. They were singing a Scottish ballad, "And with you, and with you our Johnny lad, we will be dancing the buckles off our shoes. Happy Birthday to our dear friend..." The crowd were all clapping along. Cruz and Catalina were next up. The place was really kicking into gear. The zorba music started and almost everyone in the room was up on their feet. Chloe and Maggie joined Jack and Paddy. John and Ava grabbed Danni and Rocco onto the dance floor. "We dance, we dance" was the next song and no one left the dance floor. The waiters gave out shots as the music played. All too soon came the time for Jimmy to gather his group and head back to the boat.

They laughed all the way back on the boat after too many ouzos. John was teasing Jack and Paddy about their dancing, and even Rocco joined in the fun. They were back at corfu too soon and no one wanted to leave. They thanked Jimmy profusely and all threw in giving him a huge tip.

"Let's have a look around the old town before we go back," said Jack. They said good bye to the rest of them before they all took a leisurely stroll back to the boat.

Jack took Chloe by the hand and they went down a small cobblestone lane.

"This is beautiful, it has so much atmosphere, so so beautiful," sighed Chloe.

The streets were filled with shops selling all sorts of arts and crafts. Chloe stopped at one that sold beautiful Greek paintings. She selected half a dozen and they were rolled and wrapped for her. They wandered on and Jack stopped at a little jewellery shop. He selected a beautiful carved silver ring with tiny green stones in it. He placed it on Chloe's finger for size. It fitted perfectly.

"Do you like it?"

"It's the most beautiful ring that I have ever seen."

He could have put a beer ring pull on her finger and she would have loved it. "Good, because it belongs to you, to remind you of me, every day that we are apart. We drank the wine so this is my gift to you." He put it on her finger.

"I will never take it off," she said, staring at her hand.

He smiled and went and paid for it.

Chloe was still looking at it when he returned. He put his arm around her kissed her on the head and started to walk along the cobblestones again. She thought about Kait and the tarot cards. They had been right, this whole trip had a magical feel about it and the way the cards had described the love she would find was exactly the way she felt about Jack. Incredible. Coincidence or not, she would never boohoo the cards again.

Dinner that night was all about John. Everyone sang happy birthday and he thanked everyone sincerely, saying he had never had quite a birthday like it. Everyone cheered as they spotted the waiter bringing out a huge cake that Ava had arranged. "Thank you, baby, I love you." John had got quite emotional. The men all started to pay out on him and he picked himself up.

After dinner, they all went out to a bar for a dance and a few more drinks before heading in. There was a band on and the boys all got up to dance while the girls chatted. They had obviously had too much to drink. Paddy asked the band to play a happy birthday song and they played "Happy birthday, Helen" but sung "Happy birthday, Johnny." They were all up on the dance floor and making sure John was enjoying his birthday. Afterwards as they sat down. John was going around the table telling everyone how much he loved them. He had obviously had a great day and was getting all emotional once again. By the end of the night, Paddy and John were both locked arm in arm telling the table next to them all about the day that they had. The girls were laughing at them as they got louder; then it was time to all head home.

Chapter 13

SANTORINI

Jack woke first, needing to go to the bathroom and came back with water, feeling quite dehydrated after a big night at John's birthday party. "Don't open the blinds, yet," yelled Chloe. Jack laughed; he knew what she meant and snuggled back in beside her.

"Please tell me it is not another celebration again today. I think my poor liver has had enough."

Jack laughed. "Oh, come on, where is my little party girl? You can't stop now, I have seen you back it up again. Here get this water into you, you will live to see another day. I will make you a coffee with whisky. That will get you moving."

He left her alone for a while and then bought the coffee back to bed. "Come on, my beautiful princess. Time to rise and shine," he said as he opened the blinds.

"How are you feeling ok? You are a machine," she squinted.

"No, I am Scottish. We have a wonderful knack for bouncing back," he teased, crawling back into bed.

He got her moving after her whisky coffee. They showered and dressed in shorts and t-shirts, wearing their costumes underneath in case they wanted to swim. They headed to the breakfast room but it was getting late, so they grabbed a muffin to eat on the run. They were enjoying not having any time schedules. A slower day was needed.

Walking swiftly, they made their way to the wharf after getting off the boat. The weather was brilliant, warm, blue skies, and no wind. It can be very windy, but they were blessed with the perfect day. Everyone was doing their own itinerary. Just having a casual day to relax and enjoy the island quietly. They had huge days and everyone was starting to feel tired. Not to mention a few sore heads after John's birthday drinks the night before.

The village was at the top of around three hundred stairs. There were three options. First, a donkey ride, which Chloe refused; second, climb the stairs, which was not an option for someone who's still hung over; or third, the funicular. Choosing the third they made their way to the top. It was stunning; the chalk white buildings with cobalt blue cones and sapphire blue waters were endless. It was truly a beautiful sight.

Wandering through the little villages slowly, they looked in all the shops, picking up little gifts along the way. There was a man painting portraits sitting, waiting for a customer. "Come on Jack, this can be my present to you, to remember me after we go home." Walking over, the man graciously made them feel welcome. Sitting together closely, they let the man paint them. He added beautiful Greek scenery and it was completed in no time. Slowly, turning it around he proudly showed them. Covering her mouth as she gasped, "Oh, my goodness, it is beautiful!" He had captured them beautifully, and somehow he had accentuated all their good points and rectified their bad. "This guy is amazing. We don't even seem too tired and hung over." She laughed. "Can you repaint it so we can both could take one home," asked Chloe.

"Yes, of course!"

They thanked him and graciously paid him. "We are heading off for lunch. Can we pop back and pick them up later?" asked Jack as he put his wallet safely away.

It was lunchtime, so they found a little restaurant down a few stairs right on the water overlooking the Caldera. The table that they were given had the best views right out over the beautiful sparkling water. They drank Greek beer called Mythos, which was very refreshing in the heat. They both studied the menu.

"I want everything on this menu," said Jack, scratching his head.

"Oh, everything sounds delicious." She pushed her hair back behind her ears and leaned forward to give the menu her full attention.

"Why don't we try a couple of dish's and share so we can try different things?"

"OK but I want the octopus. It is never available in Australia."

"Alright, I want the rack of lamb." The waiter arrived and helped them. "I would definitely recommend the pork, the most popular item on the menu," he advised.

They were starving. Another beer arrived. The hair of the dog was starting to work, they were away again. "This is like we have died and gone to heaven," sighed Chloe as she sunk back in her seat adjusting her sunglasses as she looked out.

"This certainly is a post card view. I love all the white buildings that are built into the cliffs. Such a sight to see."

"I thought yesterday was the best view and now this," said Chloe, scanning the scenery.

The food arrived and looked incredible. A Greek salad came with a complimentary basket of bread. First, they tried the octopus; it was grilled with garlic and lemon and simply melted in the mouth. The ribs were next and were the tastiest they had ever had, obviously cooked slowly over a hot flame. The pork was to die for. It was all crispy skin on the outside but tender and moist on the inside, once again slow cooked over hot flames, you could see why the waiter had advised them to try it.

There were cats all walking around; one had taken residence under their table. Jack threw a few bits of meat, as he smiled at Chloe hoping no one else noticed; it gulped it down, obviously starving. They were hiding it from the waiter but as they looked around everyone appeared to be doing the same thing, and none of the waiters batted an eyelid.

Jack looked at his watch and they had been there two hours. The beers had certainly given them a buzz and they were alive again. They still had a few more hours before they had to get back on the boat. Jack spotted a quad bike hire. If they hadn't had those beers, they would have jumped at it. They turned and bumped straight into John and Ava.

"Hey, how are you guys?" said John cheerfully.

"We are fantastic. Just had a delicious lunch, we were looking at the quad bikes but we have had a few beers," said Jack, looking back over his shoulder at them.

"That's awesome, that's exactly where we were heading. We have had a dry morning. We could take you."

"Hang on, if you mean I have to drive one of those things, I think you better think again," said Ava with a worried frown on her face.

"Come on, honey, you can do this. It's still my birthday celebrations and would be so much fun to take Jack and Chloe with us for the afternoon. Come on let's have a chat with the man, if you aren't comfortable we will give it a miss." They all looked at her hopeful.

"Alright, alright, I will take a look."

They walked back to the man and John explained the situation with Ava being scared. He was a salesman like they had never seen before. He had Ava on the bike in no time and they all thanked him.

"So how far do you think we can travel on our time restriction?" asked John as he helped Ava with her helmet.

"Wait, I will get you a map."

They all put on their helmets as he circled the areas they had time to visit. "I will go with Ava," said Chloe, fixing the strap on her helmet.

"Perfect. We are having a girl versus boy ride," she said, trying to sound excited but staring at her bike with a huge concerned look.

Finally, John started the bike for her, gave her a kiss and a little hug of encouragement before getting on his bike. Everyone cheered Ava on. Before they knew it, she was off.

"Jesus, hang on Jack. She's hit the accelerator," yelled John frantically.

They were finding it hard to keep up with the girls. "Are they okay?" yelled Jack anxiously.

"They are actually doing a great job. Ava has nailed it," he yelled back excitedly.

"Stay behind them, keep an eye on them."

"I'm trying, but she's a hoon."

They followed the map, which took them around the rugged coastline of the island with views of the beaches and landscape. The water was stunning and the cliffs, which dropped into the water supporting gorgeous white buildings with blue dome roofs, were so impressive. They passed the airport and a plane flew over them; they all ducked laughing.

The landscape was what amazed Chloe, reminding her of back home, so dry and barren, with what looked an awful lot like gum trees. There were also lots of olive trees and bougainvillea in full bloom trailing up the beautiful white walls.

Unfinished buildings were everywhere; it looked like they simply ran out of money. Some were small houses, while others were huge mansions. She remembered the stories on the news about the financial crisis and how Greece had been hard hit, and here she was experiencing it for herself. It was incredible to witness.

The Greek people were all so lovely. What a horrible experience they must have gone through. She had to buy some more things to take home, help the economy a bit. She thought about the man who painted them and how lovely he had been. This trip was certainly opening up her eyes up to the rest of the world. You don't pay attention when it's on the news, but once you have been here, it really hits home.

They had arrived at a beautiful beach. It was rocky with lots of beach lounges with straw umbrellas. They stopped and got off, taking off their helmets.

"Far out, Ava. You are the sweetest girl that I have ever met, but bloody hell, you get on that quad bike and you are wild," yelled Chloe, excitedly scruffing her hair.

Everyone was laughing. "You took off like a wild child alright. We had trouble keeping up with you, baby, you were amazing," said John, excitedly giving her a kiss.

Jack hurried over to Chloe after taking off his helmet. "Are you alright?"

"I am fine, it was a lot of fun," she assured him.

"This water looks too good, let's have a quick dip," said John as he eyed off the best spot. "Over here." He pointed to an area away from the beach lounges. Being such a hot day no need for towels and lucky enough, they had all worn their swimmers. "The water is so warm and crystal clear," yelled out John encouraging the rest to hurry up.

They frolicked around for a while, swimming and chatting. Jack found an old ball on the beach and they played a water volleyball game for a while. Jack knew time was getting away and got out and checked the time.

"Time to go, guys," he yelled out to them. No one wanted to leave but they knew they had no choice. They stood around and dried off a bit, which didn't take long in the hot Mediterranean sunshine.

"Are you ok to stay with Ava, Chloe? I would be ok to ride now."

"Hell, yea she is the best. Come on, Ava, let's show them how it is done."

Jack just smiled and said, "Okay, okay, I know when I have been dumped," laughing as they all put on their helmets and got back on the bikes.

They made it back in good time, thanks to Ava. She had a new talent; they had found the wild child inside a complete angel, which had been so amusing.

They set off to find the man with their paintings. He was sitting there still waiting and had them all rolled and wrapped for them. They thanked him and Chloe gave him a tip and they headed back to the boat. It had been the best day ever, quad biking with John and Ava was awesome, not to mention the stunning scenery. It was a day they would remember forever.

Today, their sunset spritz cocktails would be the most spectacular. A sunset at Santorini is something that you would never forget. They stood and leant over the deck railing watching. The sights of Santorini at sunset was world-renowned as breathtaking. Jack held her tight as Greek music was played softly over the deck speakers and she hummed along enjoying the moment. Jack turned to Chloe. "I have gone all soft since I left Scotland. The boys at the pub would laugh at me, but I am falling for you in a huge way, you make me want to run away with you forever." He smiled.

"I feel the same way; I think we have both known it for a while now."

"Aye, then we are in a bit of trouble then, aren't we?" He smiled at her lovingly.

They stood and stared out as the sun set, each lost in their own world.

"Has anyone ever told you about the Greek love story, Psyche and Eros?" he whispered softly.

Chloe nodded. "No, I don't know the story, please tell me." She loved hearing his stories, he would make his voice all soft and romantic and made her all gooey inside.

"Aye, well, you are in for a treat. Well, according to Greek mythology, Psyche was an exceptionally beautiful woman, just like you," he added. "She only wanted to marry a man who truly loved her, a bit like me," he said, smiling cheekily. "Aphrodite, the goddess of love, was so jealous, so she asked her son, the young master of love, Eros, to poison the men's souls so no one would find her attractive. But he fell in love with her himself. He was sent away, and imprisoned by the jealous goddess."

"Oh, that's just awful," said Chloe with a worried look.

"Aye, well, Psyche found out where he was and asked the goddess for his release. She had to do three tasks, which she accomplished. But it was a trap. The goddess's spell sent her to sleep and Eros went to Zeus and begged him to save his beloved Psyche. He was so impressed by their love that he granted Psyche the gift of immortality so that the two lovers could be together for eternity."

"That's such a beautiful story. How do you know so many beautiful love stories?"

"Well, I happen to be a true romantic at heart; I could give Cruz a run for that title any day." He smiled proudly. She stared quietly, mesmerised out towards the sunset. He was built like an ox with a heart of a gentle lamb. *How am I ever going to leave him*, she thought.

At dinner, everyone talked about the day that they had experienced. Mostly just relaxing around town, and shopping for souvenirs. John and Jack were telling the stories about the quad bikes and how proud John was of Ava riding like a maniac. No one could believe sweet little Ava could ride like that.

They were all starting to tell stories and laughing about the night before, and told John how much they loved him, laughing. "Ok, ok, Ava filled me in this morning. I loved you all, I know it was my birthday and I am supposed to have a good time."

After dinner, Cruz and Cat invited them to all join them in a Greek dancing party. Everyone thought it sounded like fun. There were lots of things happening on the boat that night as it had been a quieter port. There was a show, another Greek movie night and the Greek dancing that they had all decided to take part in. They all learned how to do the Zorba and other Greek dancing and then danced the night away to wonderful Greek music. They all agreed that dancing would do them good after all the food they had been eating. John was entertaining everyone as usual with his outgoing personality and Paddy and Jack were not far behind. When the band finished, they all reluctantly had to leave.

Chloe had too much ouzo and Jack helped her home and carried her through the door and placed her on the bed. She was laughing hysterically as he was teasing her while undressing her, ready for bed. He then did a strip tease for her while humming the Zorba music. Finishing, he slipped into bed and they made love under the light of the moon as it came through the window.

Chapter 14

SICILY

Once again, they woke the next morning dehydrated and with a bit of a sore head. It was all starting to be a bit of a routine now, waking up with a sore head. They needed water. Jack grabbed two bottles of water, made two coffees, and jumped back into bed. Lucky it wasn't such an early start for them. They needed a quieter morning. Only six of them taking the journey to the scenes of *The Godfather* today.

They had some wifi so they sat in bed checking and sending off emails. Chloe noticed one from Kait.

Dear Chloe,

How are you? Things are all well here. I bumped into Bob the other day and he told me Craig has gone on a three-week surfing safari with his mates. He must have had that all planned that is why he could not go to Europe with you. What a loser. So happy you have met someone new. He seems to be really nice and both Mum and I are hoping it is more than just a holiday romance. The photos all look like you are both having a wonderful time. Don't hold back waiting for Craig, Bring home Jack.

All my love,
Kait

She smiled, thinking of her sister; she knew she would be jumping up and down waiting to hear every single detail from start to finish, without missing out on a single thing. But that would have to wait; she did not have time for that. Just a quick reply will do.

Hi Kait,

Having the time of my life. We are in Sicily today and going on a tour, with some of our friends from the boat. Yes, Jack is lovely, I will fill you in with all the details when I get home. Don't worry, I am not waiting for Craig. What a loser he is, I am so glad he is not here. I am having way too much fun without him, especially now I have met Jack he he.

Gotta run,
Chloe

The port was right in town. All they had to do was disembark and walk through a gate and they were in the city of Messina. There was a mini bus waiting for them at eight-thirty. The tour guide, Gino, introduced himself and gave them a quick run-down of the day. Paddy was very excited and told them about the movie, and the guide also gave Paddy lots of information on the location. "The church was built in the 13th century and then rebuilt again in the 15th and 18th centuries. The church now looks completely different from how it looked when originally built. It now resembled a fortress. It's perched high up on the hill and will give you panoramic views over the Ionian Sea. The views are breathtaking, I am sure you will love it," said Gino.

"Even if you are not a fan of the movie, *The Godfather*, you will still be glad you came. We will also walk down to the Bar

Vitelli as they did in the movie and we will have some refreshments. I am sure you will all have a great time," said Gino.

"I remember watching the movie with my dad," said John excitedly. "This is fantastic. We are going to actually be here, where all the greats were filming. Can't wait to tell Dad."

"Paddy has put me through that movie so many times, but he loves it so I don't mind coming to see it with him," said Maggie. "I will get my turn. I want to do a cooking class."

"Oh, I would love to do a cooking class," said Ava. "I love entertaining, even John would enjoy."

"Oh, count me in, sounds like fun," added Chloe.

"Ok, I will organise something. We will drag Jack and Paddy along also," laughed Maggie.

It took about an hour to travel to the little town of Savoca.

"Here we are, the village of Savoca. We are three hundred metres above sea level and Savoca is classed as one of Italy's most beautiful villages," said Gino.

Paddy recognised the church straight away. "Oh, aye, there it is," said Paddy, leaning over Maggie to get a better view.

"That's it, that's it," squealed John.

It stood high on the hill and looked like a fortress, just like Gino said.

"It's absolutely beautiful. I love old churches, don't you, Ava?" asked Chloe and she agreed.

"I love old pubs," said John with a chuckle and the boys all agreed.

They were all out of the vehicle and started to head up the long brick path, lined with old lanterns that would light the path at night. The scenery along the way was beautiful. Once they arrived at the top, the views were breathtaking.

The inside was spectacular with old tiles, stone floor, and lead light windows. The stunning altar along with statues and chandeliers finished the look. They took time to take it all in, both inside and out, and everyone took numerous photos.

They started on the walk as they did in the movie from the church through the village to the Bar Vitelli, another famous landmark from the movie.

"Here we can have some refreshments. What would you all like to drink? I will get it for you," said Gino. They all agreed on a beer as it was so hot. Jack and John followed him to help carry the beers.

It was old and rustic, made of stone and with a beautiful courtyard trellised with vines. The famous arch, at the front, was still there. The courtyard was filled with wooden tables and chairs and they decided to take a seat at an outdoor table to admire the scenery. The music from the soundtrack of *The Godfather* was playing gently in the background. They returned with drinks, nuts, and chips.

"How often do you get to sit in a famous movie location in Sicily enjoying a beer? I have to pinch myself to believe it," said John.

Everyone agreed how truly incredible it was.

Gino sat, giving them the history of the bar and the story of Michael and Apollonia's wedding. They spent a good hour chatting about the story and taking in the stunning scenery, before making their way down the winding skinny roads back to Messina. Gino dropped them at the main piazza and told them if they were quick they would catch the show that the bell tower and astronomical clock do every day at midday. They all thanked Gino and he was off.

Finding their way to the bell tower, they arrived at the cathedral square. They found a beautiful fountain in the centre and it was crowded with lots of people waiting patiently for the show to begin. They had made it just in time.

There it stood before them, so grand and tall, so incredibly stunning. The bell tower, of the Cathedral of Messina. The highest cathedral in Sicily. The clock struck midday and the bells rang twelve times to announce the show was about to begin. They all stood mesmerised, staring.

Two golden heroine statues rang the bells. The four-metre-high golden lion that stood proudly at the top sprung to life. His tail wagged and then he waved a flag that stood on top of a long golden pole he was carrying. He turned his head to the crowd and roared; he did this three times. Just below the lion was a golden rooster. The two-metre-high rooster stood between two heroines. He flapped his wings, raised his head and crowed. This happened three times. Music began to play, it was "Ava Maria," and it was incredibly moving. In the window below, a golden angel appeared and gave a letter to the Virgin Mary, followed by St Paul and the ambassadors. They all bowed as they passed Madonna the patron saint of the city, which was standing in the centre. In the window below, a dove flew as a grand church rose from ruins. It lasted twelve minutes. As it finished, everyone clapped and cheered. It had been an incredibly moving experience and they were so glad that they did not miss it.

"I am starving. Anyone up for a pizza?" said Jack, who was always thinking about his belly.

Everyone thought it was a great idea and they found a nice trattoria that had outdoor seating with views across the ocean to the boot of the Italian mainland. There were little fishing boats tied up on the shore and the setting was so simple with wooden tables and chairs and red table cloths. The waiter came and they were served drinks while they looked over the menu. He suggested that he could bring them some typical Sicilian dishes that were popular and they all agreed it sounded wonderful. John teased Jack about missing out on his pizza.

But as it turned out, they were glad they had let the waiter decide as the dishes that he bought out were amazing. Things they would never have ordered but glad as they were delicious.

First was a seafood appetiser platter with stuffed sardines and squid and rolled swordfish and arancini balls. Next bought to the table was a platter of natural oysters and raw red prawns on ice. Then a huge platter of spaghetti vongoles was loaded with mussels and clams with raw red prawns drizzled with lemon and olive oil, so fresh caught only hours earlier by local fishermen. Apparently, they were shipped to Michelin-starred restaurants all over the world.

"Glad we all like seafood. They seem to eat an awful lot of it in Europe," said Paddy, filling his plate from the platters. "Wait till we tell Rocco and Cruz about this feast," said John.

"I like to sit next to Danni when platters are brought out. She never eats a thing," teased Jack.

The waiter gave them time to digest then bought out a beautiful chocolate cake called *setteveli*. It was a traditional Sicilian seven-layered cake with chocolate sponge, mouse, hazelnuts, and Bavarian cream. The men all took a slice but the women declined. He bought them out a lemon granita instead, which was a shaved frozen ice drink flavoured with lemon. After lunch, they thanked him for their truly authentic Sicilian lunch.

Waddling out, they all went their separate ways. Jack and Chloe wanted to take a walk around the town to walk off their lunch and explore the city. The rest went back to the ship. The city was old but stylish, the people all seemed to dress very well, men all in suits. It had a feel about it. You knew you were in the city of *The Godfather*; it just had that mafia feel.

The ship was so huge you could see it from every part of the town. They spotted a taxi and asked him to take them up the top to get an aerial view. First, he took them for a tour of the city, showing them all the sites and giving them a lesson on the history of the town. The city itself was beautiful. The streets were lined with, lots of fruit trees, laden with oranges and lemons, making it all appear so beautiful.

They reached a lookout at the top. The first thing that they noticed was the sheer size of the ship compared to other boats in the port, which made them gasp. They did not realise the size of it until now. The town of Messina was stunning; a mass of cream buildings with terracotta roofs and the water surrounding it was breathtaking.

They took in all the sights once again as they came back down, totally in awe. The city was incredibly old but exotic all at the same time. Once again, they wished that they had more time. They loved the sounds of the city with church bells and step-through motor bikes that were everywhere.

Arriving back at the port, they had one last treat to have before getting on the boat, a *cannoli*. They found a little place famous for all sorts of sweet treats with outdoor tables. A local white wine was served that the waiter recommended. They ordered some *pistachio cannoli* and sweet *arancina*. There were so many sweets she had to hold Jack back. The white wine, called *malvasia*, was light and quite refreshing; it tasted a lot like *moscato*. But it was the sweets that stole the show. Simple little Italian treats that were delicious. Now that Jack was happy that he had tried all the Sicilian treats, they slowly wandered back to the boat.

That night at dinner, everyone told their stories of the day. Rocco, Danni, Cruz, and Catalina had done a tour to the volcano. Their stories were so very interesting. You could spend a few days touring Sicily, which was the drawback of being on a cruise, but the set-up was incredibly handy as you were being taken to a new country as you slept.

After dinner, they all went to see Cruz and Catalina perform at the karaoke grand final. They did a Spanish number and their costumes were in true Spanish style. Catalina had a beautiful dress with all the layers and frills. Cruz's guitar work was incredible and Catalina's voice was as magnificent as usual. The crowd roared when they finished, and they did their bows and courtesy and came back to the table where everyone was waiting. They all sat and watched the other acts but it was easy to see Cruz and Cat had it in the bag.

Jack and Chloe were once again the first to leave. They went to Chloe's cabin to grab a few things before heading back to Jack's. They shared a whisky on the veranda, before turning in. Jack had noticed that Chloe's anxiety had been almost nonexistent lately and was curious how she was really feeling.

"Your anxiety levels seem to be quite good lately."

"Yes, I can't believe it myself. I feel amazing."

"Were you ever on medication?"

"No, Mum would never allow it. I only had mild anxiety so she wanted to treat it naturally with diet and exercise. I had it under control, I knew my boundaries, as long as I stayed close to home, had routine, ate well, did lots of yoga and meditation. I was fine, but this trip really sent me off the edge for a while. I am ok now, thanks for asking." She smiled warmly at him. She liked the way he genuinely cared about her. She had found a wonderful friend and an exceptional lover.

Chapter 15

MALTA

The distant sound of a marching band made Chloe stir. She lay still for a while, happily listening as she waited for Jack to wake. They had docked. A carnival must be nearby; she enjoyed the faint melody of music as Jack slept. He looked so beautiful as he lay asleep. He had stirred feelings in her that she had never realised existed; he was going to be hard to leave. Just looking at him sent her body into goosebumps; she had never been stirred that way with Craig. She had never felt the fear of losing someone quite like this. Why did she have to fall in love with someone who lived so far away? Was there a way to fix this, was it possible, and could it ever work?

Jack started to stir. He leaned over, smiled, and kissed her. "I love waking up with you, it's the highlight of my day," he said, stretching out. "Come and lie here with me. We don't need to rush today." He leaned towards her and pulled her in closer. "So it appears I have found the love of my life and she is a wild little beastie," he teased as they fell into each other and made love. Rising above everything, nothing else mattered to them except the ecstasy they shared. They finally came back to reality, still entwined in each other's arms after a little doze. Jack sat up, putting his ear to the air. "What's that noise?"

Chloe got up and drew the blinds. "Good morning, Valletta." Markets and festival-style marching bands lined up outside the terminal along with numerous buskers. Being docked right in the city once again meant curious locals coming to take photos and look in awe at the ship's size and beauty. Staring out, Chloe realised how lucky she was and how she had almost thrown it all away. She made coffee. "Another glorious morning full of sunshine," said Chloe, handing Jack his coffee before climbing back into bed. "Both inside and out," he smirked.

They sat and had their coffee while they woke up properly. "I can't help but thinking we are coming close to the end of our cruise and it frightens me," said Jack. "It's going all too quickly."

"It frightens me also, but let's not talk about it now," she smiled sadly. So far they had avoided the subject. It was like a taboo subject, but both were well aware it was inevitably going to happen.

Another action-packed day lay ahead, catching up with everyone for some laughs along with the cooking class Maggie had arranged. Being a lunchtime event, they had time to relax and enjoy their morning. Jack went off to the gym and Chloe went back to her cabin to shower and dress for the day.

Arriving at the meeting spot on time, they greeted everyone. A mini bus arrived and they were ushered onboard by a friendly man. The city was hot and dusty so they were pleased to climb aboard the air-conditioned vehicle. It took them way up into the hills, to a grand farmhouse with a winery attached and stunning views down to the town and port. It was a restaurant at night but closed at lunchtime so the owner ran small cooking classes in the generous country-style kitchen.

The day started with a tour of the winery where they tasted the local wines to get them in the mood for cooking. The chef put on his apron and hat and they carried their drinks as they followed him to the kitchen. Lessons included bruschetta, how to brine olives, make a lasagne and a meatball dish. Everyone had a wonderful afternoon teasing each other and having a great laugh. Afterwards they all sat around a spacious outdoor table and enjoyed their feast with more wine to wash it down.

"What's that noise? Asked Chloe. An alarm was going off, alerting them something was wrong. They watched as the staff appeared to be panicked.

"I would not worry, they will tell us if we are in any danger," said Jack reassuringly. Everyone nodded and shrugged their shoulders.

"It is probably that crazy husband of yours, Ava, up to no good as usual," laughed Paddy.

"Yea, where is he?" asked Ava as she looked around concerned. They listened as sirens appeared to be getting closer.

"Here he comes now," yelled Maggie. A very humble-looking John was walking towards them.

"Where have you been? I was starting to worry," said Ava.

He threw his arms out to the side and said, "Well, Chloe, you need not be embarrassed anymore about your toilet dilemma. I just trumped you."

"What did you do now?" asked Ava.

"I told you it would be all John's doing," roared Paddy.

He sat next to Ava with a sheepish look on his face and took a long sip on his wine. "It's all a bit embarrassing."

"Come on, John, we are all friends here," encouraged Chloe.

"Promise we won't laugh" said Jack, leaning over to Paddy, already both grinning.

"Aye, come on, laddie, what did you do?" he looked around the table and had another gulp of wine before he started.

"Well, with all this rich food I had to go to the bathroom. There was a string hanging from the roof and thought that was there to open the vent. So I pulled on it. Nothing happened, so I pulled it again and again. All these people came rushing into the bathroom, yelling something but I could not understand what they were saying. I didn't want anyone to know it was me that made that horrible smell so I hid in there and stayed quiet, hoping they would leave but next thing you know they broke down the door. Apparently, I was pulling some sort of distress alarm," cried John, horrified.

Everyone roared with laughter. Crazy, how it always seemed to happen to John.

The bus took them back to the port, and Maggie was thanked for organising a beautiful day and everyone went their separate ways.

Chloe and Jack went back to the boat and enjoyed a swim after a hot and dusty day. Drying themselves off they spotted a table. "Go and relax at the table, I will get us a drink."

He arrived back with spritz. "Great choice, Jack," said Chloe sipping on her cocktail. As she watched Jack, she could see he had something on his mind.

"What's going on in your head over there?" she asked, stirring her drink with the cocktail stick.

"We have been dodging this subject but I had to ask, when are you flying home?" Jack asked quietly.

She stared at him for a moment before answering. It was like hearing a bullet that had been shot straight towards her.

"I need to change my flight."

"What do you mean?" he asked carefully, knowing he was treading on dangerous grounds.

"I was originally going to do a ten-day road trip after the cruise and fly home from Paris but that's obviously not happening now," she sipped on her cocktail.

"No way. Wait a minute, you're telling me your flight home isn't for another ten days?"

"Well, I wasn't, no. But now I am, so I will check flights when I am back in Barcelona and change it, I will fly home from there."

"Chloe, hang on," said Jack, speechless, putting down his cocktail. "Why can't we do the road trip?" he asked, leaning in towards her.

"Don't you need to go back to work?" Butterflies were starting to form in her belly.

"No, I am in no hurry to go home, my brother and his new girlfriend seem to be handling everything now, plus imagine how happy my mother would be. Can you imagine her face when I tell her about you?"

"You mean you could stay with me and have an extra ten days together?" squealed Chloe.

"'Yes if you think you can put up with me for another ten days that is exactly what I am saying."

"Hell yea, but I am not sure about my waistline, though," she laughed.

"Why did you keep that a secret for so long?"

"It never dawned on me you would be free."

They were ecstatic. Jack picked her up and twirled her around. "You fool, of course, I am free. If you are hanging around, so am I."

"Tomorrow is a day at sea. Let's buy some WIFI and plan a trip." They clinked their glasses together. "To our road trip!"

Chapter 16

THE FAREWELL

Sitting on the bed in Jack's room, the trip planning had begun. The sun was streaming in. It was a beautiful day outside and the waters were calm and smooth. They just spent the morning doing their laundry. Now she had taken time to send Kait an informative email as she had been brushing her off a bit as she was so busy. She told her all about Jack, and how they met and how crazy she was about him. She filled her in on the private cruisers they took around the Greek islands and Cruz's proposal to Catalina. She finished by thanking her, for giving her the push to get on the plane in Sydney. She imagined Kait reading it, and it made her smile. She would be pretty jealous of her spending another ten days in Europe with the man of her dreams. But she would also be extremely proud of her. She pressed send and thought about home for a while.

Her life was so different now. In two weeks, it had totally changed. One minute she was hanging out at the surf club with a boyfriend who didn't give two hoots about her, and now here she was lying on the bed with Jack planning a road trip in Europe and dining with friends from all over the world. Yes, life does take some strange turns sometimes. She remembered what Kait had said about the cards: "You are in the right place, right where you should be, for the events that will show you a path, and change your life forever." She didn't understand it before, but totally understood what it meant now. She had ventured outside her comfort zone and survived. Even her anxiety had stopped.

She remembered the words of a doctor, which had rung in her ears for years but never understood what it meant either, until now. "It is not until you find yourself that you start to totally understand yourself and start to be comfortable with yourself and who you are, then your fears will leave you." How true, she was a completely different person than the one she was before. She respected herself now and the way she looked at things, happy to be just her. She sat amazed with her thoughts. Had she finally overcome her anxiety?

Jack's voice brought her back to the present. She was sprawled out on the bed, Jack stroking her long blonde hair with one hand while he intently studied his phone. "So Paris is our end point. Where were you going to start the road trip? I can get a one-way car rental here that doesn't seem too expensive," said Jack.

"Well, we hadn't planned anything so I guess it is up to us. It is our trip now," she smiled up at him.

"Wait, I owe you a trip to Tuscany, remember?"

"Oh, aye, you do. I could finally take you on that romantic drive."

"So you 'were' looking at that trip romantically," she teased.

"Yes, of course."

"Even all the way back then?"

"Even all the way back then, I told you I am a true romantic at heart."

"I kind of knew we were going to get together back then also," she smiled, thinking back.

"Tuscany it is!"

"We could fly into Florence."

"Ok. Let me see…yes, we can fly from Barcelona and pick up a car at the airport."

"Sounds like a great place to start, and the flight is only one and a half hours."

"That's perfect. Can we get a flight tomorrow afternoon?"

"Yes, the afternoon flight is at one in the afternoon. We are off the boat early so that would work."

"Great, lets book it," she said excitedly.

With their flights booked and the car rented they needed to find a motel.

"Now a place to stay, with free parking," Chloe advised.

"Oh, aye, and a big breakfast," he added, giving her his cheeky look.

Chloe laughed. "Always thinking of food."

"Not always," he admitted with a sly little smile. "And thinking about that, a good bed."

"And a big pool, so we can spend some time relaxing."

The list was growing, but they were having fun, it was becoming difficult to find one that catered for all their needs.

"Wait, I think I have found the perfect place. How does this sound. Free parking, free breakfast, free nibbles and drinks in the evening, a huge pool, and a bed that looks extremely inviting?" He winked.

She laughed. "Let me see, how can it have all that?" He passed the phone to her and she sat up as she read. "Far out, Jack, it's perfect, the pool is massive."

"Aye, and it is available on our dates. How long do you want to stay?"

"What about three nights and another stop before Paris?"

"Yea that would work. I will book it for three nights. Where else would you like to go?"

"What is halfway?"

He studied his phone, bringing up a map. "Well, Dijon looks nice. It's a long drive from Sienna to Dijon, so we can have a stopover for a night somewhere along the way."

"Great plan." Jack booked the hotel they found in Tuscany in the town of Sienna, and selected a special they were offering called the "romantic stay," with free wine and chocolates in the room with rose petals scattered on arrival. He wanted to make it nice for Chloe, if they only had a small amount of time left together; he wanted something she would never forget. "Booked," said Jack as he put the phone down. "Well, a good start, anyway. We have our flights, the car and accommodation for the first few nights."

"No, wait, you booked and paid for everything so far. Let me book Dijon and Paris."

"Ok I will leave you in peace and go to the gym for an hour. After that, the day is ours."

Jack organised his things and left her as she pondered over her phone. First, she started on Dijon. She put in all their requirements and it narrowed it down to a few. One stood out, The Grand Hotel. *Wow wow wow!* It was grand, alright. She entered her dates, expecting a grand price to go with it but was pleasantly surprised. It had everything that they needed. She quickly booked it.

Now, it was Paris. Easy. There was only one hotel she wanted to stay in, Le Bristol, from so many movies. She entered the details and pressed go. She gasped at the price. Cross that one off the list. She put in their requirements and pressed go once again. One instantly stood out. It was romantic and pretty, walking distance to most places of interest with a gym, a buffet breakfast, and half the price. She selected their dates and booked it. It was too easy something had to go wrong. She checked her emails and found the two confirmation letters had already arrived. Happy with herself, she changed and was ready when Jack returned.

"All done?" he said, looking surprised.

"All done! Let's hit the pool!"

They found a large double day bed, complete with a canopy over the top.

"You're very good at remembering to put sunscreen on. I am afraid to say I hardly use it," he said as he was rubbing lotion on her back.

"Well, it gets drilled into us in Australia. No hat no play. Slip, slop, slap. It's just how we grew up. You won't find too many Aussies not wearing sunscreen or a hat."

"What's slip, slop, slap?"

"Slip on a shirt, slop on some sunscreen, and slap on a hat. We have a hole in our ozone layer so the sun is very strong and burns you quite quickly."

"So even your sun bites you in Australia. I think you are very brave living with all the snakes and spiders."

Chloe laughed. "It's not that bad. I really think you would love where I live. I will take you one day."

"Tell me more about where you live."

"Ok, well I grew up in Umina Beach. It's a small surf town, a friendly town. Everybody knows everybody. Where I live now, is the next little town around the headland, called Pearl Beach, as you know. There is only a cafe and a restaurant. But that is what is so special. Not like Umina, that town gets crazy busy in summer season. If you go around the headland a bit further, you come to a small fishing town called Patonga. A lot of trawlers work off Patonga so we are lucky and have fresh seafood. You would like it there, Jack."

"Aye, but you have sharks and beasties that bite."

"And wallabies, koalas, and beautiful birds, don't just think about the bad things. It really is a lovely place, you need to come and visit one day."

"Have you always lived on your own?"

"No, I had a flat mate, my best friend Angie. We went through school together and have been at the surf club since we were in Nippers together. That's a surf training school were each Sunday we all get together and do activities in the water and learn safety and survival skills.

We shared a place together for a couple of years, but then she got a job in the city and shared a flat down there with other girls. I moved to where I am now, so have lived alone for about a year. My anxiety levels hit sky high when I first moved in alone. I found it hard but I soon got used to it and I had Mrs Whitaker, which helped a bit. Angie is back home again with her mum now, working back on the coast. We are still close. I have told her all about you." She smiled.

"And what did she say about that?" He leaned forward eagerly, waiting for her reply.

"She said you are very good looking and sounded like a dream."

"I must read those emails one day. You now have me intrigued." There was that cheeky smile again that always tugged at her heart.

"Tell me about you. Have you always lived at home?"

"Aye, I have. My mum's the best cook, and I had it pretty good. I would go to the trawlers early in the morning with Dad and my brother, and after work I would meet up with some friends for a pint of beer. Pat, my best friend, worked on a trawler also, so we kept the same drinking hours. I led a pretty simple life. I am not sure how I am going to cope going back after all this and especially without you."

"And what about Mary? You never mentioned her. How long did you go out?"

"Well, there isn't much to tell. We went out after school a bit then broke up. I was busy with the boats for years, didn't worry about girls and then a few years ago, she started hanging around again. But it was nothing serious. Like I said before, we just became a habit."

"Hey, you guys, you have a great spot here."

It was John and Ava.

"We have been enjoying the pools and the spa. It is a perfect day. How did you go with your planning?"

"We have a flight to Florence booked for tomorrow," said Jack, looking at Chloe excited.

"Oh, Tuscany. So jealous. You can fill us all in over dinner tonight. Don't forget dinner is at the Italian restaurant tonight," reminded Ava.

"No, we won't forget. We will be there, our last dinner together. It is a bit sad," sighed Chloe.

They all agreed it was sad coming to the end of such a great time. John and Ava were heading back to their room for a rest. Chloe and Jack wanted a swim and then a cocktail while they dried off before heading back for a rest before dinner.

"John, what happened to your knee?" Chloe had noticed it was all grazed and starting to bleed.

"Oh, darn, it's starting to bleed again." John got a hanky out of his pocket and started dabbing it. "Well, you wouldn't believe it." Everyone started to laugh; you just knew when he said those words you were in for a funny story. "No, wait, this is serious. So here I am just walking along the deck to the pool, chatting away with Ava, and this little kid pushed his chair back right in front of me. I tripped on the leg of it and went flying towards this poor woman sunbaking, landing straight on top of her. I must have scraped my knee on the deck on the way down."

"Oh, my God, John, you are a fair dinkum, walking disaster," laughed Chloe. "Are you alright?"

"Yea, I think so, but she wasn't. She was all winded or something, people came running from everywhere, it was frigging hilarious. Here I was trying to apologise, Ava had walked away and left me. I felt pretty bad, but she was ok, a bit of a sook, needs to toughen up a bit."

Ava was laughing hysterically. "I am so sorry. I shouldn't be laughing, I know, but it was pretty funny, that's why I had to walk away. Just imagine the look on this poor woman's face when John landed on her. She didn't know what had happened."

They were all laughing by now. "It could only happen to you John."

"So is the woman ok?" said Chloe, trying to compose herself.

"Yea, she will be fine. She was whining something about a cracked rib, but I can't see how that would happen, can you?" cried John, trying to sound sincere. But everyone was in hysterics again and no one could answer.

Everyone looked happy when they arrived for dinner; you could hear Paddy roaring with laughter from outside the restaurant. They could see John standing next to him carrying on, waving his arms around. Hand in hand they walked over to the table.

"What is going on here now?" enquired Jack.

"This laddie is crazy," laughed Paddy. "How he gets on in life is a mystery to me, Ava come and control him for God's sake."

They had obviously missed what had happened, but knowing John, there would be plenty more before the night was over. They took their seats. Chloe looked around the table. There was John. He was such a funny guy, always getting himself in trouble and being mischievous. There were always plenty of laughs when he was around. Then there was Ava, so sweet and so easy going, nothing worried her which was lucky with John by her side. They were like two kids that forgot to grow up. Danni and Rocco! Never a hair out of place, always dressed with complete sophistication, and looking like a grand New York executive couple. But put a champagne glass in her hand and she became more fun than you could handle. Cruz and Catalina slightly sophisticated but in a more relaxed way than Danni and Rocco, they had their own style, they were always the first ones on the dance floor, and always the last ones to leave. How lucky they were to witness Cruz's proposal to Cat, it had been so special. Paddy and Maggie, the fun never stopped when those two were around. Always arguing, but in a nice funny way that always made you laugh. Paddy the matchmaker, you could hear him roaring with laughter from miles away. Here they all were, for their last meal together. Such good friends in such a short amount of time.

Never in her wildest dreams would she have thought when she got on that plane at Sydney airport that two weeks later, she would be sitting here with all these beautiful people, they were her new comfort zone. She turned to look at Jack, and how did I ever live without Jack. He turned and looked into her eyes as if he too was thinking exactly the same thing. They smiled at each other; he squeezed her hand and winked. Yes, she certainly was a very lucky girl. She was definitely not the same girl who left Sydney. She had somehow matured and gained a wealth of knowledge about not only herself but the world.

They had a wonderful dinner with lots of laughs and then everyone went dancing afterwards. It turned into a huge farewell party. The cruise director was leading the party, dancing on the bar and everyone was having a wild time. They started a Congo and snaked their way around the pool area and back. Everyone would have sore heads tomorrow but no one cared.

After a while the party started to slow down, people were leaving. It was a big day ahead for lots of people packing up, getting off the ship, and travelling to new destinations. It had finally hit all of them: it was over. They all embraced each other, saying their goodbyes. John was crying again, telling everyone that he loved them and the boys were bantering and teasing him. They all promised to keep in touch and they planned to get together again somewhere the following year. It was a promise that each and every one of them was determined to keep.

Chapter 17

THE START OF THE ROAD TRIP

They stood back and took one last look at the boat. Jack had his arm around her shoulder. It had been an emotional morning with last-minute quick goodbyes over breakfast and getting off the boat. They all managed to bump into each other at the breakfast bar and most were cradling sore heads.

But now, that was all behind them, and they had ten days of peace and quiet together which they were both looking forward to. They grabbed a cab to the airport and before too long were landing in Florence.

The car rental office was easy to find. They got the keys and headed to the parking bay. It was parked in J45. Walking over, they managed to find it. It was a small Mercedes Benz. They were both excited as it was practically a brand new car for them to drive through Europe. It had an enormous boot so their luggage fitted with ease. Chloe set up the GPS and they were off. It would take them an hour along a main freeway.

Jack was coping well with driving on the wrong side of the road. The traffic was light and the weather was good. Before too long they came to their exit and Chloe helped guide him to the gates of Hotel Garden. It was a grand three-story building which sprawled out over vast parklands with multiple outhouses and an enormous terrace with tables and chairs covered halfway with a pergola, and other areas to enjoy the sun. To the left, they noticed a massive pool area with a pool house and sun lounges.

"What a find. Check this place out. It's beautiful." They parked and wandered inside to check in. The staff were warm and friendly. Jack got the key and led Chloe down the pathway that was adorned with rose gardens. The sweet smell lingered in the air. They arrived at their room and Jack opened the door and stood back for her to enter before him. She walked into the room and gasped. Speechless, she turned to Jack. "You did this."

"Aye, and it was worth it just to see your face." Tears were streaming down her face as she looked around the room. The bed was covered in rose petals, which made the whole room smell divine. There was a small table with a bottle of Prosecco in an ice bucket with two wine glasses and a small platter of chocolates and fruit.

The room itself was beautifully decorated, the king size bed was draped in a beautiful mint and white duvet and the windows had matching floor-to-ceiling tie-back curtains with a pretty lace sheer. A wooden desk had the tea and coffee for the morning with a matching chair and a mint colour tub chair in the corner. The bedside tables looked like antiques.

"Nobody has ever done anything like this for me before."

Jack handed her a tissue. "I didn't mean to make you cry," he said quietly.

"Far out, Jack, I can't believe you did this for me."

He sat her down on the tub chair. "Well, if we only have ten days together, I want them to be the best days of your life. I want you to remember me for all the right reasons."

"If you keep this up, I may never want to leave." She laughed still half blowing her nose.

"Aye, well, the plan is working then," he winked.

She took photos to send to Kait and Angie, while Jack poured them a glass of bubbles each. They sat on the bed and ate the fruit, washing it down with the wine. Jack got up and put the do not disturb sign on the door and they spent the afternoon wrapped up in each other's arms and then gently nodded off for a nap. They were both still feeling the effects of the night before.

They woke feeling refreshed and just in time to get ready for dinner. Jack had booked a table for dinner on the outdoor terrace.

The table looked beautiful, and the panoramic views over Siena at sunset were breathtaking. The waiter brought out a bottle of prosecco, poured them a wine and placed the bottle in a standing ice bucket.

"This is all so beautiful," she said, scanning the room slowly.

"Aye, it is, I think we have made the right choice here," said Jack as he opened the menu.

"I like the sound of a selection of Tuscan cold cuts, pickled vegetables, crostini and cheese starter," Chloe smiled over the top of her menu.

"I thought you might."

"Oh, and they have Tuscan steak. Sounds like you and I will have the braised veal cheek."

The waiter arrived and took their order. "And for dessert I would recommend a Bacio di Siena, it is a local favourite made for two to share."

"Oh, thank you, we will definitely try that one."

They sat there for hours reliving the days of the cruise and Chloe ended up with the giggles again.

"I can't help it," she laughed. "It's these bubbles, they do something to me, it doesn't happen when I drink beer."

Jack was sitting back in his seat, head cocked to one side, smiling while he watched her. She looked beautiful, the fairy lights and moonlight created a magical scene. They were just about the last couple on the terrace and thought they should thank the waiter and head home. "Don't rush. You stay as long as you like, if you don't need anything else we will close up and leave you here to enjoy the evening. We will see you for breakfast in the morning, we have very beautiful handmade little Italian pastries, make sure you try one."

Chloe laughed at the look on Jack's face; she could almost see his mouth start to water. He would be dreaming about them all night.

They finished their wine and wandered back to the room. It had been a perfect evening, but they were both starting to feel very sleepy. When they got home it was Chloe who had perked up. She went to the bench and poured them out a couple of whiskies. "I can't let you go to bed without your dram," she handed Jack his glass and went into the bathroom to freshen up. She slipped on her French camisole she knew Jack loved. "Plus, I haven't thanked you properly for my flowers," she teased. His eyes lit up seeing her all sexy. He had got undressed and was sitting on the tub chair in his underwear. She sat on his lap and kissed him as he explored her body with his hands.

"You're driving me crazy, do you know that?" he whispered.

"Good, it's my job to do that," she answered as she slid onto the floor between his legs and gently caressed him with her tongue until he was groaning. He picked her up and placed her on the bed, undressing her now with an urgency. She had him wild with passion. He was kissing her body. "Mo leannan falaiche, mo Chloe…" He couldn't wait any longer. He gave in and wildly made love to her until they both lay panting. "I have never met any girl like you. You're an angel in the day and turn into a wild devil at night. You bring the devil out in me, too," he laughed.

"I like it when you're a devil" she said softly as she fell asleep.

Chapter 18

SIENA

They woke the next morning late. They still had their unfinished whisky glasses sitting on the table. Jack got up and made them coffee and poured the whisky into them. "What are you doing? That is last night's drinks," said Chloe, surprised. "I know, but you can't waste a fine whisky. It will be ok, lucky we had them straight."

He brought the coffee back to bed. "You were like a little jaguar last night, you feisty wee thing," he said to her lustfully.

"I know. I am sorry. It must be that prosecco," she said, rubbing her head and squinting.

"Aye, well today, I will buy a case of it."

They decided to just stay at the hotel and relax by the pool for the day. They needed a few quiet days. It had been pretty full on the last few weeks and they both needed to slow down. They showered and strolled down to the breakfast room. It was a huge spread. There were tables laden with every food you could desire and an enormous display. Italy loved their sweets in the morning and so the lines of cakes and pastries were endless. Jack loaded his plate with every type of pastry available and came back with a huge smile.

They grazed for an hour and then walked it off with a stroll around the gardens. By mid-morning they were ready for a swim; they went to the pool house and got issued towels for the day then found two sun lounges to spend the morning on. They swam, sunbaked, dozed, and chatted the morning away.

Lunch was on the terrace. The waiter arrived to take their order. "We only need a light lunch. We have had a big breakfast," said Chloe, looking at Jack who had a disgusted look on his face.

"I know exactly what you need. Leave it to me." He turned and disappeared. "What is this light lunch you are putting me on?"

"We are swimming. We can't have a big meal, plus we ate way too much this morning," she smiled, watching his sad face.

The waiter returned and placed some plates on the table. "You will like this. It is called a *vitello*. It is sliced meat arranged on a platter with a sauce made from tuna capers and lemon, plus bread and olive oil with a plate of tomatoes and olives."

Jack looked it over and started to dig in. "Mmm different, but it is delicious, you should try," he said with his mouth full.

She layered her bread with all the different things and nodded. "It is yummy and all that we needed." She let Jack eat most of it as usual.

The next day, they went for a walk into Siena spending the morning doing all the tourist things looking at the Piazza Duomo and all the wonderful old buildings of Siena. After a five-minute walk from Piazza Del Campo they found a lovely little restaurant that looked interesting. It resembled an old cave. They went inside to see if they could get a table and luckily they had a cancelled booking. "Please follow me," said the waiter, who took them down a small set of stairs leading them down two levels. They arrived at what could only be described as a small cave dug out into the side of the building lit by a small Tuscan style chandelier.

The waiter handed them the drinks menu. "I think we will start with a beer and we will order a wine to have with our meal, a Tuscan wine, chianti classico if you have it," said Jack.

"Of course, excellent choice," said the waiter, impressed with his order. He took the menu and left.

"Jack, where are we?" Chloe giggled quietly. "Is this one of your romantic surprises?"

"No," Jack whispered back. "I would love to say I did this but I seriously have no idea where we are either. It's so Medieval, it's spectacular."

The waiter returned with food menu.

"This is an interesting place, the interior of the restaurant looks so Medieval," said Chloe.

The waiter looked pleased that they had taken some interest in it. "Yes, I am glad that you have asked. The restaurant was built within antique Etruscan catacombs caves built over two thousand years ago. You are seated in a tuffaceous niche. It is very romantic, you are lucky to get this one, it was requested especially by the man who booked it, but cancelled, so it is your lucky day," explained the waiter with a happy smile.

The interior was all stone and brick with huge Tuscan paintings on the walls. There was no doubt that you are in an old Medieval restaurant in Tuscany. It was simply beautiful. The table looked like it was set for royals with beautiful silverware and white linen tablecloth and napkins. The napkin holder was silver entwined vine leaves. They studied the menu while they had their beer.

"They have Florentine steak for two, Jack, your favourite" she smiled.

"Oh, aye that sounds wonderful, and I guess you will have the octopus and scallop appetiser," he looked up at her with a grin.

"Yea that does sound like me, but I have always wanted to try a truffle and they have a truffle risotto," she said, still intently looking over the menu. "They would be local truffles. I have watched a show where truffle puppies collect them," she said, pushing her hair back.

"Then that's it, we will try the truffles also," said Jack, closing the menu and taking a sip of his beer.

"So Siena is turning out to be interesting. Look at this place," said Chloe waving her hand in the air at all the interesting sights of the place.

"Oh aye, it would be spooky at night. I can half imagine a wild animal coming out of one of these caves, like you my little wild beast dressed in your French lace negligee."

Chloe giggled. "And you, my wild Highlander dressed in your kilt coming to find me."

"Aye, and I would take off my kilt and lay it on the ground and make love to you in the candlelight."

They were both starting to feel giddy with desire as the waiter returned with their wine followed by the food. "We have a promotion on at the moment. Because you came for lunch I will give you a coupon to return for dinner for a free entrée. It is really very beautiful at night, extremely romantic."

They both stared at each other with wide eyes and Chloe blushed.

"Thank you," said Jack as the waiter smiled and left.

"He heard us," whispered Chloe.

"He could not have. How did he hear us? It's just a coincidence." They both giggled as they drank their wine.

The presentation was first class. The octopus and scallops were served looking so beautiful, you dare not eat them, but they soon got over it and enjoyed every mouthful. The steak and risotto arrived and the waiter sliced it and divided it onto the pair of waiting plates. The scalloped potatoes and risotto set on the centre of the table. Chloe was glad Jack was a big eater.

After lunch, they walked around the town a while to walk off some food. There were plenty of piazzas and fountains and, yes, churches and the sounds of bells ringing were constant. Pigeons were everywhere, mostly living near the fountains, and had made quite a mess on all the stone walls and paved floors. It had such an ancient, almost Medieval look about it. They strolled around taking photos before heading home. They stopped at a shop and bought some wine and whisky to keep with them to enjoy a few drinks at home if they didn't feel like going anywhere. The afternoon was spent around the pool and then they walked up to reception and with the help and guidance of the reception staff they booked a wine tour for the next day.

They woke up early after a good night's sleep. The minibus arrived around lunchtime and there were three other guys already on the bus. They all introduced themselves and Chloe noticed they were Aussie. It was so lovely to hear the Australian accent again. They were from Queensland and were there for a family wedding in Tuscany. Two of them were brothers and it was their sister's wedding and the other guy was the groom's brother.

"We met a couple in Rome that had been to a family wedding in Tuscany. Surely, it's not the same one. Their names were Natalie and Matt," said Chloe.

"You met Nat and Matt. Nat is our sister," said one of them. It was incredible. What a small world. Jack was all of a sudden excited. He had liked Matt a lot. "We met them in a restaurant and then they took us to a craft beer bar for drinks, it was a great day," said Jack excitedly.

The driver came back to the bus and informed them of the day ahead. She was a crazy blonde Italian called Gina and drove like a bat out of hell. They were making their way to the first winery in Chianti. She took them through the most spectacular scenery along the windy roads towards Grieve. Jack put his arm around Chloe and they watched the scenery from the window. It was truly breathtaking. "This is the romantic drive you wanted to take me on," smiled Chloe dreamily.

"Oh, aye, but it's not exactly what I had in mind. I didn't realise I would be hanging on for my life. If I don't keep a firm grip I am sure I will land on the floor any minute." His knuckles were white as Gina manoeuvred the little van around the bends at speed. Not fun for anyone who gets car sick, he thought.

Gina finally stopped at the little town of Grieve and they had free time to wander the town. Chloe bought beautiful porcelain salad servers with wooden handles painted with Tuscan scenery. Gina was hurrying them all back on the bus. Soon after they arrived at their first winery, Castelino. They were seated at a long table outside. The views were spectacular as they looked over the rolling hills of the vineyard.

Wines were brought out and placed on the table. It was the wine that they had fallen in love with on the cruise, the one Jack opened for them on their first night together. They loved it and both bought a case to be sent home. The next was another rooster wine. They gave them the history of the wines of the region and explained that a rooster on the neck of a bottle determined it was from the Chianti region. Everyone enjoyed the story and the history behind it.

They sampled more wines accompanied with cheeses, olives, cold cut meats, and bread. They spent an hour sampling before Gina arrived and started yelling it was time to get back on the bus. "Right O, time to hit the frog and toad," said one of the boys with Gina right on his heels. Everyone laughed and rushed back on the bus. Jack looked at Chloe and whispered, "He doesn't like frogs all that much, but I didn't even see one, did you?"

Chloe laughed after catching on to what he was saying. "Oh, Jack, I am sorry I forgot you would have no idea what that is. It means time to hit the road, you know, go, leave."

"Oh, well why didn't they just say that?" he whispered.

The guy seated in front of him turned around, laughing. "I did. I could have said, let's do the Harry Holt or right O, on ya bike. It is all the same, mate." He laughed. "Yea, it is Aussie slang. The Harry Holt is the bolt. On ya bike, let's go, time to shoot through, all means the same thing," said the other guy as everyone laughed. "I will make an Aussie out of you by the end of the day, don't worry."

They made their way to Montalcino. There was more stunning scenery along the way. Beautiful castles and towns built right on top of the rolling hills. The next winery was just as impressive as the first and they sampled the different wines that they showcased. All were incredible. They were sat at another large table outdoors and four bottles of wine were opened and placed on the table. "Lunch will be served here, please enjoy our wines while you wait, and please ask questions. We love to talk about our wines," said the lady from the winery in broken English.

The boys introduced themselves as Mick, Matty, and Tom. "So what is your story?" asked Mick.

"We met in Barcelona. We were both on the same cruise and now we are on a road trip to Paris," said Jack, popping an olive into his mouth.

"Are you coming back to Australia afterwards? We could catch up," asked Matty.

"I would love to take Jack back to Australia one day," said Chloe, smiling at Jack, elbowing him in the rib.

"Ouch, I can't speak the lingo," said Jack in defence.

"Don't worry, Jack, we will teach you the lingo. We'll give ya the mail, mate, that's, we'll tell ya what's going on, you know, give ya the news," laughed Mick.

"We loved our day with Matt and Natalie. They took us to a hidden bar and the beers were fantastic."

"Yea we have all been in Tuscany for the wedding and went our separate ways. We have been up to Lake Como and now were heading to Greece to do some island hopping and then will fly home from there. Natalie and Matt were heading north to Venice and had no plans after that, so funny you met them."

"We went to Santorini on the boat. You will love Greece," said Jack, as he poured another wine for Chloe.

They all got on well, and teased each other all the way through lunch. The more wine they drank, the louder the laughter. Jack started telling stories about Scotland and the one the boys loved the most was the referees in Scotland were sponsored by spec savers. They almost fell off their chairs with laughter with that story. The lasagne and tiramisu were devoured. "Oh that lunch was a dead set ripper, mate," said Mick, wiping his mouth.

"Bloody oath." yelled Jack back at him.

They laughed. "See, you're getting the hang of it," yelled Tom from the other side of the table.

They bought wine from the cellar door to take home and it was time to move on. The ride home was full of laughter and they were all sorry to see the end of the day. The bus pulled up at their hotel and they said goodbye. Jack leaned back into the bus. "Hey, can you give Matt a message for me. Tell him I took his advice and he was right. He will know what I am talking about," and got off. They waved as the bus took off.

They went for a swim to freshen up after the wine and the heat of the day. They sat on the sun lounges to dry off. "I had fun with the Aussie lads. They made me keen to maybe come to Australia for a visit one day."

"You would pick up the Aussie slang in no time. I will teach you some food ones. A dog's eye is a meat pie. The dead horse is tomato sauce."

"How do you know all this?"

"Because it's the way we talk, it's easy. I have been bought up on it. My grandfather was a real ocker and spoke like that all the time and Bob at the surf club is a classic example. You would like him."

The more she told him the more shocked he started to look. "Maybe it's not such a good idea after all."

"You'll be right. You have me beside you all the way," she assured him, slathering on more sunscreen. What's some Scottish slang, then?"

"Oh, I am not even going to go there. You Aussies win hands down when it comes to slang. I still can't stop thinking about what you do, with smuggling poor budgies," said Jack, astonished.

Chloe laughed. "Have a guess. What I mean if I ask you to strip off to your reg grundies?" said Chloe.

He sat back and thought for a moment then a sparkle came to his eye. "Your undies."

"You got it. See, it's not that hard. You really did have a fun day with the Aussie guys, didn't you? I will take you back to Australia one day, you will have a ball."

Chapter 19

DIJON

They woke up early and drove for a little while before stopping for a break at a rest house-style café to have a coffee and donut, then had a quick stopover at a small town, which was halfway, before heading off again, early the next day. After a few hours, they found their way to the Grand Hotel. Impressive was an understatement, standing five stories high with every front facing room featuring a Juliet balcony with wrought-iron balustrades.

They pulled up out the front and a valet was waiting. The luggage was taken inside and they handed him the keys.

"This is quiet upmarket, Mademoiselle," Jack said quietly.

"Well, Monsieur, you certainly had the bar quite high for me to follow," she whispered back.

They arrived at reception. The staff both quick and professional and they were in their room a short time later. The room was beautiful with a little balcony overlooking the Place Darcy. The bed was king-sized, which Jack sat on, bouncing up and down with a smile. "Oh la la, comfy bed, Chloe."

She just smiled, already checking out the large, clean, marble bathroom. "No spa, Jack," she called back.

"Aye, lucky the bed is comfortable. We don't need anything else." He kissed her on the neck as he poked his head in to take a peek. They had a decent size sitting area with a small lounge. Chloe walked over and opened the French doors and stepped out onto the little balcony as she watched the passing parade below.

It was still early in the day and seeing they only had a few nights, they decided to head straight to the old town to take a look around. Reception advised them to take the Owl's trail, and gave them a map to follow. A tourist's guide took them all over town showing them the sights and the history of the town. The markets were on in town also. They thanked them and headed towards the start of the Owl's trail.

They happily followed the little owl markings and read the plaques along the way. They bumped into the markets and decided to have lunch. Local produce was in abundance, fish and French cheeses galore to choose from. They bought a bucket of non-shucked oysters, some cheese, cold meat cuts and a baguette and sat at a table to share their feast.

"Have you ever shucked an oyster before?" she asked, looking at the bucket of oysters.

"Oh, aye, I have shucked hundreds. Here, let me show you."

She watched intently as he picked up an oyster in one hand and a knife in the other.

"You put the knife under here and gently turn it and it will pop open, then run the knife underneath the oyster to loosen it." He threw his head back as he tossed the oyster into his mouth. "Here you have a go."

She did exactly as he showed her while he watched on, making sure she was doing it right.

"There, see, it's easy as long as you are careful, that's all." She sat back, proudly handing him back the knife. "Oh wait, I will be back."

She had spotted over his shoulder a stall selling wine by the glass and brought back two glasses. "What would you like to do while we are here?" Chloe asked, sitting back down.

"Maybe a wine tour. We had fun in Italy on the wine tour," he said as he cut a large piece of cheese, placing it on his bread.

"Ok, maybe reception can book us one," she replied, stuffing her mouth with another large oyster. "But tomorrow I want to do more of this. Just hang out and have fun."

The next day was spent doing anything they wanted, a relaxed morning and then a walk into town.

"Jack, would it be OK with you if I find you a nice bar, while I go to the store?"

"Really, of course. Why didn't I meet you years ago? You Aussie girls are so easy going, we are in lots of trouble going to the pub in Scotland. Well, I did anyway, and many others do also."

"Well, I keep telling you this, but you have been hanging out with the wrong girls," she laughed.

"Well, I am working that out quickly."

They started walking and Chloe saw the pharmacy she wanted to go to, and the department store was close by. "Well, this is where I want to be. Let's see what's around here for you."

They looked around and spotted a bistro with outdoor seating and people were casually having a quiet drink.

"This is a perfect wee watering hole," winked Jack.

"I will grab us a beer before I set off for the shops."

Jack got the seats and she returned with the beer.

"1664, I see," admired Jack as he pulled out her chair and she placed them on the table.

"Yes, I forgot we are back in France, it gets so confusing."

Ava had told her how every girl needs a visit to the pharmacy in France, it's a wonderful treat. Different to the larger department store she had visited in Marseille, being far more intimate and had lots of little goodies. She had been extremely excited to check it all out. Ava was right; the shelves were lined with all the best brands. Heaps more than what she had seen in the department store in Marseille. She grabbed a few things from her dream brand skincare range and some perfumes and headed off.

Next was the department store. She wanted to buy Sophia some little French dresses. The department store was huge. She wandered through, looking around. Turning a corner, she found herself in the lingerie section. It was a show stopper, the sexy negligee, baby doll pj's, bra, and panties sets, and they all looked so enticing. "Sophie," she reminded herself, "Sophie." Leaving that behind her she found the children's section. It was laden with gorgeous outfits, shoes, and accessories. She chose three little dresses and some matching accessories and started to head out.

Walking past the lingerie section, she stopped; she couldn't help herself. She looked over everything with admiration. She had become a French lingerie addict. *I have to buy some,* she thought. Jack will love them. A girl could never have enough lingerie. She selected a few bra and panties sets and some sexy nightwear; they were even more beautiful than the ones she had bought before. He had definitely sparked something in her that she never knew existed before. She, all of a sudden, wanted to be sexy. He made her feel like a princess and she really wanted to impress him. First time ever that she felt that way. Happy with her purchases, she set off to find Jack. He was waiting for her right where she had left him. He was instantly smiling when he saw her.

"How was your shopping, my love? Looks like you have had a great time," he said, gazing down at all of her bags.

"I had a lovely time, thanks. Did you enjoy your watering hole?"

"Aye, I did. Never did I think I would enjoy a girl going shopping. A whole new world has opened up to me."

Chloe laughed and went to buy them a beer. They sat for a while. She told him all about her shopping experience and they watched the world go by.

On the way home, they decided to stop by reception and book a wine tour for the next day. The lady at reception gave them lots to choose from but recommended one that was very popular that took them through the Burgundy region.

Jack rang his mother; it was her birthday and everyone was having dinner. She wanted to hear all the details about the trip and how Chloe was. Jack then spoke to Jeannie and told her all about their day and the wine trip they were taking the next day. He found it hard to catch up with his family, as he thought about them all sitting around the table. He was glad he wasn't there; he loved his mum and sister very much, but the thought of sitting at the table with his brother and his ex was something he could do without. Instead, he was sitting in Dijon with a beautiful girl. He stared over at Chloe. How life takes you on some strange turns.

They waited outside their hotel to be picked up by the minibus, which was to take them to the wineries of Cote de Nuit and Cote de Beaune. An English couple were already seated on the bus and they had to pick up two more passengers along the way. They drove around a few blocks before stopping to pick up two girls. As they got on the bus, one of the girls turned to Jack. "Oh, hello, we meet again." They sat down the front of the bus and Chloe instantly recognised a Scottish accent.

"How do you know those girls?" asked Chloe, concerned.

"I will fill you in later" he whispered. He overheard the bus driver talking to them and saying they were a late booking and he only got advice an hour ago he had to pick them up. The girls agreed it was a last-minute booking they made.

The scenery along the way was beautiful, and the driver was extremely educational on the area and the wineries as he spoke to them with great passion. The English couple were extremely interested and seemed to know a lot about wines. They quizzed the driver about the region and he spoke in great detail about the Burgundy wines and region. They laughed together, it certainly wasn't the same sort of day that they had in Tuscany, with crazy Gina, driving hell bent through the winding hills, and the Aussie boys laughing all the way. Gee, they had enjoyed that day. The French were far more serious about their regions and their wines.

They arrived at the first winery and were ushered inside to a table where they were supplied with tastings of a few of their best wines. Each wine was accompanied with a thorough explanation of its region and make. The Scottish girl kept staring at Jack. Chloe was aware Jack was feeling uncomfortable, and she was starting to feel the same way. They moved onto the second winery and sampled more wines. Jack seemed to sit a lot closer to Chloe and had his arm around her shoulder the whole time, which made her feel a bit better.

The Scottish girl started making remarks about the two lovers up the back of the bus, but with venom in her eyes. She had green eyes that were wicked, nothing like Danni's beautiful eyes. Her hair was curly brown shoulder-length and she wore a very revealing dress that if Chloe didn't know any better she was dressed to attack. If Jack knew this girl, why wasn't he saying anything?

"Let's take a walk around outside, get some fresh air," he whispered. They both let out a sigh of relief as they made it out the door. They walked towards a fence a few meters away in the distance, which gave an outlook of the sweeping valley below. A cat came along and started to rub itself on Jack's leg. "You seem to be very popular today," said Chloe sarcastically. "Who is that girl? I get the feeling that you know her, maybe even some history there also."

Jack was looking around to make sure they were alone. "I know her from back in Fraserburgh. What are the chances of bumping into her yesterday, and now her being on our wine tour today?"

"You bumped into her yesterday."

"Aye, while you went shopping. I was sitting there, and she walked past, saw me and stopped."

"You never mentioned it to me."

"No, I didn't think about it again. It wasn't important, until she got on the bus."

"Who is she? Do you two have history? And she seems to be sending me daggers all day."

"Well, sort of. I went out with her a few times at school, that's all."

"So who ended it. I am guessing you, am I right?"

"Aye, I was a bit like Craig. Too interested in hanging out with the lads than spending time with her. She was whining, so I ended it."

"How long were you with her?" Chloe asked curiously.

"Just a few months," Jack said, casing the joint, scared she might be around.

"That's a bit longer than a few dates. That's quite a long time for a school romance."

"Aye, but we never did anything, and I just wasn't interested, but too gutless to end it. After I did, she hounded me for ages and then I met Mary, so she finally dropped off."

They heard the door open and turned to see her coming out the door and towards them. "Well, this is a lovely view, isn't it?" she said casually. "I don't think we have met. My name is Shauna."

"No, I am sure we haven't. I am Chloe."

"So you have a new girlfriend, Jack. I only heard the other day that you and Mary separated. Is this one a rebound affair?"

"That was a few months ago now," he said squirming.

"Oh, well if I had of known sooner, I would have looked you up," she spat, staring at Chloe.

"Well, I am now with Chloe, and very happy, indeed," said Jack sternly.

"So, I see. And where are you from, Chloe? You don't sound like you're from Scotland."

"No, I am from Australia," she answered proudly.

"I didn't know you went to Australia, Jack, where did you two meet?" she asked curiously.

"We met in Barcelona."

"Ohhhh, so it's a holiday romance. I will be able to catch up then when you get home, won't I?" She smiled sarcastically at Chloe. "They never last, holiday romances."

"No, I don't think so, it's not just a holiday romance. I have met the girl of my dreams, and I am planning on going home with her to Australia," he said strongly.

"Oh, off the market again. Oh well, let me know if it doesn't work out and maybe we can pick up where we left off." With that she walked off, glaring at Chloe.

They both turned back to the view. "I am so sorry, Chloe. I never meant to put you in this situation."

"Don't worry about it. You set her straight," Chloe said gently as he leaned and gave her a kiss. The guide was calling them to get back on the bus.

The last winery was a quick drive down the road. The pair of them had fun being all lovey dovey in front of Shauna, and they could tell she was starting to fume. She was getting more and more sarcastic as the day went on; the more wine she drank the more fire she breathed. They were happy when it was time to order take-away wine and get back on the bus. They bought a few bottles of wine to share over the next few days and then they were finally dropped off. They took the wine up to their room and then set off for a walk. They stopped at a little tavern near their hotel.

"I am so sorry you had to go through that today, Chloe," Jack said sincerely as he placed the beers down on the table.

"It's ok, you put her in her place, but I am glad to be leaving for Paris in the morning," she said cheerfully. But there was something hidden behind the visage of her cheerfulness. She was totally freaking out on the inside. She tried to hide it. "Mmm French beer. Thanks, Jack."

It was a relief to be sitting there unwinding after a stressful day; she loved the slow pace of the area after a hectic day. She had played it down in front of Jack, but if the truth be told, it scared her a lot. It was something that she had not even thought of before. Was it just a holiday romance? Those words had been ringing in her ears all day. What if he went home to Scotland and forgot all about her? He probably had women lining up to date him. He was so good looking and a really nice genuine guy. Shauna had said herself that she would look him up when he got home. She knew one thing for sure; he was no holiday romance for her and she was trouble.

"You are very quiet today." Jack had interrupted her thoughts.

"Oh, I am ok. It's just been a long day."

"As long as that is all it is, you do know that you have nothing to worry about, right?"

"Yea I know that. It's all good, Jack."

But in fact, she was a little bit suspicious. How did he just happen to meet that girl by chance twice in two days. Something just wasn't adding up. It was uncanny, she just finds out Jack is separated, then bumps into him in the streets of Dijon, and then happens to incredibly be on their wine tour the very next day. Coincidence, Chloe wasn't so sure, but one thing she did know, she didn't trust that girl as far as she could throw her.

They decided to go to a little restaurant near them that night for dinner. It was known for exceptional meals, by an unknown up-and-coming chef. France was full of them. In fact, it seemed that there was one on every corner. They had certainly nailed the food industry in France. Turning a corner, they strolled down a little cobbled side lane and spotted it at the end. It was a cute little restaurant with only half a dozen little tables and it was full. The waiter escorted them to a small table set for two in the back corner. It was simply decorated, with red and white chequered table cloths and French music playing quietly. It was very cosy and had a lovely relaxed atmosphere. Menus were brought out and the waiter spoke to Jack in French. Jack ordered some wine for them, and he was gone. Chloe was reading the menu.

"It's in French," she whispered.

"Here, I can order for you. I know what you like. I ordered us a rose wine to start. The waiter recommended it from a local winery where we were today," he said quietly as he went back to studying the menu.

Just the thought of the wineries dampened Chloe's mood instantly. The wines arrived and the waiter spoke to Chloe in the best English he could about the food and the regions the produce came from. She listened carefully and thanked him.

"There is escargot on here. We could have some for an entree and there is a corn-fed chicken here, I know you like that, or fish," stated Jack.

"The chicken sounds delicious, thank you," she said quietly as she scanned the room, half expecting that girl to walk in. Jack looked at her over the top of his menu. She was quiet. He knew why. He instantly felt guilty. Today had been a total nightmare and he had no idea how it all had happened. But he knew he had to try and lighten Chloe's mood.

The waiter came back to take their order. Jack ordered the meal in French, the escargot for an entrée, chicken for Chloe and a beef in Burgundy wine for himself. The meals came out quickly and were delicious. They had been plated with extreme care and not one tiny herb would have dared to be out of place. The chicken came roasted with scalloped potatoes and baby carrots on the side. The beef dish was a rich red colour with chat potatoes and a baguette to mop up the jus. Jack was trying hard to keep Chloe entertained all through dinner. She was very quiet. She knew she was ruining their dinner and it wasn't his fault after all. He had been so lovely trying to pick up her mood.

"You have been sitting there all night with a wee sad face. You're not planning on running away on me again, are you?" he said. She instantly laughed. He always knew how to make her laugh. If it wasn't something that he said it was a smile or a silly face he would pull.

"I am so sorry. I am feeling a bit flat tonight, after today," she said, still looking around every time the door opened.

"Aye, I understand. It played with me head also. Don't worry about it, let's not let it ruin our night. It's over now."

"You're right. Do you feel like dessert?" That was a silly question. What did she ask that for? She smiled and then they both burst into a giggle. It lightened the air and he grabbed the menu and opened to the dessert page. "Oh a caramel Gateau sounds like a treat. What about you?"

He looked over at her but she was shaking her head. "No, I am too full."

"Well, you can have a few mouthfuls of mine."

The dessert came to the table and it looked incredible, Jack started devouring it instantly and gave her a spoon so she could share. She had a little chuckle to herself, watching him offering her to have more. He was feeling guilty, she had better lap it up that wouldn't happen again in a hurry. They were starting to have fun again and enjoy the meal. They went for a stroll after dinner taking the long way home. It was a perfect evening; they stopped at a fountain and sat for a bit before making their way back.

Finally, home after a lovely walk which had made them both feel better. Jack found a movie to watch while Chloe went and had a shower. She hardly ever had a shower on her own anymore. She started to panic about their relationship. He didn't even ask to join her. She decided that tonight she would surprise him with her new super sexy baby doll pyjamas. She knew he wasn't interested in Shauna but she wanted to make sure he was still interested in her.

Her self-esteem had taken a bit of a battering today. She had to be sure, so she shaved, exfoliated, and moisturised and then slipped into it. It really was super sexy, she checked her look in the mirror. It was very low cut, backless, and the beautiful French knickers scalloped at the back to show off her nicely tanned cheeks. Perfect for what she needed tonight, a pick-me-up for them both. She took a deep breath and opened the door. She had never done anything like this before in her life. It was the new Chloe coming out in her again. She stood looking down at Jack. "Would you like a drink?"

As he looked up, the look on his face was so cute. He looked like a little boy who just saw his presents under the Christmas tree for the first time.

"Where did you get that?"

Chloe went over to the bar fridge and leant over to fetch the beers. When she turned around, she began to laugh at the way he was staring.

"I bought it yesterday when I went shopping. Do you like?" she asked with a sexy smile, handing him a beer.

"Do I like? We are never leaving this room again as long as you are wearing that. On second thought, I hope you didn't pay too much for it, because it won't stay on you very long." He still looked wide eyed.

"I couldn't resist it, I walked past the lingerie section and thought it would be an idea to have some fun while in France. I loved the ones I bought in Marseille so much I thought I would buy some more."

"I like your ideas, and they get more and more revealing every time you go shopping. I must find another watering hole again tomorrow."

"I bought more than this, and underwear as well," she said cheekily.

"You're driving my imagination wild."

"That is the idea," teased Chloe.

Needless to say he couldn't keep his hands off her that night and her self-esteem was starting to come back. The movie never came on, but the wine was shared and they opened the French doors to let the moonlight in, as they made love continuously through the night. They were back to their usual selves again and both of them were very relieved.

Chapter 20

PARIS

They slept in the next morning and were grateful check-out wasn't until midday. They tidied up the room as they laughed together, saying it looked like they had a party. Jack picked up Chloe's pj's and folded them neatly, putting them in her bag.

"You can't leave these behind," he said with his cheeky grin. "Would you like to do some more shopping while we are here?"

"No, I still have a few more little surprises in store for you yet," she teased.

Jack went to the gym while Chloe got ready for the day and then they went to the buffet for breakfast. They were both quite hungry after the night's events, and had a bit of a drive ahead, so a decent breakfast was needed.

They were relieved they were leaving the car at the outskirts of town. They were already feeling stressed by the traffic. The man at the car rental called them a cab and told the driver where they were going. He soon pulled up out the front of their hotel. It was on a side street so it was a lot quieter which they liked. The building itself was extremely elegant, the façade dated from the 17th century. It stood four stories high with crisp white walls and fancy French windows, moulded window frames, and once again little Juliette balustrades they were beginning to realise they were extremely common in France. However, there was no valet or doorman running out to get their bags here.

They lugged them inside, and were met with a pleasant girl who spoke with a plum in her mouth and advised them their room was ready and gave them the key. They were on the top floor. The little lift was handy and they squeezed themselves in with their luggage only just fitting. It wasn't much bigger than a phone box.

They had a front room, overlooking the road, but as it was a side street, it seemed like it would be quiet. The room itself was large and decorated in true French style, with raised mouldings on the wardrobes and features on the walls. They also had a vase of sweet-smelling white roses on a small table with two red love heart chocolates.

It was so beautiful. She had been secretly a bit worried, as she had found this hotel at a price that was a steal compared to some of the places she saw, and thought it might have been quite shabby when they got there. But it was just what they needed. They had free minibar in the fridge and downstairs in the courtyard they had free drinks and nibbles available all day. The courtyard was an outdoor space where guests could go to sit to read books, play cards or games which were on a stand near the door.

They had limited days left together, they would go quick. They sat on the bed and read all the tourist information. They wanted to do a river cruise, see the Eifel Tower and Moulin Rouge other than that they were happy to enjoy the city. They went down to reception and booked Moulin Rouge for that night and the river cruise for another. They had a quiet afternoon looking around their local area.

They walked to the Louvre and the Arc de Triomphe and found a little bistro on the Seine. Sitting enjoying the outdoors, they ordered a beer and watched the view. Not needing to be anywhere, it was nice to linger a bit longer. Jack ordered a few small tapas-style plates and happily grazed for hours.

After lunch, they went back to the hotel for a rest before going to the show.

"This is a lovely hotel you chose for us. I am extremely impressed," he said.

"Well, it's a bit of a fluke," Chloe admitted. "I really wanted to stay at the Le Bristol but it was way too expensive."

"No, this place is much nicer than the flash ones, it has more character."

Moulin Rouge looked stunning as they arrived, all lit up, with red and white lights and the crowd made the atmosphere electric. They were shown to their seats, which were great seats at the front. The girl with the plum in her mouth actually did a great job. While dinner was served, a band played and the singers performed in both English and French. They were served champagne, which was exceptional. The best that they had tasted or maybe it was the location making it so special.

The show started as soon as the meal was finished. It was very French, indeed, with mild nudity and erotic dancing at times.

"They have been shopping at the same shop as you," whispered Jack.

"But you look so much sexier, especially with your wee seductive look you give me."

"Shh stop it people can hear you." She giggled; the bubbles were starting to work.

"I don't care, I want the world to know how lucky I am."

Sipping his champagne, he smiled at her. "You're blushing."

"Between you and the champagne, what chance do I have?" she whispered.

"I love it," he smirked, having a chuckle.

It was over before they knew it and they walked to find a bar to have a night cap on the way home.

They enjoyed a wonderful sleep in the next morning. Jack ordered room service and had croissants and crepes delivered to the room, and then put the do-not-disturb sign out as they had breakfast in bed. Chloe was wearing her sexy outfit as requested and he couldn't keep his eyes off her.

They laid on the bed and scrolled through their photos, laughing and reliving the memories of their trip. "Have we really only been together a few weeks?" sighed Chloe. "I feel I have been with you forever."

"Oh, aye, I feel the same. It feels so long ago I met you at that bar in Barcelona, but it feels like time has gone so quick at the same time."

They were both far off in their thoughts. Then Jack said, "It's crazy but when I met you in Barcelona there was some strange pulling inside me, something telling me to protect you, to look after you, it's almost as though we were destined to meet."

Chloe sat up on one elbow "I am going to tell you a story, but don't laugh at me, ok?" she said, unsure if it was a good idea telling him.

"I tell you stories all the time. Now it is your turn to entertain me." He sat up, eagerly listening.

"When Craig decided he didn't want to go, I was too scared to do the trip on my own. I went to my sister's place for advice. She got out her tarot cards and done a reading for me. I pulled out all of the most favourable cards, which meant I should take the trip, nothing bad was lurking. But then, the last card I drew was the lovers card. That card, Jack, means you are about to meet someone, you will form a strong bond with, an unconditional love, someone that could be the one you will love, for the rest of your life."

Jack was staring at her. "Well, if you told me that story a few months ago I would have laughed at you, but after all I have encountered over the last few weeks with magical moons and crazy leprechauns, I think I honestly believe that story, Chloe."

She laughed, relieved he hadn't told her she was nuts. "Plus, I had asked my nanna to guide me. She is Scottish. I honestly think she sent you to me."

"Well, I sure hope Granny isn't watching now. Come here my wild beast let me show you how much I appreciate what she has given me."

They had been putting off organising their flights but the time had finally come and it needed to be done. They chose a lunchtime flight for Jack, the same as Chloe's, so they could check out and go straight to the airport together. They showered, dressed and headed outdoors for a walk. They went to the Eiffel Tower and sat on the banks of the river and chatted. The afternoon was spent people watching and embracing the atmosphere of the city.

The night of the cruise on the river was a perfect evening. They were shown to their seats and with the large windows had incredible views. It was light but the sun was soon to set. Champagne was served as soon as they were seated, and dinner started to be served soon after the cruise began.

"Now we are on a very sophisticated French river cruise, so keep your champagne giggles down," teased Jack.

"I will do my best, Monsieur," she giggled.

It was the most romantic dinner. The sunset was incredible and as the moon rose, the city of lights came to life. There was a band softly playing French music, and each course of the meal was matched with the appropriate wine. It went all too fast and soon they were back on the docks of the river.

They found a spot on the river to watch the Eiffel tower shimmering as the lights danced in the moonlight. Jack held her tight as they watched. "You know that I love you, Chloe. It is breaking my heart leaving you, but I know in my heart it won't be forever. If I could marry you tomorrow I would, and be by your side forever. But unfortunately, that is not an option for us at the moment."

"Promise me, Jack, you will always remember us. Please don't go home and forget me." She was so scared of him going home and just going back to his normal life and forget all about her.

"I promise you with all my heart that I will never, ever forget you. And one day, I will return to you and marry you."

Chloe was crying. "I hold you to that promise, Jack."

"That's good because I meant every word."

"I will be waiting for you. I will never forget you, either. I have never been in love like this."

It was a promise to each other that they both needed to hear. Leaving each other the next day was breaking their hearts.

As they woke up on their last day in Paris, they were all over each other. They ordered breakfast and Jack didn't even go to the gym. Chloe finally got him to agree to get on Facebook so it would be easier for them to stay in touch. She set up his profile and gave him a name that only people that he wanted to know would be able to contact him. He chose Jack Mac. They finally ventured out of the house around lunchtime. Holding hands, they happily wandered the streets.

"I am taking you out for dinner tonight, our last supper," Jack said proudly. "I know that you wanted to stay at the Le

Bristol, so I have made reservations for us at their restaurant Le 114 Faubourg."

"You did?" She gasped like an excited child.

"Yes, I did." He laughed. He loved seeing her so excited. "I knew you would like to go there, so I called reception to make us a booking for 7 pm."

"You spoil me so much, thank you, I am so excited."

"Well, it's the last time I can spoil you for a while and you deserve it." He smiled.

Chloe was ready on time and Jack could not take his eyes off her. "My God, you look amazing!"

She wore the dress that she had worn on the elegant night on the cruise. The night that they had got together and he wore his suit. Letting his hair hang loose, he looked very sexy.

The taxi was waiting downstairs and they arrived in no time at all, even with all the Parisian crazy traffic. The restaurant had a warm and cosy atmosphere; they were shown to their seats immediately. The table was elegant with white linen and sparkling silverware and crystal glasses. The table had been decorated with scattered rose petal. You had to hand it to the French, Jack thought; they certainly think of everything. Chloe would be thinking I arranged these petals. He glanced around; it appeared that every table for two had them. He hoped she didn't notice.

"Wow, this is so beautiful, I hope it's not too expensive, and such beautiful rose petals, you really are a true romantic," she smiled.

"Aye, I do keep telling you this."

Jack was handed the menu. He realised that Chloe would have a pink fit if she saw the prices. She looked so beautiful and happy, it would make her uncomfortable. He decided to order for her. He knew her well enough by now to know what she liked and didn't like. He ordered a bottle of wine, entrees of octopus for Chloe and sea bream for himself. Mains of roasted veal fillet and sea scallops for Chloe. Desserts they would decide on later. Chloe just sat watching him as he ordered in French.

"I hope you don't mind but I ordered for you, but I got all the things you like."

"Thanks, I appreciate it. I would eat anything. I am sure it will be scrummy, look at this place it looks just like it does in the movies."

She could not stop scanning the room, wondering if any stars were there, and noticed at least two women eyeing off Jack. She was not the only one noticing how good he looked that night.

When they got home, Jack dropped the keys on the bench and walked towards her with desire in his eyes. "You have been driving me crazy all night. Let me slip you into something more comfortable."

He unzipped her dress and it fell to the floor. She followed his lead and slowly undressed him. He stood there naked as Chloe slowly looked him over. My God, she adored his body. Using her hands, she gently felt every muscle that she never wanted to forget. He started to do the same; he loved her body and wanted to touch every single inch of her. No words were spoken, no words were needed. They were in complete adoration for each other. He picked her up and laid her on the bed and as they looked each other over once again as they began to make love, it was different that night, slow, sensual and extremely moving for them both. Then sweating and panting, they lay together quietly.

"I want to do that for the rest of my life with you," whispered Jack.

"Don't forget me, Jack."

"How could I ever do that?" They held each other tight as they fell asleep for the very last time together in each other's arms.

Chapter 21
HOMEWARD BOUND

The dreaded day had arrived. Lying in bed as long as possible, Jack rang room service for breakfast then the packing began. "Can I keep one of your negligees so I can put it under my pillow and sleep with it every night?"

"Only if I can have a t-shirt that I can wear to bed to remind me of you also."

They did the exchange with a smile.

The cab ride to the airport was silent, they checked in, and went to the bar and ordered a couple of whiskies, needing something strong.

"I wish we were back in that bar in Barcelona and start again," said Chloe.

"We had a great time, hadn't we? And met so many wonderful friends."

"Friendships that will last a lifetime, I am sure."

"We will last a lifetime also, Chloe. Just think of this as an organising stage, but once everything is all fixed, I will be back with you, I promise."

The boarding sign started to flash for their flights.

"Well, this is it, Chloe," said Jack as he finished the last of his scotch.

"I wish we didn't have to do this. Thanks for everything, Jack," her heart was pounding so fast she thought it would leap out of her chest.

"I love you, Chloe. I won't forget you, like you keep saying I will, I will be knocking on your door sooner than you think."

"I hope so. I am going to miss you like crazy."

"Me too, take care of yourself, my wild little beast, I will stay in touch." He kissed her long and slow and turned, looking back one last time as he waved.

She started for her gate holding back her tears as they welled in her eyes. She could hardly see where she was going. Arriving, she turned back, hoping Jack had changed his mind and was walking towards her, but he was gone. That was the moment reality hit. She felt like her legs had gone from beneath her, she collapsed on the chair in the boarding gate and started to cry, feeling as though her heart had broken in two. "I can't do this." She sobbed uncontrollably, as people started to stare, she didn't care. Jack was gone, possibly forever. *What if he gets home and forgets me?* Or even worse, Shauna knocked on his door. Oh God, what a horrible thought; she pushed it from her mind. What if I leave now and get a flight to Aberdeen? Yes, that would work. She would fly and meet Jack, he had told her enough about his town to find her way there. Her thoughts were interrupted by the announcement that boarding had commenced. She realised that it was all too late she had to board the plane.

Jack sat on the plane heartbroken. How did he let the love of his life walk away? Was he crazy? The thoughts of what lay ahead of him once home depressed him. It was now all too clear. He had to go to Australia. There was no way he could live without her. He still had some of his dad's money saved. If he sold his share of the business to his brother, that would give him enough money to start a new life. It was possible, it could definitely work. He would make it work, he had to keep the promise that he had made to Chloe at the Eiffel tower.

Jack was walking down the street to his home in Fraserburgh. Nothing had changed. The overcast and dreary skies looked the same. The grey stone two-story cottage came into view as he turned the bend. The smell of the sea hit him first then the different smells of cooking coming from the little cottages all the way along the street. He knew that walking in this door to his life would be hard to do. He had been through so much in the past few weeks, life would never quite be the same again. He didn't want to be home, that was for sure. As he walked up the path, he could hear his wee dog Jock, barking. A smile crept onto his face. He had missed him a lot.

As he opened the door, his mother squealed with delight. Jock jumped up and down all over him. "Oh, my bonny laddie is home, come here and let me take a look at you." He threw his arms around her. "Hello, Mum, how are you?"

She had missed him so much. Jock was still going crazy so he leaned down and patted him on the head; he rolled over for his belly to be rubbed. "Hello, buddy, good boy. Have you been missing me? Hey, hope you have been looking after the women while I was away."

"He hasn't been too well, actually; this is the most active I have seen him in weeks. I think he was fretting for you. I will put on a pot of tea." She ran to the kitchen, screaming out, "Jeannie, Jack is home." His younger sister came running in and threw her arms around her brother. He gave her a cuddle and they sat at the table. His mother arrived with the tea and some homemade shortbread and started giving him all the news of around town and what he had missed.

Jeannie was more interested in what stories Jack had to tell, and butted in asking him about the boat. He sat for a good hour giving them all the details of the trip, in true Scot style, stretching the truth slightly to make it funny or interesting. But they seemed to enjoy it immensely. They were hanging on every word he had to say, smiling and laughing, loving having him home.

"And what about this girl you met, Chloe?" asked Jeannie curiously.

There it was, the sound of her name; just hearing it made him smile. He told them all about her, where they met, how she was scared and lonely and how much fun they had together.

"Oh I can see I made the right decision, getting you on that boat," said his mother happily. "She seems like a nice girl. Jeannie has been keeping me up to date, showing me all the photos. She is very attractive."

"Aye, she is very beautiful," he said with a dreamy look in his eye. His mother studied him carefully as he said the words. She saw something in him she had never seen in him before. "I think we should let him get tidied up a bit, he hasn't been home for weeks, I have put a clean clootie on the end of your bed," she said as she started to clear the table.

"I think she is very beautiful also Mary is a bit funny with it all," warned Jeannie.

Jack smiled. "I wouldn't worry about her." He gave her a kiss on the top of her head as he headed for the Stairs to his room.

Nothing had changed, the yellow and tan checked wallpaper, and his bed with the tan colour doona cover looked the same. He dropped his bag and lay on the bed, staring at the ceiling. He was home, back where it all started but this time he was not staying. He needed Chloe by his side, he didn't belong here anymore. He had to put his plan into action. The sooner he got things organised the sooner he could go to Chloe. He had never felt so empty before in his whole life. He lay on the bed feeling gutted, unable to move. He had to pull himself together. He couldn't just sit there, his mind was going crazy.

He decided to unpack. As he did, every item told a story. He found the portrait they had painted in Greece together and just the sight of it made him long for her terribly. She would still be out there flying around, how he ever let her take that long flight on her own; he had promised to protect her to look after her. What had he done?

A knock at the door startled him. It opened and Jeannie peered in. "Come in." She came over and sat beside him; he still had the portrait in his hand.

"That's a lovely painting, you both look very happy, you got on well together," she said. "You must miss her a lot."

"Aye, I do, I want to go to Australia and see her again one day soon," said Jack sadly.

"I think that is a good idea. Things have changed a bit around here since you have been away. Mum has been quite anxious about you coming home," she said cautiously.

"What things? You mean, Jimmy and Mary?"

"Aye, they are planning a wedding. Mum didn't know how you would take the news," she softly said. "I wanted you to hear it from me first, before you heard any gossip around the town."

"Thanks, Jeannie, but that really doesn't worry me, I don't care what they do," he said honestly.

"Mary has been a bit spiteful. Mum says it's because of all the talk about you looking happier than you have ever looked before, made her a bit mad," she explained.

Jack just nodded. "Well, it's true, I am the happiest I have ever been."

"I don't know what she is up to but she came here the other week, with that girl that you used to go out with before her, I think her name was Shauna."

Jack's head spun around, eyes wide-open with surprise. "Shauna was here? When?"

"Aye, the other week. Why? I thought you loved Chloe, I didn't think she meant anything to you."

"No, of course she means nothing to me. I know what Mary has been up to, that conniving cow."

"You do? How?" asked Jeannie surprised.

"Have you been keeping Mum and Jimmy up to date on the details of my trip?"

She nodded. "Yes, every day we would discuss you around dinner. If I got an email I would tell them everything. I thought that was ok." She looked worried.

"No, you did nothing wrong, Jeannie. It's all starting to make sense, that's all. So Jimmy would tell Mary, of course. I knew it was too much of a coincidence."

"Yes, sometimes Mary would come to dinner also…what was a coincidence?" Jeannie said, confused.

"She turned up in France, trying to come onto me, in front of Chloe making quite a scene. It wasn't the most pleasant situation to be in, plus it ruined our whole day in the wine region."

Jeannie gasped. "Who? Shauna? She was on your wine tour? I heard her and Mary talking one day about her going on a long weekend away with a girlfriend but I thought that she was going to Barcelona."

"Well she probably was, until Mary got in her ear. She was aware of my every move, that's how it all happened."

It was all beginning to become clear, what was going on. Mary was upset over everyone being happy for me that she had to try and sabotage my happiness. He was fuming. It took a lot to get Jack cranky but when he did, look out.

"Thanks for the information, Jeannie" he kissed her on the head as he got to his feet. "But there is something that I need to take care of."

"Be careful, Jack, think about what you do first," said Jeannie, knowing exactly where he was going and what he was going to do. He was angry; she hoped he didn't make matters worse.

He knew where to find them; he headed straight towards the trawling yard and office. It was windy and the smell off the sea spray which he usually loved annoyed him. Everything about being home annoyed him. Jeannie was right. He decided to take a walk, he needed to calm down. He walked down to the rocks and watched the fishermen for a while. Everything looked grey and misty just like his mood. He had to think about this carefully, he couldn't go in and rip his brother's head off and then ask him to buy him out of the business. He decided to think about how he was going to approach the subject. It needed to be done right. There was nothing Mary could do now, to destroy what he had with Chloe. He could see what she was up to now; he was more prepared to handle the situation.

Chapter 22

AUSTRALIA

Kait was at the airport waiting for her when she got out of the terminal. Tossing her arms around her sister, she hugged her tight. "Oh, it's so good to have you home," said Kait excitedly.

They tossed the bags into the back of the four-wheel drive and headed off. "So tell me all about it? My cards were right, hey," said Kait proudly.

"Yes, they were right. I would never have believed it but they were," admitted Chloe.

"He looks like a catch. You two look like you have had a blast. Where did you meet him? I have been busting to hear all the details." Kait was more excited than Chloe.

She told the whole story of meeting him in the bar in Barcelona and then how she got scared on the boat and wanted to come home and how he done everything he could to make her happy and safe and then how he totally knocked her off her feet.

"He was my knight in shining armour that came to my rescue, my beautiful highlander," said Chloe dreamily.

Kait was blown away. "Tell me more, I need to know everything," she said excitedly and Chloe laughed.

"I knew you would be busting."

"So when did you finally get together?"

She explained how they met all of their friends, and met for dinner every night, and became very close. She told her how Paddy had been trying to match them from the start, and then finally while they were dancing under a huge Sorrento moon he kissed her.

"That is so romantic, far out, Chloe. You can't let this guy go. Hang on to him." Chloe was laughing and they were having such a great time they hadn't noticed they were already at Pearl Beach.

Kait helped her take her luggage inside and Chloe made them a coffee. "Oh, wait I have something in the car for you." She returned with a basket of goodies. "Bread milk and some homemade meat pies and biscuits, compliments from Mum. We thought you might have a craving for some Aussie food. They are fresh so you can freeze them."

They sat down with their coffee and biscuits in the courtyard.

"I was hoping you were bringing home Jack," said Kait sipping her coffee.

"Yes, I was, too. That would have been perfect, but he said he has things to take care of back at home, and he will come over," Chloe sighed.

"So he said he would come over here," she asked surprised.

"Well, he sort of made a promise to me. He would come and stay with me."

Kait was wide eyed. "Stay here? For how long?"

"Well, he kinda said he wanted to marry me," she said quietly with a smile, dunking her biscuit in her coffee.

"Get out of here!" Kait squeeled. "That's pretty serious, Chloe. Do you love him?"

"I have never felt anything like what I feel for him, ever before. What we had over there was incredible. Yes, I am totally a hundred percent in love with him."

"Well, if he is going to be my brother-in-law, I need to know all about him," demanded Kait with a smile.

"Ok, ok, let's see. Where do I start? He is a fisherman, his family owns fishing trawlers, his father recently passed away and left him money so his mother encouraged him to go on the cruise. She wanted him to travel."

"Well, that all sounds wonderful, but I was more interested if he was good in bed."

"Kait, my God," she squealed, spilling her coffee, putting it down.

"Well," she smiled, waiting for an answer, grabbing another biscuit.

"Well, as a matter of fact, he's dynamite," she said with her cheeks glowing quite red.

"It is pretty important in a relationship, you know. I was just checking what sort of a relationship my baby sister was getting into, that's all."

"I understand that now, but I didn't know it back then. It's an awesome relationship. Well, that's if it lasts."

"What do you mean, if it lasts?"

"You know…holiday romance and all that."

"Well, if it doesn't, you have had a wild time, and if it does, which I think it probably will, you have found the man of your dreams and he will be knocking on your door any day."

"So glad Craig didn't go," they both said at the same time. They both burst out laughing.

They happily chatted, while Kait filled her in with news around town before she had to go. She thanked her for everything and told her the stuff that they spoke about today was to be kept under her hat for a while. The last thing she wanted was her parents hassling her.

She started unpacking, and found Jack's t-shirt. She buried her face in it and breathed in. *Ah, Jack.* She took a quick shower and slipped it on. Even though it was early, jet lag had kicked in and she needed to have an early night. She checked her phone, no messages. Doing the calculation, it was seven in the morning in Glasgow, that town was close enough to him, it would be roughly the same time zone. She sent him a message. "Hi, Jack, I am home, strange being without you, I miss you so much. Well, just wanted to say I am home safe, take care, love you heaps." She didn't expect anything back as she knew what he was like with phones, but was surprised when it went ping. "So good to get your message, I slept with the phone under my pillow with your pj's waiting to hear from you. I miss you heaps yea it's weird being home, so hard to deal with. Love you." It made her smile knowing he still cared. She opened a bottle of wine and took a glass out to the courtyard. It was only six in the evening, but she was hoping to be passed out within an hour. Another message arrived. "What are you doing now? Have you slept yet?"

"No, not yet, I have just poured a glass of wine, but won't be long till I crash."

Instantly, he felt guilty that she did the journey alone, if only he was there with her sharing that wine. He thought that he would give this skype thing a go that she had been teaching him. Time to find out if it worked. Chloe answered instantly. She was so excited to see him, she started to cry.

"I didn't mean to make you cry..."

"They are tears of joy!"

He asked about her flight and she told him all about Kait and how she had a million questions and wanted to hear every detail. He laughed as he listened.

"How are things at your end?"

"My mother and sister were happy to have me home, and Jock went crazy. He is a bit sick I think he fretted."

"Oh, that's not good. What about your brother?"

"Well things haven't improved between us." He didn't tell her about Mary and Shauna as he didn't want her to worry. As far as she knew, it was all over with, and Shauna was out of the picture. "I am planning to sell my share of the trawling business to him and use the money to come to Australia."

She wanted Jack to be very sure that is what he wanted to do, before he went ahead with it, but deep down she couldn't control her excitement, that he really was making plans to come and see her. She showed him around her cabin and courtyard. He was impressed how lovely it all looked. After they got off the phone, she danced around her courtyard so full of excitement she thought she was going to burst. He was coming to Australia. She couldn't wait.

Chapter 23

FRASERBURGH

Jack had made his mind up to approach his brother straight away about the business. It had been so lovely to see Chloe; it made him all the more determined to start to get things organised. He loved the look of her place and was keen to get over there with her. As he went downstairs for breakfast, he spotted his brother at the table.

"Welcome home. I have been told you had a great trip."

"Aye, I did, thank you," said Jack quietly. What he really wanted to say was and I hear you have been busy with that bitch also. But he bit his tongue. Jeannie walked into the room and almost walked back out but Jack told her to sit. "I am glad we are all here this morning, I have something I would like to put forward," announced Jack. "As you are all well aware, things are a little uneasy around here and everyone is walking on eggshells. I just wanted to say, I am happy about your upcoming wedding plans and I wish you all the best."

"I was going to have a talk with you about all of that," Jimmy said fumbling around uncomfortably.

"It's ok, Jimmy, you're my brother. You are both suited to each other, better than we ever were, and I am happy for you. However, I would ask you if you could buy me out of my share of the business so I can now move on with my life."

Everyone at the table froze as they sat staring at Jack. "Jeannie, you have the rights to the house, so I know you will be ok. If I sell my share of the business to you, Jimmy, it will give you and Mary a great start to your family life together and I can move on with mine."

Jeannie was aware what he wanted to do and she was happy for him. He had to move on; there was no way life could go on as it was here now. Too many things had changed.

"What are you going to do?" asked Jimmy surprised.

"There is no doubt you have heard I have met someone, and I will be following her and hopefully set up a life in Australia." Jimmy looked horrified.

"Australia? Are you mad? You have only just met this girl, and you're throwing away your family's birthrights and want to go halfway around the world to some girl you met on a holiday, where it may or may not work out. Think about what you are saying."

"No, I have never been more sure about anything. I can now see where my life is taking me. She is the girl I want to marry, and I will go anywhere and do anything to do just that," said Jack proudly.

Deathly silence filled the room, then Jeannie finally spoke up. "It is a great plan and I wish you all the best."

Jimmy had finished his breakfast, pushed his plate aside, wiped his mouth with the serviette, and stood up. "I will run it past Mary," as he stormed out the door. As soon as he walked out his mother walked in. She had been doing the laundry and knew she had missed something unsettling.

"Mum, sit down, let me pour you a cup of tea." He placed the cup of tea down and explained everything that had occurred. He finished by telling her he loved Chloe and wanted to move to Australia and marry her. She sat there for a while not saying anything. Jeannie and Jack were looking at each other, wondering what was going through her head. At last, she spoke.

"Well, I think this is what your father would have wanted. You have met someone that you care about, I have seen the look in your eyes when you speak of her, you have a deep love for this girl, just as your father did with me. He looked at me with those same eyes. He gave up his dream of travelling for me, and never looked back, and so I gave travelling to you so that you could spread your wings and you did. He would be proud of you, as I am. I give you blessing, laddie, but I will miss you." She had started to cry.

"I am so sorry, I didn't mean to make you sad, Mum." Jack went over and put his arm around her.

"Aye, it's tears of joy, lad. Go and find your lassie, but bring her home to meet me one day."

"Of course, I will. She may even want to come and stay here one day."

Everyone was crying now and his mother went and got the whiskey bottle and three little glasses. "I think we all need a wee drink."

They all agreed and had a little shot before going about their business.

He spent the day hanging around his town, catching up with friends and having a few pints at the local pub. He was missing his little Aussie drinking mate and told anyone who would listen all about her. It was a lovely old pub, white painted brick with tiled steep roof with a fire and a huge beer garden out the back, with fire pits which were lit on cold days. He bumped into Patrick, his best mate and he sat and told him all about his trip. He was interested as he had never left town so keen to listen to all of Jack's tales.

It was dinner time and he didn't want to be late for dinner. His mum would be waiting for him. She had made him her fish soup which he loved and some homemade hot bread to go with it.

When he got home, everyone had arrived for dinner except Mary, thank God. At least they had the decency to give him that. There was still a chill in the air and everyone felt it. Silence surrounded the table. "So I was wondering, when are you coming back to work," asked Jimmy.

"I think I made myself perfectly clear this morning when I asked you to buy me out, I am not."

"I have asked Mary and it's out of the question. We are hoping to buy a house."

"Oh is that right. Well, I didn't know our family finances had anything to do with her."

"I don't like to point out the obvious here, but she will be family when I wed her."

Jack was fuming but held it together for his mother's sake. "Well, she is not family yet," he glared at his brother furiously; tensions were rising. Jack got the whisky bottle after dinner. "Who will join me in a dram?" Everyone agreed as he poured the drinks.

His mother started making idle chat, trying to diffuse the tension. Suddenly a knock at the door startled everyone. Jimmy immediately jumped up but it was too late. The visitors had walked in. It was Mary and Shauna. Jack thought he would explode. Just the sight of Mary with her ginger tone hair and cold green eyes made him sick in the stomach.

"We are going to the movies," Jimmy said sternly and started to head for the door.

"Jack, you're home, I thought that you would be heading for Australia to visit your wee Aussie tart," spat Shauna.

Jack was losing his cool and no matter how hard he tried to control it he knew he was about to lose it. "I know all about the little games you both have been playing with me and Chloe and I am fed up with it," he said with gritted teeth. "How you two wench's managed to meet up with each other again and plot your revenge on me I will never know, but I am over it, you're wasting your time. I am in love with Chloe and as soon as I sell my share of the business I am out of here."

"Oh, now, Jack, we are not up to no good. You still have feelings for me deep down it's all just a matter of time, you wait and see," said Shauna sarcastically.

"I know exactly what you are both doing. I want you both out of my mother's house now, you have done enough damage. You're nothing but a pair of conniving sluts."

Jack turned to his mother who was starting to become quite pale and apologised. But while he had his head turned Jimmy took a swipe at him. "Don't you ever call my future wife a whore or a slut."

Jack wiped his mouth and apologised to his mother again and looked at Jimmy. "I think we had better take this outside."

They were both out the door and into it. Emotions were raw and rage needed to be aired. His mother stayed inside with Jeannie while the others went outside to watch. They were into it, no holding back until Mary finally stepped in and broke it up. They were sweating profusely and shirts looked like rags hanging off them dripping in sweat and blood. Jimmy walked off with Mary and Shauna and Jack walked inside and went to clean up.

His mother was sitting in the dining room having a whiskey with Jeannie when he returned. She poured one for Jack as he took a seat.

"I am sorry again, you had to witness such behaviour," he said as he put his hand over hers. "I never meant to hurt you, it is the last thing I would ever want to do, but there is only so much a man can take."

"I have filled her in with what they have done to you, with Shauna turning up in Dijon and all," said Jeannie quietly as his mother had a sip of whisky with shaking hands and nodded.

"Aye, it doesn't excuse my actions," he said, looking at his mother. They poured another whisky as a nightcap and all went up to bed.

He lay full of anger. What was he to do if Jimmy didn't want to buy his business? He was never going to stay here no matter what happened but he would have to stay long enough to try and make his brother agree to buy him out. If that wasn't going to happen, he had enough money put aside for at least an airfare and some cash to see him by for a few weeks, but ultimately, he needed to sell his share of the business. Tomorrow was another day, and he hoped he didn't have to break his mother's heart again.

Jack did the time calculation. He wanted to call Chloe as promised. He rang and she picked up instantly. He felt better straight away, the sound of her voice made him happy again.

"It is so good to hear your voice. How are you?" he said with a smile.

"I am just hanging in here, working most days and dreaming about the day you arrive. Have you any news yet?"

"No, not yet. I have asked Jimmy to buy me out but no answer yet." He didn't tell her anything else. He didn't want to worry her. He was going to Australia to see her, that's all she needed to know.

The days went on and on. His brother was still refusing to buy his share and Mary and Shauna were making new problems for him every day. Because of this, Jimmy and he had all in brawls most nights of the week, much to his mother's disgust; this was exactly what she had worried about.

His little dog Jock was still lying around, so Jack decided to take him to the vet. The vet looked him over and explained he had been suffering from stress and fretting for him while he was away and for a dog at his age, it would take a lot to recover. He gave him pills and told him to let him rest as much as possible.

Jack took him home and put him on his cushion near the fire and he went straight to sleep. He sat by his side as he slept. Jack felt him stir and jumped up. He opened his eyes and looked at him. "I am sorry I left you, my dear friend. I was always coming home, but I guess ya didn't know, did ya? Ya thought I left ya." Jock closed his eyes again, and he left him in peace.

Jock passed away in his sleep that night. Jack was beside himself; he was the only little bit of happiness he had left. It hit him hard. He dug a hole out the backyard in a nice part of the garden where he liked to lay in the sunshine and buried him. He called Chloe, without even thinking of the time, and luckily she was still up.

"I am so glad you answered."

"Jack, what's up?"

"I just had to bury Jock." Chloe was aware Jock had been sick and Jack had blamed himself for it, so she knew how hard he would take his death.

"Oh, Jack, I am so sorry."

"It's all for the best. He is at peace now, plus I am coming to Australia, and I won't have to hurt him again." She heard the pain in his voice. They chatted on the phone for ages and he started to feel a bit better as she spoke about anything to keep his mind off it. As he hung up the phone he saw his brother walking into the house with Mary. He certainly couldn't deal with them right now and headed for the pub.

Jack started drinking at the pub most nights to get away from it all at home. He was drinking way too much and Chloe could hear it in his voice when he called. She asked him repeatedly if everything was ok and he kept telling her he was fine. But the truth was he wasn't. His life was falling apart and he wasn't proud of himself. He was still continuously having huge fights with his brother. Both were built just like each other, full of muscles from working on the boats, and both had tempers that flared at just the mere sight of each other.

One day, he was checking his emails and was surprised to see a message from Paddy. He opened it, he was asking how things were, and if he made it home safe. He gave him a call and Paddy sensed something was terribly wrong. "Jack come and stay with me and Maggie for a while, we would love to catch up, we are lonely after getting back from the cruise." Jack thought it was a great idea, a break away from where he was at the moment would do him good. "Okay, I need a break. Is it ok if I come tomorrow?"

"That is perfect, I will pick you up at the station."

He packed an overnight bag and explained to his mum and sister that he needed to get away for a few days. He told them he was going to see Paddy. They were both relieved he had Paddy to talk to, he had told them all about him and he sounded like a bit of a father figure for him. He certainly needed someone to talk to at the moment.

Chapter 24

PADDY AND MAGGIE

He took the train to Glasgow and Paddy met him at the station. He felt better instantly as they gave each other a man hug and Paddy slapped Jack on the back. They jumped in the car and were soon pulling up in a huge pebbled driveway. The large wrought-iron gates closed behind them. It was a stunning two-story well-presented Edwardian-style home with generous secluded grounds that were immaculately kept.

"This is some home you have here, Paddy." It was nothing like the homes back in Fraserburgh.

"Aye, the hardware business has treated me quite well," he smiled. "It's all too big for me and Maggie now but we raised our boys here and we can't bear to leave all the memories behind. I guess one day a time will come to sell."

He showed him inside as he yelled out to Maggie. They walked into a large entrance before, taking a hallway leading out the back to a large family dining area with the kitchen off to the right. You could smell Maggie had been cooking all afternoon; she spotted him and came running over, wearing an apron with Italy on it. She hugged him tightly.

"Oh, it is so good to see you, come I will show you where you will be sleeping." She held his hand tight as she showed him his room and around the grand house. There were five bedrooms in total upstairs, with a huge main bathroom, which Jack had to himself. Downstairs had a formal lounge and dining the casual area out the back, which led off to a beautiful conservatory overlooking stunning gardens. They landed back in the casual lounge and opened a beer as they settled in comfortably for a catch-up. It was good to see Paddy and Maggie again, he felt so happy to be with them. In a way it made him feel close to Chloe, knowing they shared this friendship together.

Two of his sons came in, obviously wanting to meet their parents' new friend that they had heard so much about. They introduced themselves and sat down, having a drink and headed off.

Maggie went back to the kitchen to organise the evening meal, which left Paddy and Jack alone to talk. Jack told Paddy about everything that had occurred. He listened carefully and at the end offered him some advice.

"You need to try and stay calm, and go back to the trawlers to work. You need it to help pass the time while you wait for Jimmy to change his mind or find someone else to buy his share."

Jack thought about it. He remembered giving Chloe the same advice on the ship when she was out of her mind also. He had to keep busy and Paddy was right.

"Thanks, Paddy, you are right I could do with the extra cash also. I am not thinking straight at the moment."

They had a lovely catch-up together and Maggie had prepared a huge roast for them with all the trimmings and Jack enjoyed every mouthful. After dessert they made their way back to the lounge area where they settled in for the night.

They all drank too much whisky, but the night was full of fun and laughter. Everyone missed Chloe and it was clear, Jack was not coping well without her.

"Why don't you stay another night I could do with some help with the pump on the fountain out the back," Paddy said, pouring him another whisky.

Jack nodded and wiped a tear. "Thanks, I would love to, I have not been coping back at home."

He ended up staying three nights in total. He helped Paddy with the fountain the first day and some other odd jobs around the house. Maggie spent her days in the kitchen cooking and baking, happy to have another mouth to feed. She missed not having her boys at home and she just loved having Jack around. Plus, he enjoyed his food so she loved cooking for him.

The following day, Paddy took Jack to his hardware and the local pub where he introduced him to some of his friends. On his last day, they arranged a barbecue lunch. Being a Saturday, he arranged for all of his boys to come over. It was an exceptionally good August afternoon. One of those rare days when the weather was warm and the sun was shining. Maggie went out shopping for groceries and Jack helped Paddy set up.

"John would love this barbecue you have here, Paddy."

"Oh, aye, it would be so nice to have him here for a beer today, wouldn't it? He was one hell of a crazy lad, wasn't he?" said Paddy as he was thinking about his times with John. "We need to organize a catch-up for next year. You will have to get yourself sorted and bring Chloe over also."

Just the sound of her name made Jack smile. "I would love to bring her over here, Paddy, but at the moment, there are too many dramas going on. I would hate to bring her into it all, But when I get home tomorrow I will start to sort things out properly, once and for all."

"Don't go throwing your family fortune away, Jack. Don't let Jimmy walk all over you. You need to take a deep breath and make sure you get what you are entitled to. Chloe will wait. That money will set you up for life."

Jack wanted to go home, pack his bags and say the hell with the lot of you and jump on a plane to Australia, but he knew deep in his heart, it wasn't possible. Paddy was right; he had no choice but to sit tight and make sure everything was done properly. He didn't trust his brother one little bit especially with Mary pulling his strings.

Maggie arrived home with the groceries and headed into the kitchen to make the salads. Before too long the boys started to arrive. First were the two youngest sons he had met the other day, Will and Shay. Will had his girlfriend Emily in tow. They lived together in a flat closer to Glasgow city. Shay lived with them to keep the rent down. Both boys worked close to the city so it was convenient for them both and they were near the nightlife on the weekends. Will and Emily had been together for around a year. Maggie was hoping Will would put a ring on her finger soon as she was a lovely girl and they got on very well together. Shay was just a funny larrikin with Paddy's red hair, single with no intentions of finding a girl any time soon.

They all took a seat around the outdoor table. Maggie had it set up lovely. It was a huge paved area with a built-in barbecue along the wall. On the grassy area beside was a big fire pit where they would move to later as the chill settled in. James and his wife Ailsa were the next to arrive. James was the oldest son and was a bit more reserved than the younger lads. He worked at the hardware and Paddy left a lot of the daily running's up to him now, along with his brother Bobby who also worked there. James and Ailsa had been married a few years and lived locally, a few blocks away in a new suburb. Bobby lived in the same suburb with his new bride Skye. They both arrived soon after causing all sorts of commotion as they had brought their dog and it was running around madly. Paddy was yelling at Bobby and Maggie was yelling at Paddy. Finally, they put the dogs in another area with Maggie's little dogs and they all settled in.

Paddy was handing out drinks and making sure everyone was introduced to Jack. The afternoon went well. All of Paddy's boys were great fun and why wouldn't they be with Paddy and Maggie as their parents?

All the men got up to have a beer at the barbecue while Paddy cooked. Maggie and the girls went into the kitchen and brought out all the side dishes. The meal was delicious and the girls all cleaned up while the boys sat around and had a beer. The girls came back with a big chocolate cake and some ice cream. Jack looked around the table; he wished Chloe was there, he was missing her terribly. This is exactly what he hoped he and Chloe would have one day. Paddy and Maggie were very lucky. He knew it on the boat but now that he had met the family, he felt it even more.

As the temperature started to drop, they lit the fire pit and they all dragged their chairs around it. Paddy brought out the whisky while the girls made coffee. It had great atmosphere, everyone got on so well together. It wasn't like his family; they all wanted to rip each other apart. They soon all started to leave and Jack said he would be back again one day to see them all again. Maggie went inside to finish cleaning up and Jack and Paddy had a few whiskies around the fire.

"You are very lucky with what you have here," said Jack, swirling his glass.

"Aye and I do know that. I say a prayer of thanks to the Lord quite often. You will have this one day also Jack. Just give it time," said Paddy sincerely.

Maggie was back with more food for them to nibble on while they were having a drink. "If you want to drink, you have to eat," said Maggie.

"And if you want to eat, you have to exercise," replied Jack with a chuckle. "That's why I am always at the gym, I love to eat."

They all laughed; they knew how Jack was with his food. They sat there stoking the fire for hours. It really wasn't cold but it was the ambiance of it they were enjoying. Maggie was the first to leave and told them to behave and be good. The boys had a few more quiet drinks before heading in themselves.

The smell of Maggie's cooking wafted through the house alluring the men down for a big breakfast. He had showered and was ready to head to the station after they ate as he had booked a seat on the morning train home. After giving Maggie a big hug, he grabbed his bag and Paddy drove him to the station.

"Thanks for everything, Paddy, you have no idea how much I needed that."

"Oh, I think I do. You will be ok now. Just take your time and things will sort themselves out."

It was a four-and-a-half-hour train ride, so he settled into his seat and thought about the last few days and Chloe.

When he got home, he wanted to turn back around and leave. He hated the sight of the place now, but he knew what he had to do and he had promised Paddy he would do it right. He couldn't wait to Skype Chloe; he was excited to tell her all about his catch-up with Paddy and Maggie. She was happy to hear all the news. He explained to her there was still no news on the business front and she started to cry.

"I am so sorry, Jack, I didn't want to cry in front of you, but I miss you so much. I feel like my heart is broken."

Jack was fighting back tears of his own at the sight of her crying. "Please don't cry. It breaks my heart. I will be with you one day soon, I promise, all will be ok."

As he hung up he couldn't control it any longer and lay on his bed and let it all out. He felt like he had hit rock bottom. No one could make him feel worse than he already did.

Jack took Paddy's advice and started working back on the trawlers. He stayed as far away as possible from everyone, and just did what he had to. He wanted to call Chloe but feared he would break down if he heard her voice. Plus, he had no good news; it was useless, calling her. Things went on the same as usual day after day, the two brothers would brawl and Shauna was always hanging around making advances towards him. Paddy called him regularly to check on him and knew he was doing it tough.

Chapter 25

JEANNIE

It was Jeannie's birthday in a few days and his mother sat them both down and gave them a lecture. They were having a party for Jeannie and they were going to stop the fighting and behave for one night for their sister. They both agreed and their mother made them shake on it. Reluctantly they did.

The day arrived and both brothers helped set up the yard for the party and placed the tables and chairs around the fire pit, and stacked the wood. Jack was doing the barbecue and Jimmy had to look after the fire. Some of Jeannie's friends started to arrive and everyone remained civilized throughout the night.

While Jack was doing the barbecue, Liam came up to give him a hand. He was a nice lad that lived around the corner and knew the family well. They spoke about Jack's trip and how he had wanted to travel to Australia. Jack thought Liam seemed to know an awful lot, but thought nothing of it. The meat was done, and everyone started to fill their plates. That's when Jack noticed who had walked through the gate. It was Shauna; she was with Mary and Jack almost lost it. *The hide of that woman,* he thought.

He put up with it for a while, as she constantly harassed him in front of Jeannie's friends, grabbing his bum and talking all cute to him sarcastically. She really was a nasty piece of work.

Finally, he couldn't take it anymore; he went to his mother and asked if it was ok if he asked her to leave. She was making everyone uncomfortable, and it was hard enough as it was. His mother agreed and told him to do it nicely.

She was talking with Mary so he went over and asked if he could have a word with her in private. He took her over to the side away from everyone just in case there was any conflict.

"Well, Jack, I knew there would be a day when you came to your senses and realise you want me, you must be aching so badly for me."

It was obvious she had quite a bit to drink and started to put her arms around him. He gently took her arms off him and she leaned in to kiss him, grabbing him on the crotch. He instantly tried to get her off him as he saw a flash. Turning, he saw Mary taking lots of photos of them together.

"I wanted to be the one who got the first snaps of the new happy couple together," she said sarcastically.

"I was trying to ask her to leave. She is not welcome in this house anymore. She is causing too many commotions it is not fair on my mother and it's Jeannie's birthday."

Mary had also had too much to drink, as she was flying off the handle at Jack. "I will do anything that I can to make sure Chloe sees these photos of you and Shauna together which will finish your relationship with her once and for all."

She turned to walk away and stopped dead in her tracks as she saw Jimmy standing there with a look of anger on his face. "I have just been informed what you have both been up to, what a terrible deed, trying to sabotage my brother's relationship. I am disgusted with you both. Mary, get out of my sight. Shauna, I think that you should leave and I don't think you are welcome in this house ever again." Both girls staggered off without saying another word.

"Jack, I think it's time we had a whisky together and talked about the details of me buying your share of the business." Jack nodded and they walked back to the house.

Mary had walked off with Shauna and they left the party. Jack and Jimmy had a few quiet drinks together and made sure Jeannie was having a good time. They were all there to see her blow her candles out and Jack noticed Liam standing a little too close to his sister; there was something going on with those two, for sure.

When everyone left, they all sat around outside by the fire, which was still roaring and had a few whiskies. As Jimmy got up to go to bed he quietly said, "I will get the business evaluated in the next few days."

Jack nodded. "Thank you." He helped his mother to bed and came back to have a quiet talk with Jeannie. "Will it be ok if you look after Mum when I go to Australia?"

"Yes, of course, in fact I need to let you in on a little secret." She had a few too many whiskeys and was spilling her beans. "Liam and I have been seeing each other for a while and it is getting quite serious." His mother loved Liam and he instantly knew things were going to be ok.

He smiled and gave her a cuddle. "I am happy for you, Jeannie, he is a nice lad. Mum will be pleased.

"I think she already knows but we haven't announced it, yet," she said, giggling. "Mum knows everything."

Liam was a nice kid working hard and had been around the family for years. His mother would be happy if his sister ended up with him and so would he. He lay in bed that night thinking about how things were turning out for the best. And then he realised he had forgotten to call Chloe again. He would make an effort tomorrow. She would understand once he explained everything he had been through.

The next few weeks were busy getting valuations and then settling on a price. Jimmy went for the loan and it was all a waiting game now. Jack was keen to tell Chloe the news but he could never catch her. She never picked up on his calls. At first, it didn't bother him, he knew she was busy, but then after a while, he started to get a bit worried. Maybe she had moved on, maybe she had hooked back up with Craig. Surely not, but stranger things have happened. He kept trying but no luck. He sent her messages constantly asking if she was ok and he didn't get anything back from them either. Was he just paranoid or was something horribly wrong?

Jack had just finished the morning work on the trawlers when Jimmy came over and asked if he had a minute. They walked over to a park bench.

"What's up," asked Jack.

"Well I have good news and I have bad news for you," sighed Jimmy.

"Ok hit me with the good news first, so I can handle the bad news better."

"I got the loan, the money is yours, I will transfer it to you. There are papers that need to be signed, of course. I will make an appointment with the solicitor."

Jack just sat there looking straight ahead at the water. "What's up, is everything ok? I thought this is what you wanted?" Jimmy looked confused.

"No, it's not ok. I really don't know what is going on. I can't get in contact with Chloe, she has been dodging my calls for weeks, so now I don't know if I am doing the right thing selling my share of the family business. I think she has moved on. She would have men lined up now she isn't with Craig. I guess I took too long, I think I have missed out." He couldn't believe he was spilling his heart out to his brother, of all people, but right now, he had lost faith in everything and everyone, and had totally no idea what he was doing.

"Well, I might be able to share some light on that. That's where the bad news comes in." Jack looked up with a stern look. "I only found out last night, but it appears Mary sent photos of you and Shauna to Chloe, using my profile on Facebook. She knows my password, I had no idea until I saw something unusual last night and when I looked into it further, it all came to light."

"She what? Oh no, do you know what this means? She thinks I am having a full-blown affair with Shauna!" He told Jimmy all about what had happened in Dijon and he said he was sorry. He felt bad, what Mary had done to his brother.

"Yep, and I can see how she thinks that, after that story, especially after seeing the photos. I am sorry, brother. I don't understand why they are doing this to you. We had a pretty big fight last night I have put the wedding plans on hold. I sent Chloe a private message trying to explain everything but she hasn't seen it. She would have thought I was trying to warn her when she thought I sent the photos. It's all a real big mess."

"I told Chloe I didn't want anything to do with Facebook, now look what it has created. I need to call her. What time is it in Australia? Why am I asking you? I don't care what time it is I need to talk to her."

He rang but she didn't pick up. He left a message trying to explain hoping she would at least get that, but after he got off the phone he realised it sounded like he was trying to smooth things over. It was hopeless. He sat on the park bench and bent his head low, holding it between his hands.

Chapter 26

CHLOE

Not coping well without Jack, Chloe was keeping herself busy at the café and surf club. She sat down with the owner of the café and spoke to her about some ideas she had for the menu. She gave her approval to speak to the chef and together they worked out a great new summer menu. Chloe was getting more and more shifts as she worked alongside the chef putting out the new menu and it was bringing in the crowds. The French crepes were the biggest money earner and it surprised everyone how popular they were becoming.

She had also talked to Johnny about putting bloody Mary on his breakfast menu and the Aperol spritz as a sunset special. Both drinks were a hit. Chloe was working shifts with Johnny as well, as the school holidays were approaching, and things started to go crazy in the town earlier than usual this year.

She loved working in the kitchen and he always made it a fun shift. Jack called regularly and he was still keen on coming out but never any commitment on dates. She was starting to worry about whether he really meant it. She tried to push it from her mind as much as possible.

All was going well until the day she had her heart ripped out. Lucky she was at home, because she felt like she had been hit by a truck. She opened up her Facebook to find messages from Jimmy with photos of Jack and Shauna. It looked like they had been embraced in a kiss and was shocked someone had been watching and caught them. Jimmy must have been giving me the heads up, no wonder Jack had been quiet, she thought.

The photos were labelled Jeanie's party. How did she end up at some family party. Then the words Shauna had said came flooding back. It's only a holiday romance, I will catch up with you when you come home. Well, obviously she did, it was clear to see now. She started to cry, she had lost Jack, it was true, and it was just a holiday romance to him. She was so stupid. How did she fall for it? He had sounded so sincere. She sobbed and sobbed until there were no more tears to cry. Her anxiety peaking, she crawled into bed and stayed there for days.

She blocked all calls and messages from Jack. It was over. She blocked him from her phone and closed her Facebook account. Nippers started up and she threw herself into that. She worked as many shifts as possible at the café and restaurant and spent any spare moment she had, helping Bob at the surf club. A lifesaver called Steve kept asking her out, and came almost every shift she worked at the café. He was cute but it was the last thing she needed right now.

Bob had been her rock; he kept her busy at the club and was her ear when she needed a friend. She had told him all about what happened with Jack one night over a few beers and he had been supportive listening to every detail carefully.

"I can't understand how he flipped so quickly, when a man falls in love, the type of love you are explaining to me, it usually is the real thing and a man just wouldn't be able to turn it off like that."

"Well he did. He was faking it the whole time. God, I was so bloody naïve."

"I don't think so, something isn't right. I bet there's more to the story you don't know about. Why don't you give him a call, face him, let him explain."

"What, so he can break my heart again and look like a bloody fool? No thanks I have had enough of men, especially Jack."

She kept herself busy, and Steve was starting to hang around more and more but she kept telling him she wasn't ready for a new relationship and he kept saying he would wait however long it took.

It was suddenly October and the whole town had tripled in size with tourists, both the café and surf club were doing good business and Nippers was in full swing. She was busier than ever, and exactly the way she liked it. She had no social life and had hardly done a thing outside of work. She knew her life was in complete turmoil, her anxiety back and trying hard to beat it, with lots of meditation and yoga. She had a friend's wedding coming up and needed a date. She was thinking of inviting Steve. He seemed like a nice guy but she was aware he was interested in her and didn't need any ties or extra problems at the moment. Or was it time she should pick herself up and move on? She made a promise to herself she would give it some thought.

Chapter 27

JACK

The next few days were frantic. Jack couldn't contact Chloe and Jimmy tried to help Jack as much as possible but he had no success either. Jack decided to push on with buying the business. He had the meeting with the solicitor and signed the appropriate paperwork and the money was transferred into his account within days. Everything he had wanted had suddenly landed in his lap. All except one thing: Chloe.

He rang Paddy. He would know what to do. He told him everything that had happened. Paddy couldn't believe what those girls were capable of. "I have no way of contacting her we don't have Facebook, but there is only one way to fix this. You have to go to Australia."

Jack sat motionless, staring out to sea. "I know what I am advising you to do is extreme and if I hadn't met Chloe, I would never have advised that to anyone. But I know what you had with her and it is worth doing anything to get it back."

Jack took his advice and started to get things organized. By the end of the week, he was all set to head to Australia. He got cold feet at times. What if she hated him? He needed to talk to her before he got on the plane. If only she would only pick up the phone.

Mary hadn't been around much since the night of Jeannie's birthday, and Shauna had not been back at all. He was enjoying the peace and quiet. His brother had never been nicer to him and doing anything to help. He thought everything over in his head for days before making his mind up that he was going.

There was nothing here for him, anymore. His brother now owned the business and he knew it would not take long before Mary was forgiven and back on the scene. He decided to take the risk and head for Australia, hoping for a slim chance to patch things up with Chloe. If it didn't work he had no idea what he would do, but he would have to work that out later.

He bought maps online and checked the trains and accommodation and booked it all. He sat motionless when he was finished, not knowing how he felt. He was excited he was going but scared to death he wouldn't find Chloe. He remembered how his stomach was in knots getting the plane to Barcelona, and that had worked out far better than expected. He had to put all his faith into this, and hope it worked out just as good.

He organized to take his mum and sister down to the local pub for dinner the night before he left. Jeannie asked if it would be alright to bring someone and Jack knew who it would be. They strolled down to the pub and Jeannie said she would meet them after work. It gave him time to check on how his mum was really feeling about him going away.

"I don't know how long I will be gone for Mum. I may be gone for a long time or I might be home in a week," he said softly as they sat in a booth having a whisky.

"I understand. I know that you are looking at me and thinking that I am sad, and I am, because I wouldn't be a mum if I wasn't, but I am also very excited for you, Jack. I want you to go and find this lass and win her back. I will be here waiting to meet her when you are ready."

He leaned over and kissed her on the cheek. "Thanks, Mum. I will certainly do that, thanks for understanding. I want you to know that I love you and that it's not your fault that I am leaving. I just really need to find Chloe and sort all this mess out." She patted his hand and encouraged him to go as Jeannie arrived at the table with Liam.

Jack could see Jeannie was nervous. He wanted to reach out and give her an encouraging hug. He gave her a wink across the table instead. As soon as everyone was settled at the table, she blurted it out. It was as if she had been practicing every word and needed to lift it off her chest.

"Mum, Jack, Liam and I have been seeing each other and are in a serious relationship. I just wanted to let you know."

Both Jack and his mother were happy and Jack shook Liam's hand. He got up and bought a round of drinks for the table while they looked over the menu. The steak pie and haddock and chips were the order of the day.

Jack went and ordered for everyone. The meals were delicious and hearty servings as usual and everyone was having a wonderful night. It was what they had all needed after all that had happened over the past few months. Everyone was happy and relaxed and Liam had fitted in perfectly.

He had a few quiet drinks with his mum after they got home from the pub. She was encouraging him that everything was going to turn out well for him. She was starting to blurt things out after a few drinks.

"I am very happy Jeannie has hooked up with Liam, he is a nice boy, I had an idea something was going on, but I waited for them to tell me, but I hope Jimmy ends it for good with Mary. She has been trouble for years. I can tell you some tales but I won't go into it tonight. Things you are unaware of. She has been making decisions for Jimmy with the businesses that are no good. I am happy you sold the business and if this hadn't of all blown up, I was going to advise you to get out of it, anyway."

Jack sat shocked as she took the last sip of her whisky and he refilled it hoping she had more stories to tell.

"How do you know all of this, Mum?"

"I am not as daft as you all think I am. I have eyes and ears and am no fool." He smiled gently at her. "I know you are no fool, Mum. Dad used to tell me stories. You had something he called a woman's intuition, and to always listen to what you say, because you are probably right."

She dropped her head and with a smile then looked up and said "Aye, he was a wonderful man, your father. I miss him terribly. I want you to have what we shared, it was beautiful."

"Thanks, Mum, you have no idea. The confidence you have given me tonight, I thought I had done the wrong thing, selling the business but you have made it all seem right again."

"Oh, bless you, Jack, you go and find that lass. She will be waiting for you, I can feel it in my heart."

They were both wiping tears away as they finished their drinks and he helped her up the stairs to bed. As he lay in bed that night, he tried Chloe one more time. No answer as usual. He was still in high spirits from the night at the pub and was feeling excited and positive about his trip.

He was excited to say the least when he was leaving the next day. He kissed his mum and Jeannie good bye and got the train to Glasgow. He made it to the airport in good time and checked in. Sitting at the bar, he rang Paddy.

"Well, wish me the best of luck, Paddy. I am sitting at the airport about to leave for Australia." He was fiddling with his beer coaster. It instantly reminded him of Chloe at the bar in Barcelona. He had a chuckle to himself and put it down.

"Go get her, Jack, you can do this."

"Oh God, I hope you are right. I am scared to death."

"It will work out fine, mark my words. I will be here waiting for the news. Wait, Maggie is yelling out she is sending her love. Stay in touch." He hung up the phone and he drained his glass.

He was on a high as he boarded the plane. He was on his way to see Chloe.

Chapter 28

AUSTRALIA

Jack arrived at Sydney Kingsford Smith Airport on an early morning flight. He grabbed his bags and followed the signs to the train station. He knew exactly where he had to go. He had studied it at great length. He found the platform and only had to wait a few minutes before the train arrived to take him to Central Station.

He strode to the departure board and found the platform for the Central Coast train. It was already there waiting, due to depart in a few minutes. He boarded it and settled into a seat with his bags. He stared out the window. Was he really in Australia? It was a glorious spring morning. The city was turning it on for his arrival, and he was very impressed. The train started to move and he smiled. He knew what he was doing was right. It was the best he had felt since he returned from his holiday. All he had to do now was convince Chloe to give him another chance.

Looking out the window all the way, he was enthralled. They went over a beautiful old bridge with stunning waterways underneath. He watched the fishermen in boats and then further along there were lots of oyster beds. It was almost his stop so he grabbed his bags and stood near the door.

The train pulled into the station. He glanced around as he got off and spotted the taxi stand. There was one waiting; he threw his luggage in the back and they were off.

They sped past a fish shop that had lots of signs out front promoting local fish, crabs and oysters. After one very long road that had taken them into town, he saw they were heading straight towards a large white building. What was it, it certainly didn't look like a caravan park and it was definitely the end of the road. He leaned forward stretching his head to read the sign: "Umina Beach SLSC." *Shit!* Oh, what did he tell the driver? He must have said he wanted to go to the surf club instead of the caravan park? He must have been thinking about Chloe. It had been a long flight. He was just about to yell out to the driver when he made a turn to the right down a small lane. Jack leant back in his seat and sighed. "Phew! Thank God for that!" He could imagine how embarrassing that would have been, him arriving smack bang on her doorstep, bags and all. They drove to the end of that road and they were at the caravan park. He grabbed his luggage and made his way to reception where they welcomed him and they gave him the keys to his cabin.

It was right at the end, of course. He dragged his luggage all the way. It seemed like a decent park and he could hear the waves crashing over the bushes beside him. The salty smell of the ocean confirmed it was not too far away. "Christ how far does this road go for? As if a man isn't tired enough. Now I have to walk a mile with my luggage in this heat, with these beasties trying to eat my face." He talked to himself all the way as he swatted the annoying flies.

The end of the road finally came into view. He remembered the lady telling him, his was the last cabin. He had made it, and it had the most amazing views of the ocean. He was stunned how beautiful it was, he quickly forgot all about his long haul to get there. He had struck gold.

He dumped his bags and went straight back outside onto the veranda looking around, taking it all in. He looked out at the beach. He smiled; that had to be kiddie's corner. He remembered all of Chloe's stories. Now he was here looking at it. It was just as beautiful as she had described it.

He went inside and changed into a pair of board shorts and a t-shirt and grabbed a peak hat. He remembered her warning him how the sun bites. He walked down onto the beach and took a deep breath. He could smell the sand and the salt and the bush that surrounded. It all had a wonderful smell, he loved every bit of it.

Walking down to the shore line he turned to the right that was the rock face that she told him about. He was right; he must be at kiddie's corner. He noticed the road that winded up the cliff face above. "That's the road to Pearl Beach, that's where she lives," he mumbled to himself. He was so close to her. He could feel the excitement in him grow. He wanted to go there now. He was sure he could find her place if her details were as accurate as this. "This has to be done right. I canna rush it. I have one chance of winning her back and I am not going to blow it by turning up jetlagged and making a goose of myself."

He spun around and peered down the beach the other way. He stopped dead in his tracks—there it was, that was the surf club. It was an oblong building with a long veranda upstairs and a flagged walkway onto the beach. He could now see the red and yellow safe swimming area signs. "Yes, this is it, it's just as she described." He started to head that way, it wasn't far maybe five hundred meters at the most.

Kiddies' corner was a quiet area, appropriately named. The beach was full of dogs playing with sticks and balls and little children playing with buckets and spades on the shallow waters of the shoreline. As he walked, he passed lots of people out for a walk or jogging. Almost all of them greeted him as they passed by. He had arrived at the flagged area. He stood and stared up at it. There was the restaurant, Seasalt. He knew all about the place, he knew it all so well, but had never been there. It was an incredible feeling. His excitement instantly turned to fear. He was in the danger ground. What if she saw him? He wasn't ready to meet her yet.

He frantically turned and started to head back to kiddies' corner. It was a warm day, especially for him; he had just left freezing conditions in Scotland. He took off his shirt and went in for a swim. The water was a bit cool, but refreshing at the same time. It was certainly not as warm as the Mediterranean sea, but a hell of a lot warmer than Scotland. He swam out past the breakers and enjoyed his swim. He did a few laps and then stopped to admire a lighthouse that he could see across the waters. He would take a walk tonight and see if he could see it flashing. He peered back at the shoreline; his body had adjusted to the temperature of the water. He could do this every morning. What a great start to the day.

A fish jumped out of the water, which startled him; he suddenly remembered about crocodiles and sharks. His swim back in to the shoreline was of Olympic speed. He was grateful when he reached the shoreline, puffed and hoping no one noticed his frantic swim. The kids had the right idea; he would learn from them and paddle on the shoreline in the future. He had enjoyed his swim immensely, but was glad to be safe and out of the water. Grabbing his shirt, he went for a walk over to the rocks while he dried off.

There were fishermen, so he strolled over and chatted to them for a bit, asking about what they had caught. They had been so friendly and were happy to show him their catch. He loved their accent. It reminded him of Chloe. He couldn't wait to see her. He made his way back to the cabin. The swim had picked him up; he felt alive again. He made a plan to take a look around the town and get his bearings. He still had no idea how he was going to handle the situation, and meet up with her, but he would work something out. He had a shower, freshened up and walked into town.

He spotted the pub and went in for a beer. Walking to the bar he gazed over all the taps. The man in front asked for a schooner of gold. That's the beer she used to tell him about. He remembered the story about in New South Wales you order a schooner of gold or a "goldie" for short and in Queensland, it was called a "pot of gold."

"What will you have, mate?" asked the bartender as he wiped down the bar in front of him.

"A pint of gold, thanks," he said, not thinking. He went to correct himself but he was pouring it before he had time. Well, he had worked that one out pretty quick; pints were in oz as well. Happy with himself, he took a stroll around the pub. There was a beer garden out the back with a stage and a huge screen. He could imagine watching football games in thirty-degree heat drinking cold beers. He smirked to himself he was growing to like this town more and more.

The bistro was open and he was starving. He took a seat as the waitress wiped down the table.

"What is the favourite around here?" he asked.

"Well you can't go wrong with the Schnity chips and salad. Just order inside when you're ready."

He walked in, ordered his meal and another beer. He sat back down at the outdoor table and had his beer watching the sport on the big screen.

The meal came out quickly; it was huge and delicious. He ate it like he had not eaten for days. He sat back happy, wiping his mouth with the serviette and then moved on to get another beer and take a look at the front bar.

Sitting at the open window that opened out onto the main street, he could watch the town in full swing. He liked the whole vibe of it. There were buskers playing up the road and from what he could hear, they were pretty good. People were so friendly, just like Chloe had said they were. The streets were busy with people walking dogs and lots of people heading to or from the beach all chatting with friends. He finished his beer. It was time to move on.

He needed some grocery items so he headed to the supermarket. He grabbed a few items for breakfast and then went to the bottle shop and grabbed a bottle of whisky. He had spotted a club close to the caravan park that would be handy for dinner. He headed back to the cabin, looking at everything along the way. He crossed a sporting oval that had just been mowed and the smell of freshly mown grass was lingering in the air, which made him smile.

Making himself comfortable on his veranda, he poured a whisky as he watched the waves crash onto the sand.

Tomorrow, he would feel better and check out the surf club. Maybe even possibly see Chloe, now that was an exciting thought. Today, he just needed to reset the body clock. He poured another drink; he certainly did have a great feeling about this place. He sat for what felt like ages, just getting in a really relaxed zone.

He became interested in a cricket game that had started on the beach for a while, having a chuckle at it all. Starting to feel a bit weary he went into his room to have a quick nap. He needed to go to the club for dinner. He had never been at a club before, but he remembered Chloe telling him about it.

When he woke up, he could hear waves crashing onto the shore and birds chirping. There was light coming in through the window. It was early morning. He could not believe it. How long had he slept? Looking at the clock, it was half past five in the morning. He went outside. It was early dawn. He could see people on the beach exercising, jogging, and walking their dogs. He was starving. He went in and made a coffee and some muesli and took it back outside. It was another sensational morning.

Today was the day that he would head to the surf club. He felt good about it, excited, ready for it, he felt sensational after a good sleep. After breakfast he went for a walk. It was an amazing start to the day. He walked further today, past the surf club and right to the end. He stopped and chatted to more fishermen and said hello to everyone that he passed, saying "G'day" was an art that he would have to practice. He loved it; he was having a wonderful time. Walking back, he looked up at the surf club and along the beach to the rocks at the end. She was just around the corner. He was so excited, but anxious all at the same time. What if she didn't want anything to do with him? What if she was back with Craig? He pushed it from his mind. He couldn't cloud his head with those thoughts. He needed it to be clear and focused.

Mid-morning, he set off back up the beach towards the surf club. He noticed the café that she obviously worked at. He looked around quickly; she was nowhere to be seen. His heart was pounding in his chest hard. It was busy, lots of people sitting outside drinking coffee and eating. Many more were standing around waiting for take-away.

He managed to get a table at the end near the surf club entry. The roller doors were up and they were taking some boards down onto the beach. He sat and drank his coffee watching, on the lookout for her.

He felt uneasy, anxious, and extremely uncomfortable. All of a sudden he heard someone yell out, "Bob, have you got a minute?" His ears pricked up immediately. Out walked a man that was the spitting image of the way Chloe described him. He watched him as they worked on getting a jet ski organised. He walked past him. Jack wanted to stop him and ask him if he knew Chloe. It was all too daunting, he couldn't do it. He watched for a while as he was in and out of the surf club and finally plucked up the courage to approach him.

"Hi, I was wondering if you know Chloe Clarke?" Bob was not in the habit of giving out details of anyone, especially Chloe.

"Who's asking?"

"Well I am a friend of hers, and I have come a long way to see her, and really wanted to catch up with her," said Jack nervously.

Bob stopped and had a good look at him. He recognized the Scottish accent and he looked a hell of a lot like the bloke in her photos. It was Jack, he was sure.

"Your name wouldn't happen to be Jack, would it?"

"Aye, that's me."

Bob looked around to find a quiet spot.

"You had better come with me, son."

He followed him to a large deck that overlooked the water. It had stunning views right up and down the beach.

"So you're the bloke who broke Chloe's heart. You have a bit of a hide showing up here."

"I can explain, it's not how it looks."

"Well, you have a lot of explaining to do, so I suggest you start."

Jack was feeling uncomfortable. "Aye, I know I do. It's all been a terrible misunderstanding. My ex-girlfriend got very upset when I met Chloe. She was so angry because everyone kept on saying how happy I was now that I had met Chloe. Well I was trying to ask a girl to leave my sister's birthday party and she was not welcome and kept falling onto me. She had a few too many drinks. Anyway, long story short, my ex took photos that looked like I was with that girl. She hacked into my brother's Facebook account and sent them to Chloe. She obviously thought that I was getting it on with this girl. She would not even answer my calls when I tried to call and explain. She cut me off completely. So now I am here to show her that I still love her and want to be with her."

"Well, that's one hell of a story, son. Bloody facebook. I keep telling these kids it's no bloody good. Just one thing, what in the flaming hell is your ex-girlfriend doing at your sister's birthday party if you are busted up?"

"That's another long story, but she is with my brother now. It's been a horrible few months."

Bob just stared at him speechless for a moment. Then said, "Well it sounds like you've been through the ringer mate."

"Aye, I have, and I have only just scratched the surface on the story. You don't know half of it," he said as he stared at the waves.

Bob watched him for a moment, working him out. He sounded genuine and he remembered Chloe's stories and it all seemed to add up.

"Well, any man that travels halfway across the world to set things straight with a Sheila is alright in my books, but I am giving ya the mail now. If you hurt her again, you will have me to deal with."

"Aye, I understand what you are saying. I am giving you my word. I hope that she will hear me out, give me a chance, I am not planning on going anywhere now, not without her anyway."

"I don't think that I introduced myself. I am Bob." He held out his hand and Jack shook it.

"Pleased to meet you, Bob."

"Chloe will be here tomorrow morning. She is helping out with the Nippers, she finish's up around half past eleven."

"I can't thank you enough. I promise, I won't let you down."

"Well, let's see what your 'man's word' is really worth then. See you tomorrow."

He turned and walked away. Just as he was about to walk off, he noticed a sign on the front of the deck: "The deck of excuses." He had a chuckle to himself. How ironic is that. He had just stood on the deck of excuses, telling Bob all of his excuses why he should get a second chance with Chloe. He walked off down to the beach towards the caravan park.

He was more than happy with the way things had turned out. He had met Bob, wow, and he was a really nice bloke. But the best news that he had all day was that he would see Chloe tomorrow. Things were finally starting to work out for him. All he had to do now was convince her.

It had been a busy morning with Nippers. Bob called Chloe aside after the events were over and they were starting to pack up. "I just wanted to warn you. There was some bloke here yesterday hanging around asking if I knew you."

"What bloke? Who was he?" asked Chloe, still trying to brush the sand off her.

"Well he looked a hell of a lot like that bloke in your holiday photos, and he had a Scottish accent."

Chloe froze. "Jack" was all she could say. She was so excited. Jack. It had to be Jack. "What did you tell him?"

"Well, I wanted to tell him that he had a hell of a hide to turn up here, and to get on his bike, but I am a good judge of character, and he looked sincere and lost and thought that if he came all this way to see you, you should hear what he had to say," explained Bob.

Chloe pulled up a chair and sat down; she thought that she was going to faint. Could it be Jack? She felt sick. Was he really here? "You spoke to him?"

Bob nodded.

"So what did you tell him?" asked Chloe again, shakily.

"I told him I knew you, and that you worked in the café. You need to face him, Chloe. No man travels halfway across the world if he doesn't love a girl. Give him a chance. I think that he is fair dinkum and he deserves at least that."

She couldn't stop shaking, her legs were like jelly. "I need to go, I have to go home, I don't know what to think right now," she said as she walked towards the beach. She was still in her bikini and surf club rash vest. She walked down onto the sand staring at the waves as if they had the answer that she needed.

She was lost, mesmerized as they crashed over and over onto the shore. He was here in her town. How was she going to handle this? She still had to remember how he had hurt her, that he had hooked up with that girl as soon as he got home. No one had ever hurt her the way he did. Did he really deserve a second chance? It must not have worked out with that other girl and now he was crawling back to her. How dare he. She was feeling pretty cranky and upset with the whole situation.

"Bloody hell, Jack, what are you doing to me?" she yelled to the waves.

"I have come to get my secret love. Mo leannan falaich mo Chloe," a voice came from behind her.

She was too scared to look. It had to be him, only he knew those words, those words, that meant so much to her, but did she just imagine those words, was he really standing behind her? She turned around and Jack was there, he was really there.

"Jack," she whispered as tears started to stream down her face.

"It's me, Chloe."

"What are you doing here?" She was trembling.

"You wouldn't answer my calls." He smiled. "I know you seen those photos but they were not as they looked. I love you Chloe, I always have and I always will. I promised you that I would come for you and I have."

"I want to believe that, Jack."

"Then don't stop believing. Trust me, it's true, give me a chance to tell my story. I never had anything to do with that girl or any other girl, you are the only girl for me. Those photos were of me throwing a girl out of a party who had way too much to drink, that's all."

She ran to his arms and he pulled her in close as she cried. She looked up at him and tears were streaming down his face also. She wiped them away and kissed him, it was a hard passionate kiss that seemed to last forever. "I missed you so much, Jack."

"Aye, I have been lost without you, Chloe, can't believe I have you in my arms again," he smiled excitedly.

"I don't know if I could handle it if you hurt me again."

"That is not going to happen. Give me a chance to explain, that's all I ask."

She nodded and hugged him tightly.

"Let's go somewhere and talk."

"I was hoping to hear those words. I want 'us' back, the way we were, the way we were always meant to be."

She nodded in reply, unable to speak. It was exactly what she wanted also.

Walking down the beach , Chloe could not believe what had just happened. Jack the man she thought that she had lost forever had appeared out of nowhere, and here she was now ,with the strong arms she knew so very well wrapped around her shoulder. Jack the man who had stolen her heart, the one who picked her up in her darkest hour and comforted her, protected her and swept her off her feet, making her feel alive for the first time in her life.

Her highlander, her huge gentle giant that had taken her heart so easily but then broke it like it had never been broken before. The voice in her head was warning her 'Chloe what in the bloody hell are you doing, he broke your heart, remember that excruciating pain that he had caused, can you play this game again. He had left you so badly broken that you never thought you would ever recover. But you did, and now he is back'. Two dogs chasing a frisby came dangerously close to colliding with them. Jack snuggled her closer to him.

Feeling her body so close to him again was the best feeling in the world. He thought she would hate him, hit him, tell him to get back on that plane and never come back. But she didn't, she kissed him. It wasn't just a kiss either; it was just as intense as the first kiss on the boat.

He remembered it well. It was something he would never forget. That feeling he knew he would never feel again if he didn't win her back. That erotic flame that had burned for her was ignited into a fierce blaze that night. The way her eyes looked up at him, had burnt into his memory forever, and then that kiss. The hot wet touch of her lips sent him into ecstasy that he could not control. His playful little kitten had turned into a fierce jaguar that night.

The kiss today was just as passionate, she still loved him, he was sure of it. But she was hurt, he had to win her back over, he had to explain everything to her and hope that she would understand. He felt her stiffen in his arms, what was she thinking, she had been so quiet.

He was so worried that he would ruin everything. If she told him to get back on that plane his life was over. He wiped his brow; it was so god damn hot. He could not believe how much he had sweated since he had arrived. "Chloe come here, sit for a minute, I need to explain something to you, before we go any further" he felt her stiffen as he turned her towards him and gently helped her as they sat on the sand. He cleared his throat and wiped his brow again.

"Chloe those photos that you were sent are not as it seems" Slowly she pulled away from him finding a stick, she doodled in the sand, one knee up as she cradled it with one arm resting her chin on it. "I can understand how you thought I was getting it on with Shauna, now that I have seen the photos myself, but it's not true" She didn't say a word she did not move she just kept drawing lines in the sand "Chloe I was throwing her out of the party, she was drunk and falling all over me, I was trying to keep her upright and that's when Mary , took the photos." Jack was clawing his fingers through his hair " I spent the last four months , going through hell and the only thing that mattered to me was finding my way back to you" she never moved.

"He put his hand on her hand and threw the stick away with the other "Look at me Chloe I need to know what you're thinking" He pulled her face towards him gently. "It was wet with tears; they were streaming down her face. Just the look of pain in her eyes sent a dagger through his heart. Looking at how much pain it had caused her. Tears began to well in his eyes at the sight of her. "Chloe I can't tell you how much I love you or how I feel because there is no words for it, but I have come a long way to tell you to your face what happened and hopefully spend the rest of my life 'showing you' how much I love you"

He smiled gently at her as he swept the hair from her face with his finger and wiped her tears"You can't tell me that you don't feel the same way, look at you"

It was the smile that she could not resist, the smile that turned her legs into jelly and melted her heart. She wanted to believe him so much, she loved him and wanted them to be the way they were in Europe. She had no reason not to believe him, he had travelled such a long way and the kiss, it was so full of passion and desire, and there was no way he could fake that. She watched him staring at her; she wiped his tears from his eyes and smiled gently.

"You better not be telling me one of your wild stories Jack Maclean" His heart missed a beat, she was coming around. He wanted to do cart wheels all along the beach "Just give me a chance to prove it to you, that is all I am asking, what we had was special Chloe, you don't find that every day, someone just tried to wreck it for us and they nearly did, but what we have, can never be destroyed, we are forever" he smiled at her again wiping her tears away. She was sobbing now but smiling. He pulled her in close and snuggled her into his chest as he comforted her while she sobbed.

Her highlander had returned and wanted to stay with her forever. It felt so good to be back in his arms, her great big security blanket, she felt safe, calm, relaxed. In an instant she knew that everything was going to be alright. She smiled gently as she whispered the words from Cruz's song.

'Stay with me forever, and walk this path called life'